Under Dark Sky Law

Tamara Boyens

Supposed Crimes LLC • Matthews, North Carolina

This book would not have been possible without three critical things: my friends, the Arizona desert, and way too much coffee. Many thanks to Abby Fox who watched me bang the keys over many long, dark, heavily caffeinated nights. As my partner in crime, she provided essential feedback throughout the whole process and harangued me whenever I wanted to quit. I was also fortunate to have the support of my glam squad: Jason, Hope, Ty, Jane, Yoshi, Dani and Merica.

An author is only as good as their caffeine supply—much of this novel was written in the wee hours of the night at Lux in Phoenix and Black Crown in Tucson. I am grateful for their tolerance of excessive profanity.

Writing this book taught me to love the desert in all of its terrible beauty. Thanks to the strange city of Tucson, Arizona, and the Sonoran desert for sharing their dark secrets with me.

CHAPTER ONE

SCORCHED EYEBROWS and toxic waste wouldn't keep me from saving my best friend. Only one night we had to stay here, but even one minute in the Breakers was too long. These defunct biodomes were nothing but a permanent deportation station for all the unlucky souls who lost the genetic lottery. My Zone Pass and my supercharged lungs made me a free woman, but both my jobs forced me here for business.

Now Trina was dying. Ugly business.

Night fell over the River Slums, and light trickled into the bedroom from an illegal street lamp. The air tasted like refrigerator mold, and the shack had no soap.

That was a problem.

Filthy from a long day of traveling, sweat and dirt mixed into a gritty paste on my skin. Argon lay on top of me, his hips digging into my waist.

I touched my chest and got a palmful of mud. "Nope, can't deal. Move your dick so I can shower."

He propped himself up, and a curl of orange hair fell over his eyes. "A shower? Here? Haven't had enough punishment for one day?"

"Cleanliness is godliness." I pushed him back, and he rolled off me.

"And you want to be the god of this place? Look around. A

swimming pool of bleach couldn't save this shack."

I sat up. "A kingdom is a kingdom."

He pressed dirty palms into dark eye sockets. "Wipe yourself down with a washcloth or something and come back to bed. Big day tomorrow."

"Washcloth? Really? Setting myself on fire again might be safer."

He yawned and stretched out on his side. "Your funeral. Call me if you need help exterminating any alien life forms in there."

"I thought creating alien life forms was your job."

"No aliens in my labs, just good strong drugs."

I dragged a finger across the grooves in his abs. "Gross." I held the sticky finger up to his face. "I'm not sleeping next to you like this. Shower with me."

He laughed. "If you survive, I'll consider showering."

"Some bodyguard you are."

"Like you need a bodyguard."

I folded my arms. "You're supposed to be the hired muscle on this trip."

He shifted to his back and flexed his biceps. "Muscle, I got. Energy, I don't. I want to sleep so we can finish this job. I want Trina back. With both of us gone the lab's going to fall apart."

He made it sound like Trina had a cold, but it was worse than a common virus. Much worse. And he couldn't know that. We needed wishful thinking.

My stomach rumbled. "I can't believe those assholes confiscated our food. I'm fucking starving."

"If I don't fall asleep, I'll see if there's anything remotely safe to eat in the pantry, but I doubt it—unless you're into mystery mushrooms," he said.

Gag me. Here in the Casa Grande Breakers, one of the worst abandoned biodomes in the region, the fucked up climate control was good at growing fungus. On everything.

"I'll pass. Just try not to let anyone kill me while I'm in the shower. Some serious shit is going down. Stay alert."

"Aye aye, Captain," he said and rolled onto his stomach. He'd be asleep in minutes.

I shook my head. Fieldwork didn't suit his lazy habits, but working with him was safer than using an underpaid stranger. Couldn't trust him to watch my back, but at least he wouldn't stab it.

I left him alone and made my way to the bathroom. River

garbage and mildew crusted the windows above the tub, blotting out any stray light. I touched the slick bands of scar tissue that spun around my neck like Saturn's rings. Call me paranoid, but it wasn't paranoia if someone was actually gunning for you.

I needed more light.

Even with active power circuits nearby, none of the wiring in the shack worked. We hadn't used this base in months, but we might still have candles and matches. Gangs wouldn't bother stealing those—fire and toxic gas make for a fun game of candle roulette.

We'd lost more than one flophouse that way.

Catching my face on fire wasn't a favorite activity, but the military confiscated our solar lamps at the border. Besides, I already burned my eyebrows once today, so why not roll the dice again? Better than having my throat slit. If there's one thing I've got, it's priorities.

I skimmed the bathroom sink, whacking used tea lights into the basin before I found a box of matches and new candles. The flames cast weak light across the wall—a small improvement. Nothing exploded either, so that was a bonus.

I leaned into the rusty mirror and put my left eye up to the fractured glass. Below a mangled eyebrow, the iris shone a clear green, but smashed capillaries stained the white parts a murky crimson. A mottled bruise, halfway through healing, decorated my cheekbone. I hated getting punched in the face, but it came with the job.

I ran a hand over the sides of my overgrown Mohawk—didn't need a mirror to know it had faded to the color of expired pea soup. Out in the Voids, the wild lawless lands without biodomes, fashion was armor. Just like a poisonous animal, my neon green hair, spiked high to the ceiling, was a warning signal for predators: don't fuck with me. I'm the boss.

I'm Xero, ruler of the Tucson Voids.

But I'd let myself go to utter shit. Trina was dying, and suddenly everyone wanted a piece of my territory. No time for personal maintenance on the battlefield. With a limp dick of a dirty Mohawk, I looked more like Xero, ruler of the broken toilets

At least my tits still looked good.

I sighed and tried to untangle my wilted hair before braving the shower, but my fingers caught in the strands, stuck in something warm and sticky. Very sticky.

Oh, hell no. Not the sacred Mohawk.

Soap. Must find soap.

I thrust my head under the cabinet, grimacing as slimy things brushed against my fingertips. Creepy crawlies couldn't breed in this poisoned district, but it still reeked of dead things. No stench would stop me. The soap had to be mine.

I clawed through the dank mess, flinging aside slop until I reached a hard rectangle. With the soap case clenched in my fist, I raised my hand in triumph. After such a fucked up day, I almost cried happy tears as I cracked open the plastic shell and snatched the prize inside with my greedy little fingers.

Then the thing in my greedy little fingers went squish.

Mold. It had been soap at one point, but only curdled scum remained. A black mess covered my hand.

"Fuck!" I yelled and flung the nasty shit at the wall.

The heavy blob splatted into the bathroom mirror, and the direct hit destroyed it. Glass clattered into the sink and shards scattered, tinkling like a broken music box on the tile floor.

I may have overreacted.

"Everything okay in there?" Argon said, his voice sleepy. Figured.

"It's fine. Place is just falling apart," I said, and he grunted.

More glass stabbed my heels as I moved toward the sink. Great. No soap or antibiotics, and now I had to worry about catching flesh rot. Dark blood spotted the tiles. Nice deep cuts. Just perfect.

I rerouted to the bathtub and hoped the solar tank still worked. The shower taps were stiff and crusty, but after a minute of swearing and twisting the handles, a rush of icy water smacked me in the face. The spray went up my nose, and water that smelled like sulfur and rusty iron dripped down the back of my throat. Goosebumps jumped across my skin, and the cold shock sent a wave of nausea through my stomach.

I've had bullet wounds that were more pleasant.

Screw this trip. I planned everything out, had each step perfectly timed, like I always do. Then we checked in at immigration and found the whole district on lockdown. Riots. Big riots. Quick riots. They started before we reached Casa Grande and were out of control when we hit the checkpoint.

I liked a good riot as much as the next bitch, but having my supplies confiscated was over the line. Immigration took everything, including our clean water. In the state of Arizona that was illegal. The biodome wasn't the only thing falling apart in Casa Grande, and I hated that outdated government policies still required us to pass through this nest of corruption. I'd file a complaint when I reached Phoenix, which still had a functional biodome and a supposedly functional legislation, but that didn't help us now.

Annoying as it was, having our supplies taken shouldn't have been such a big problem. I'm organized. I have backup plans. I'm a fucking desert pirate—a supply god. Then we got to our main outpost, and it was on fire from the riots. Spectacularly on fire. We kept the place packed with heavy munitions, and I'm surprised the explosion didn't blow a hole in the Dome ceiling.

The blasts destroyed the neighborhood. Along with my eyebrows.

So we were stuck in this hellhole until morning when our official processing pinged and we could move on to the Phoenix Dome. The River Slums was the worst district in the Casa Grande Breakers, which is why this shack was only an emergency base. Still. It shouldn't have been this disgusting. We were slipping. Too many wars, not enough money, and not enough time.

When I was as clean as I could get without skinning myself, I cranked off the stubborn taps and jumped out of the shower. Water pooled around my feet and broken tiles poked my toes. No towels. A hard breeze came through the bathroom, and I shivered. It just got better and better.

Once the water was off, I heard muffled shifting and grunting in the bedroom, like Argon was having an intense nightmare. He usually slept like a corpse. I nudged the door open and peered into the dusky room.

My eyes dilated, the bedroom coming into soft focus in the flickering light. The candles paid off—not paranoid after all.

A Skeleton was straddling Argon's bare ass, choking him with a garrote wire.

It mashed Argon's face into the pillows, muting his screams. Argon pushed himself away from the wire around his neck, but the Skeleton had leverage. Locked in a seesaw battle, they struggled against each other, a tangle of bulging arms and legs.

I reached behind the bathroom door to find one of the many weapons we kept stashed around our bases. My hand struck blank wood. Splinters dug into my palm as I flailed for my gear. Nothing.

Naked. No weapons.

Calavera's Skeletons—mercenaries wearing black armor stamped with white bone patterns—were no joke and bare-knuckle boxing one wasn't a good idea. What else could I use as a weapon? The broken mirror—a long, fat shard still glittered in the sink. My feet crunched over more glass slivers as I dashed to grab it. The shard, long as my forearm, was sharp on both sides, and I had nothing to wrap the bare edges.

This was going to hurt.

I stampeded into the bedroom and sprung onto the bed. My knees struck the Skeleton in the ribs, and I landed behind it with my legs hugging Argon's ass. With the wind knocked out of it, the Skeleton released the wire. Argon flopped forward, gasping, wriggling and trying to escape or flip over, but he was trapped beneath me and the Skeleton.

Before the Skeleton could recover, I grabbed its head with one hand and dug my fingers into its unprotected eye sockets. It screamed, and I pulled back, exposing its throat.

The Calaca suits—their custom armor—had a weak point at the base of the neck between the collarbones. I rammed the glass into the thin space, waiting to feel it slide through flesh and into its trachea.

I missed.

The shard hit solid armor, and the edge slipped up my hand, cleaving flesh before shattering into smaller pieces that spiked into my palm. Thanks to adrenaline, I felt no pain as my blood showered onto the Skeleton.

I shook off glass and clutched its head with both hands. Blood from my mangled palm smeared across its white skull markings, and I jammed another knee into its spine, keeping it off balance.

The Skeleton struggled, and Argon kept thrashing beneath us. My arms slithered around the Skeleton's neck, and I wrapped my legs around its waist like an anaconda smothering prey. The armor protected the Skeleton from chokeholds, but I had another plan.

I locked my arms, tensed my body, and flung all my weight at the wall behind us.

The Skeleton flipped over my head, and I held on. We rolled together, flopping off the bed and hitting the floor before the Skeleton's face smashed into a wooden dresser. The shock rattled my skull, but we landed exactly where I'd planned. Before the Skeleton could recover, I stood up and stomped its head into the floor. The fragile wood exploded, and its face sank into the boards.

With its head pinned beneath my foot, I reached behind the dresser and pulled a long machete from a hole in the wall. Jackpot. Using both hands, I clutched the hilt, jumped straight up, and rammed the blade through the gap at its throat. Layers of bone, flesh, and flooring crunched as the machete slid through its neck.

Blood pooled around my feet, and the warm ooze flowed between my toes. I couldn't stand dried blood under my nails. Looked like another arctic shower was in my future. I backed out of the expanding pool, my feet making sticky slap slap slaps as they stamped bloody prints across the floor.

Panting, I called out, "Yo. Argon. You okay?"

"Yeah—thanks for that," he sputtered.

"You were seconds from being ghosted." I moved in front of the bathroom door to get more candlelight.

Argon sat up on the bed. He cleared his throat and rubbed the purple and red wounds on his neck. Blood trickled down his chest.

"Way too close. Took that one up the ass." He kept rubbing, smearing blood on his chin. Some of that blood was mine.

I bit the corner of my lip. "I'd pay to see you take it up the ass."

"We can play that game later when we have more soap."

"Next time I see a real bar of soap, I'm going to kiss it." I flipped damp Mohawk strands out of my face and eyed the blood creeping toward the bed. "Damn it, that's going to ruin our only mattress."

"I think that's the least of your problems—you already trashed the sheets." He peered at me from the shadows. "You hurt bad?"

Right. The adrenaline was running dry, and things hurt. Glass in my feet. Splinters in my back. Knees bruised and raw. My hand looked like I'd run it through a paper shredder. A hit of Alphadrine or Vinicodone would really take the edge off, but I didn't allow anyone in my crew to use our products. Including me. Especially me.

I brought my hand closer to the candles. "Fuck. Yeah, I've got a situation here." A big date with a razor blade and some tweezers was in my future. Even worse, I had nothing to sterilize the wounds. No hot water. No soap. No bandages.

No antibiotics.

Argon came to my side and examined my hand. "Crap, that's not good. I'm sorry."

At least he had the decency to feel bad.

"Remind me to revoke your guard card." I pulled my hand away.

He touched my shoulders. "Never wanted that job anyway. Just glad we're both alive."

I breathed out and couldn't help but smile. "Can't argue with that. Keeping everyone out of the graveyard is getting more challenging by the day."

He stepped back again, looking at the corpse. "So what's with this fool trying to dust me? Thought you hashed out a truce with Calavera." He coughed several times and gagged as he tried to adjust his squashed Adam's apple.

I knit my bushy brows together, fat lips pursed. "No idea. Calavera's a total asshole, but she honors deals. Maybe this is some copycat dressed up like a Skeleton for a piñata party."

"No way. You know what happens if Calavera finds people wearing her threads. Bitch is serious about style. I dig that."

"You got a crush on her or something?"

"Hell no, she's psychotic," he muttered.

I gave him a look but let it go. "If Calavera was going to violate our treaty, she would've sent a whole Skeleton army, not some wannabe ninja loser like this dude."

"Hey now, that loser almost had me snuffed from behind like a bad porno."

I smirked. "No comment."

He clucked his tongue. "You're just jealous."

"I'm jealous of cartels that have their shit together. My weapons are missing from the bathroom. Good thing I remembered that machete tucked behind the dresser—almost forgot Neptune hid it back there."

Our security officer, Neptune, loved machetes. And grenades. I found them stashed in the oddest places. Nothing like a surprise grenade to liven up a boring afternoon.

"I know why the weapons are gone. Trina and Neptune—they came out here to clean and restock things, but that's when Trina got jacked up with the Lung Zaps. I bet they took everything out to inventory and didn't finish. The weapons are probably in one of the back rooms."

I cringed. "Right, I was on a run when that went down."

He hesitated but continued, "Security's not my usual gig, but I should have swept the property when we got in tonight. Riots threw me off—I was brain dead."

"Well, at least one part of you was still working."

He waggled his eyebrows. "That part is always working."

We both laughed. Sometimes laughing was better than crying. Or stabbing someone. Actually, I usually preferred stabbing as long as it didn't involve mutilating myself in the process.

"We should save the corpse, or at least the head, to show

Calavera," he said.

"Man, I don't want to cut off any heads tonight. Let's just drag this thing to the shed and send her a message. First thing in the morning, she better get here and explain this shit."

"This isn't in my job description, but you're injured, and I owe you one. I'll move the body and call Calavera's people about making amends."

"Think you can manage not to screw it up this time?"

I'm tall—way over six feet, but Argon still had several inches on me. He came forward and leaned over until his nose was level with mine.

"You are far too scary to let down again."

I grinned and pinched his nipple. "Lucky for you, you're far too pretty to kill."

CHAPTER TWO

IN THE River Slums, nothing lasted. Built against an old overpass, our shack was one of the few abandoned buildings left standing. I leaned on a concrete pillar outside the front door, nudged a rusty can with my combat boot, and grimaced—still had glass in my feet.

The river echoed off the dead highway, and I hoped the stench wafting from the water didn't seep into my pores. Skin peeling off? Strange growths? Sudden death? This neighborhood had it all, and the morning fumes prickled my skin like boiling drops of fat.

"Christ, it's fucking foul out here," I said. Cement dust fell on my face, and I rubbed my eyes. I had the apex of the resistance gene, giving me the strongest protection against toxins, but the vapors belching up from the river still made my eyes blur.

Argon scrutinized the overpass. "Do we need to tag this district?"

He wore a ripped pair of heart-studded boxers and no shirt. I had slipped into saggy, gray underwear and a stained white tank top. Not much protection from the elements, but we had to keep our other clothes clean for the run.

"We don't need to advertise, and I won't be sad if another gang invades this turf. Save the tagging for a permanent base. Our spray paint went up in the fire anyway."

He nodded and walked around, turning his head, still searching for rival graffiti.

I kicked the can, and it flew into the chunky river where garbage washed downstream from the Phoenix Dome was decomposing. "Besides, there's a tag in the living room just in case someone makes it that far. Anyone sees our mark, they'll steer clear."

"You mean like last night when a Skeleton steered right into our bedroom?"

I shot him a look. "That doesn't count—something's up. Stop critiquing street art over there and come help me check out that body."

Just getting to the old toolshed was difficult, and I was grateful for my heavy boots—the acidic river slowly eroded everything along the banks, and I didn't want any of that muck splashing my skin. Spongy ground squished under my feet, and with high knees, we picked our way across piles of decaying trash.

The shed, made from some aluminum alloy, was lopsided, crumpled on one side, sunk into the mire on the other side, and covered with gang tags. The overpass shaded the small building, and I squinted through the bright sunlight. Looked like the crooked doors were open.

I stopped. "Oh for fuck's sake."

The Skeleton's black and white boots were hanging out the front door.

Argon shrugged. "It was dark and late."

"You might be the worst employee ever. I didn't say put the body halfway in the shed. I said hide it inside the shed."

He put his meaty arms behind his head. "Worst janitor, best chemist. Can't have it both ways. You know how hard it was to drag that body out here without falling into a pile of toxic waste?"

I tapped my foot. "Forget it. Let's get this over with." I held up my mangled hand that was wrapped in bloody sheet scraps. "You do it." I couldn't sanitize the gash until we escaped the Breakers, and I didn't want to grind more bacteria into it by fondling dead things.

"If I must." He pulled the body out, trying to avoid the slimy trail it left behind.

I motioned with my head, and he ripped off the armored Skeleton mask. Beneath the helmet was a Hispanic man, his face tattooed with an intricate sugar-skull design.

"Shit," I said. "This isn't an impostor. Those tattoos didn't get there overnight."

"He's a decorated enforcer too. Check out those layers of tats."

He turned and pointed at me. "See—he wasn't just some loser flunky."

"Whatever makes you feel better, buddy."

He glared but continued, "We may have a real problem here."

"We'll have an even bigger issue if we don't get moving. Where the fuck are Calavera's goons? We need to beat the seriousness of this incident into their skulls."

He touched my arm, and I shied away.

"I don't care how sexy you are—dead Skeleton cooties are a deal breaker. Wash your hands before you put your mitts on me again," I said.

He rolled his eyes. "Then let's clean up and get dressed. Maybe they'll be here by then."

"Shove this asshole back in there, but don't get messy. Use a stick if you have to. I can't handle another shower out here."

"Good thing being respectful to the dead isn't in our code of ethics."

"Fuck respect. Nothing's more serious than a cold shower."

CHAPTER THREE

BACK INSIDE, sun warmed the shack, and it smelled like dust and burned mushrooms. I coughed and stared at the congealed pool of Skeleton blood. Mold had already bloomed in the center of the puddle.

Matches and gasoline might be the only way to improve the decor.

I gagged a few times before heading to the bathroom and splashing cold water on my face. The cracked porcelain sink dug into my waist as I hung my head over the basin, trying to shake it off.

"When will we get cool gear like the Skeletons?" Argon sat on the bed and rummaged through a duffel bag.

"We're not superheroes. You don't need a costume." I dried my face with my tank top, and my pale skin glowed through the wet fabric, white as the sink.

"I don't want a costume. I want a badass armored uniform like the Calaca suits."

"Armor is for pussies. Go join Calavera if you want to parade around in a retarded outfit. She's just a lame chola drug dealer—stick with the Grease Weasels if you want fame and fortune."

He folded his arms. "Fortune, huh? Where is it? And what about minions? Why don't we have an army of minions to do our bidding?"

"We've got piles of capital, and we've got minions aplenty. That's who does our grunt work." Lucky I was still anemic from the stab wound and dehydration, or I might have flushed with embarrassment. We'd lost epic cash fighting Calavera, Albuquerque, and Juarez. Attacks all around. Payroll was tight.

"This *is* grunt work. I almost died last night, I'm hungry, I'm tired, and I should be back in the lab, not out here pretending to be a two-bit thug," he said.

"Come on, this trip will be fun. We get to fuck with the Dome drones and take a hike out to Yuma."

"Yuma's always been a shit hole."

"How would you know? You were out sucking dicks in Phoenix when Yuma got a Dome. That place was a swinging underground hideaway before it domed up, and the Voids are still awesome. Dome's laid back too—we can stay somewhere amazing like the Super 88, and we won't even have to forge our Zone Passes."

The more I talked, the more I convinced myself. Good. I needed an energy boost to push through the day.

"You call that a good time? The Super 88?"

"The Super 88 has clean showers and tons of hot water," I said. "You're missing out. Phoenix and L.A. can't regulate Yuma because of the dead zones. Every time I do a run, new shit pops up. We'll have a blast. Best of all, the dunes are still controlled by the Voids, and I'm on good terms with the territory boss. You ever been off-roading in the Imperial Dunes?"

He wrinkled his eyebrows. "You're weirdly excited about this run."

I bit a fingernail, peering at his expression. "And you're shaken. Look, dude, yesterday was totally fucked up, but you lived. I lived. Move on. We've got slots and sluts waiting for us in Yuma."

He frowned. "That's not it."

It wasn't like Argon to be so glum. For all his faults, he was calm and analytical in a crisis. Helped him keep the lab from exploding.

I eyeballed him. "Ah, I know what it is. Trina."

"What if we can't get the Ketacillin?"

"We'll get it."

"Isn't it stored under maximum security? Can we really pull this off?"

We were the best in the business. You wanted it, I smuggled it, but this was a tall order, even for me. With so many mutant bacteria strains cropping up, rare antibiotics sold like liquid gold on the black market.

I pushed aside my doubts and forced a smile. "Absolutely. Get dressed."

He shook his head. "I hope you're right."

We dug into the disguise bag, and I squeezed into a light pink miniskirt and blazer with a white blouse underneath. Pearls flashed at my ears and neck. Black pumps, a puffy blond wig, and a touch of makeup completed the outfit. From cartel boss to corporate whore in three minutes.

If we looked clean and proper, we might avoid a decontamination shower when we passed through Dome immigration. I hated risking our only clean outfits so early in the trip, but if one of my inside guys wasn't on duty, we wouldn't even make it through the first Breakers checkpoint without the right clothes. Usually we had several sets of gear for this—the ride out to the Phoenix Dome would be messy.

Still. We had to try. Avoiding a decon rinse was no small thing—sometimes they forgot to calibrate the sterilization acids. Quick way to find yourself dumped into a fertilizer bin.

He whistled. "Freaks me out when you dress like that. You look so innocent."

I smiled with sickly pink lips. "I like it. People assume I'm a harmless girl." People in the Domes, that was. In the Voids, fancy clothes meant trouble. They'd see my poison lipstick from a mile away.

Dressed as a bodyguard, Argon wore a simple black suit, and a dark wig covered his neon orange hair. When he stood tall with mirrored shades over his eyes and his shoulders squared, he definitely looked the part. As long as he kept his mouth shut.

I looked him up and down. "Not bad. I'd fuck you."

He scratched his head. "I hate these wigs. Gutter glue itches like hell."

"Don't knock the gutter glue. That wig's on so tight even a decon shower won't get it off." I looked over his shoulder. "Your ass looks nice in those slacks."

"Don't even think of kissing me."

I smirked. "No time for monkey business." I walked around the bloodstain, snagged a black clock off the dresser, and thrust it in his face. "The military caravan is leaving in an hour. Get Calavera on the horn right now."

"I'm on it." Argon slunk outside to use a transmitter. The broken Domes of the Breakers created a natural radio barrier—making a call indoors was impossible.

He reappeared a few moments later. "I contacted the nearest enforcer crew, and they've got trouble at the border. The riots-squads can't get here until evening."

Calavera could be lying, but we had the same problem yesterday. Not good. Military patrols should have stopped the riots by now.

"We need to split up. You don't have clearance to trigger the supply order on your own, but once I'm through Dome security, I'll get papers for you to follow. Can you handle this?" I said.

"Got it. I'm a smooth talker."

"If shit gets hairy, call for emergency back up and bail. Head straight for the military compound."

A horrible plan, but I couldn't let this incident slide—showing weakness was fatal.

"You've still got connections to local gangs?" he said.

"Yeah, they're not usually reliable, but they owe us. After last time, they won't let me down."

"Talking about torture while you're wearing that wig is creepy."

"That's part of the fun."

He put his hands in his pockets and rocked back on his heels. "Better go before the convoy leaves without you."

I fluffed the blond wig. "I'm counting on you to rectify this. Another war with Mexico will seriously fuck up our groove."

CHAPTER FOUR

BEHIND THE helm of an ATV, I zipped over mounds of smoking debris. The wind tore at my wig, gutter glue pulling at my scalp but holding fast. I clutched the handlebars, standing with bent knees as I bounced over dead cars that hid like land mines beneath the garbage. I grinned and stomped on the accelerator.

Speed and destruction were my friends.

I needed a covered vehicle to protect my clothes, but our mini-crawler was another casualty of the big explosion at our main base. The motorcycle was faster than the ATV, but Argon might need the extra juice if things went sour. I would have sent him on to the Domes ahead of me while I dealt with Calavera, but his Zone Pass couldn't clear immigration without going through the back end.

And this wasn't a back end job.

Time was burning faster than the smoldering trash piles crunching beneath my tires, but there were no gang choke points along the river corridor. Lucky—plowing through flaming rubble at kamikaze speeds in a bright pink suit wasn't exactly stealthy. Stealth wasn't my style anyway. I preferred to come in the front door, guns blazing, and I didn't have time for a shootout with the local crews.

Those vicious gangs practically ruled the Breakers, but I felt sorry for anyone living there, even the hardcore thugs. They had just enough of the resistance gene to get stuck in limbo—lungs too weak to survive the open air of the Voids but too strong to earn Zone Passes for the Domes.

Funny how that worked. When the government ran out of money, and the working Domes blew capacity, the genetically gifted got a one-way ticket to exile. People like me, with lungs of steel, won the prize of wandering the wastelands. We had a chance. The others weren't quite so fortunate. Trapped in the Breakers, their lives were miserable, but they made perfect customers for Alphadrine. And for that they held a special place in my heart and in my wallet.

I rounded a corner, the powerful ATV munching through trash like breakfast cereal. The engine's whine jumped in pitch, and I downshifted, scouring the gauges for problems. Everything looked fine.

My gaze swung back to the field. Some asshole was lying in the road directly in my path. Sprawled between a concrete pillar and a burned out shack, I had nowhere else to maneuver.

I swerved and hammered on the brakes, but it wasn't enough. I slammed into the edge of the shack. Glass shattered—headlights destroyed. I cursed and beat the steering wheel hard enough that blood seeped through my bandaged hand. I sighed and got out to survey the damage.

Someone was screaming.

Fuck. Still ran him over.

I jogged around the front, jaw tight, arms at my side, ready to punch someone. "What the hell are you doing out here?"

Then I saw him.

It was a kid with red hair, his pale face streaked with grease and mud. He held his wrist and cried.

"Oh Jesus," I said.

Little bastard could have been Argon's kid brother. He wore an oversized button-up shirt, like he'd stolen Dome clothes to play dress up. He wasn't wearing pants, and his bare calves and thighs had deep chemical burns that marbled his legs with dark purple streaks. Shiny white ribbons of shinbone peeked out from the ruined skin, and his feet were already black with flesh rot.

My worst nightmare.

I squinted at his face—some of the filth wasn't actually dirt. Puncture marks crept across his neck, and another line of dead flesh marched up from his collarbone. Kid was a junkie, probably been lying there for days.

He smelled like a corpse.

"Hey, kid, I'm sorry I yelled at you," I said.

He kept holding his injured wrist but stopped crying and stared at me with giant blue eyes, his pupils swollen from drugs. Strange how pain worked—a broken wrist was nothing compared to the massive tissue death eating through the rest of his body, but those pain sensors were already blown out. At least he had smack to keep him company while he died.

"And I'm sorry about your wrist." It was a stupid apology, but I meant it. Would have been better if I'd just crushed his head.

He said nothing, but I cringed. He stared at me, and it was clear part of his brain still worked. He understood what was happening to him. No ten-year-old should live through that.

"Water," he said through cracked lips that stuck together at the corners.

"Let's move you out of the road. Then I'll get you some water."

I couldn't just leave him there. Looking at my pristine outfit and back over to the rancid kid, I scowled, but came around, snatched him under the armpits, and dragged him toward the shack's doorway.

I took dainty steps but lost my footing in the unstable dress shoes. His greasy head flopped back and left a giant mark right in the middle of my skirt, bits of slimy skin clinging to the fabric. Great. The stain would be tough to remove, but if we had enough time before leaving for the Domes, I might get it clean and still avoid a decon shower.

I leaned him up against the front door. He was visible and off the path, so he wouldn't get run over again. Maybe a family member was looking for him. Doubtful, but sometimes even the worst junkies still had people who cared about them. I remembered what that was like, knowing a person I loved had overdosed for the final time. Wouldn't wish that on anyone.

I moved in front of him, trying to get his floppy body into a more comfortable position. He started crying again, sobbing so hard that he gulped air and trembled. I bent down and tried to comfort the kid before he suffocated to death.

He opened his mouth, and I thought he was going to say something. Instead, a waterfall of black vomit gushed into my pumps.

The warm puke smelled like rotten eggs roasted inside a septic tank.

So much for good deeds.

I thought of all the open cuts on my feet. I imagined the dark vomit, teeming with germs, slithering into the puncture wounds. When I looked at his legs, black and dead with flesh rot, in my mind I saw my pale feet, still wearing these ridiculous business shoes, morphing into his rotting stumps.

I gagged once and shook my head to clear the image. Back to work. I had a job to do.

After dumping the puke out of my shoes, I went back to the ATV and grabbed a water bottle out of an armored tackle box mounted above the back seat. I poked around until I found the hinge of a trick lid inside the deepest compartment. I fished out a bag of white powder from the secret space and emptied the whole thing into the bottle.

When I got back, the kid's sobs had quieted, and his eyes were closed.

"Hey, look at me," I said. I shook the bottle until the powder dissolved.

His eyes fluttered open.

"I know this isn't your usual stuff. I don't have any needles, but if you can hold this down for five minutes, you won't feel anything else. It's pure. Five minutes is all it will take," I said. "Got it? Blink once if you understand."

It was a promise I could keep. Only the finest products came out of my cartel. Trina and Argon were geniuses in the lab.

He blinked slowly, eyelids moving like clouds across the dark moons of his pupils.

"Good." I opened the bottle and put it by his uninjured hand.

I wasn't sorry I didn't have the five minutes to sit with him.

Back in the ATV, I raced over the jagged terrain, ignoring the vomit squishing between my toes. Life was ugly in the Breakers, but that kid was bad, even for the River Slums. At least I'd put him out of his misery. The first one's always free, but sometimes that first one is the last.

I followed the river, and within twenty minutes the exit compound came into view. Armed soldiers and tactical vehicles surrounded the small facility. Spools of razor wire twisted around the tops of the red brick walls like savage bird nests. Felt just like home.

I hurtled over one last epic garbage pile, and the ATV went flying, catching wicked air.

"Woo, yeah!" I shouted as my feet levitated off the floorboards.

The thrill was just what I needed to get my juices going again.

The ATV's giant wheels crashed down and couldn't handle the shock. I whipped forward, the handlebars punching me in the stomach. I grunted, lost control, then jumped on the brake pedal with all my weight. Metal screeched, and I jerked the wheel hard to the left. I skidded sideways, and the ATV stopped a few feet from the compound's gate.

Perfect landing.

I took a few seconds to straighten out my clothing, trying to ignore the oily stain on my skirt and the smell rising up from my shoes. When I left the vehicle, five armed soldiers in camouflage gear rushed me. Couldn't blame them after that spectacular entrance. I held up my hands.

"I'm a Class Ten Supply Executive. Name's Petrovna. I'm on your roster for today," I said as the soldiers came within firing range.

"Get down!" the first soldier yelled.

Gas masks clung to their faces. Not locals. Locals didn't need gas masks. The two in the front wore full desert camo gear, but the three in the back wore mismatched uniforms that looked like they'd been fished out of a dumpster. The three ragtag soldiers had name badges and rank stripes safety-pinned on, and they held their rifles awkwardly. Recruits so raw they were sent out into the field without real uniforms or firearms training. Not good.

"No reason to get crazy. Check your roster," I said, leaving my hands up. Getting shot would be a bad way to end the morning.

"Ma'am, you're on fire," the second soldier in desert camo said, his voice fuzzy over the gas mask intercom.

I twisted around. Smoke tendrils floated off the back of my skirt.

"Son of a bitch." I spat on my hand and swatted out the flames. It singed my fingers anyway, and I grimaced.

The burn distracted me for a second, and that's all it took. A bullet ricocheted off the ATV, inches to my right. It was the fourth recruit in the back, wearing a ratty uniform and clutching his rifle with shaky hands. He tensed to squeeze off another round.

The soldier hesitated, and before he could make his move, I snatched a rusted hunk of iron from a trash pile. The sharp metal sliced through my palm, blood flowing down my wrist and soaking the pink jacket sleeve. So much for my suit and my good hand. I hurled the iron at the soldier. It hit his rifle with a solid thwack and swung the muzzle off course.

He fired anyway, and another soldier to his left screamed as the bullet landed in his foot. I rolled behind the ATV. They squabbled over their intercoms, and I couldn't make out what they were saying. I reached over the top of the vehicle, fumbling until I found a round object inside the metal box. Just in case.

My hand was still bleeding, leaving dark smears across the front of my suit. The back of my skirt was wet and clinging to my ass. Fumes burned my eyes, and I didn't want to know what I'd rolled through.

I waited, clutching the object, a burning wetness creeping into my ass cheeks as I listened to their muddy intercom speech. The yelling escalated, and another round of shots pinged against the ATV's grill. The direct attack was enough to give me a green light for self-defense.

I pulled the pin and threw the grenade.

CHAPTER FIVE

A LONG walk down a dirty corridor lit by fluorescent lights brought me through a battered door covered in chipped tan paint. A recruit shoved me into an army-green metal chair and pushed it in front of a matching desk. I wobbled forward and caught myself on the edge. Blood seeped through the dirty rags wrapped around my hands, leaving a stain on the metal.

I killed for less, but the recruit was already gone.

A dark-skinned man wearing desert camo pants, a drab olive shirt, and a military cap walked into the small room and put his hands on his hips just above an impressive array of laser holsters.

"Well, if it isn't Anastasia. Damn, you look like hell," he said and laughed, his thick mustache twitching. "But that outfit is priceless. You could be the secretary of my dreams if you weren't so jacked up. Get on your knees and give me some sugar!"

Dead eyes.

He swallowed and pulled at his shirt collar. "Shit girl, don't take things so seriously, lighten up a little."

A broad smile crept across my face, and I stood up. "Had you there for a second, didn't I?"

He released a lungful of air and laughed. "Bitch, you fucking scared me. These noobs are clueless, but I've seen the shit you've done. That grenade was child's play."

"Sanchez, you never change," I said, and we hugged each other like old army buddies, which wasn't far from the truth. I was half a foot taller than him, and I gave him credit for not making a crack about getting his face stuck in my cleavage.

"Good to see you. You saw the riots? They'll get it under control, but I'm damned happy we've got you on the convoy today. I did a stint out in Texas earlier this month, and some of them runners are just useless. Thought I'd never make it back to Arizona in one piece with those assholes along for the ride."

I stepped back and rested my wet ass on his desk. "Speaking of idiots, what kind of operation are you running here?"

Sanchez put his hand on the back of his head and ruffled the buzz cut poking out from under his hat. "You mean the new recruits? I'm not happy about this either. I've told HQ not to put raw soldiers out at this post, but you can see how well that worked."

"Glad you're not pissed at me for blowing up a chunk of the base."

"Let's get it straight—you aimed away from those fucktards. You don't miss. Hell, you did us a favor by blowing off all that garbage."

"Good. I've had enough trouble for one day—I've already been puked on, stabbed, set on fire, and doused with toxic waste. My ass is burning. If I can't hose off, I'm going to get an unwelcome STD Blaster for a mysterious rash." I held up my hands and thick strings of clotted blood flicked onto my skirt. "And I need to clean these wounds or I'm in for a serious case of flesh rot."

He cringed. "Damn that's nasty—so that's what the lovely smell is."

"Yeah, it's eau du junkie, the latest from the Breakers fragrance collection."

"You can shower off, but there's nothing to change into. No inventory. We're at a record low for supplies."

I stared at him.

"Goddamn it, you know better than I do—you can't wear military gear until you clear Dome inspection, and official digs are all I've got."

"Total bullshit. I'm in for the decon shower from hell." I looked down at the ruins of my burned suit, painted with ash, blood, vomit, and rotting skin. The lingering puke in my shoes was drying, my soles sticking to the inside of the pumps.

I shuddered. A scalding decon bath was starting to seem like a good idea. It would burn like hell, but it would kill bacteria.

Nothing was going right, but I tried to stay positive. At least my wig was still on.

"You're the supply maven. Bring us some new shit," he said.

"I'll get right on that," I said. "Just as soon as someone puts me in charge of the Breakers."

We laughed, and it echoed off the gray walls. Like the government would ever let an outcast get elected into an official position. In any event, I was perfectly happy ruling the misfits.

"The air is getting worse. It may as well be the Voids in here—I have to wear a mask if we're in the field too long," he said.

A few stray soldiers walked through the hallway behind us, the fluorescent lights yellowing their already jaundiced skin. I could almost smell the liver death.

I motioned toward the door. "What gives? We're about to a leave for a major run. Where's all the staff?"

He bared his teeth and jabbed with a stiff finger. "Lazy bastards— they're all from the Domes. Pampered fucks run to mommy and daddy if you take their masks off for one second. They outlawed field shock runs—say they're inhumane. How am I supposed to train them if they can't even spend five minutes in unfiltered air?"

"Makes for a jumpy trigger finger. Jackasses made me waste a perfectly good grenade. You know how hard it is to get grenades out here?"

He took a step toward me, jaw tight. I didn't move. He smelled like ammonia and cigars.

"You know how hard it is to make a grenade explosion disappear on an incident report?" he said.

I put a single finger on his chest and cleared my throat. "Excuse me for not wanting to get shot in the face by a bunch of rookie assholes." I met his eyes without blinking.

He stepped back, and my finger left a perfect oval blood print on his shirt. I rubbed my wet fingertips together.

He coughed and put up his hands. "You're right. It's just...things are tight politically. It's impossible to recruit Breakers kids into the service, even if it means getting them out of this cesspool. That's how we end up with this huge riot and a mess of useless Dome kids pretending to be soldiers. Can't even hold a rifle without pissing their pants." He stopped and stared at me.

I shifted, and the wig fell across my face. A slimy plastic wrapper dangled in the strands like a trapped fly. "What? You think I know something?" I fished out the plastic with two fingers, grimaced, tossed it on the floor. It landed on the dusty gray linoleum, an inch from his tan combat boots.

"I know you run in a lot of circles, and I know you're one clever bitch, so yeah, maybe you do."

I rolled my eyes. "I run with the Voids crews. They hate us out here, and I'm recognizable."

He gave a small, awkward laugh. "I was just wondering if you'd gathered some intel."

"Nothing. I was hoping you had more info—transmitters work for shit down by the river," I said. "By the way, there were some major violations at the immigration gate. We had everything confiscated on entry. Water included."

He walked around the desk and sat on the ripped green padding of a slightly comfier looking office chair. I swiveled and dumped myself back into the hard steel chair.

"That is a load of donkey cock," he said. "But immigration's another jurisdiction. I don't have any sway over what happens at that outpost. You'll have to file an official complaint when we get to Phoenix."

"Figures."

He folded his hands and rested his elbows against the table. "Hell, I don't know what I could do even it was my jurisdiction. This base is chock full of morons. But don't worry, we'll have some old timers on the convoy back to the Phoenix Dome." He leaned forward. "Which reminds me, where's the rest of your crew?"

"Didn't you hear? HQ approved a run with reduced staff since we're just heading out to Yuma. I've got one more guy that's supposed to join us. We had a little trouble down by the waterfront last night—probably related to this uprising. He'll follow after business is taken care of."

Sanchez gave me a sideways glance but nodded. Some things were best left unexplained. I trusted the man, but only so far. He was a Breakers kid, but as a military commander, he was still a Dome drone, even if he was one of the better ones. The recruits from the Breakers always had more perspective, but they were unstable. Hard to trust someone who didn't really understand the concept of loyalty.

"Tough night for everyone?" he said.

I gestured to my clothes. "What do you think?"

He leaned back again and put his feet up on the desk. "Well, Anastasia, even banged up like that, your transformations never cease to amaze me."

He'd seen me out in the Voids, in my natural environment, in my normal clothing and make-up. Almost shat himself when he saw the fluorescent Mohawk.

"Weirds me out when you use my real name," I said.

Military personnel weren't supposed to know my code name, but Sanchez and I had spent major time in the trenches together—still felt strange to have him use my legal name.

He stretched his arms farther over his head. "I have to go by the books around here. Can't let them think we're fraternizing or something like that."

"Heaven forbid," I said sarcastically, but it really was a big problem. They basically lopped off your dick in the decon process if you fucked someone from the Voids.

He widened his eyes at me, half kidding, but there was some genuine fear.

I smirked. "Don't worry, I don't kiss and tell."

He dropped his feet back to the floor. "I know." He paused. "All right, we're running behind schedule as it is. Go clean yourself up so we can get moving."

"You sure the showers in this hellhole still work?"

He raised an eyebrow and smiled. "Sure, they work. There's just no hot water."

CHAPTER SIX

SANCHEZ HUNKERED over the wheel of an armored black cruiser, a full-face gas mask jammed on his head, his squashed mustache poking into the visor.

"You know these budget cuts are murder—can't even get the clearance to oxygenate and filter the whole cabin anymore. Total bullshit. I can barely see the road with one of these things on," he said over the mask's intercom.

Budget cuts. Sure. More like large-scale government failure. My territory might expand after all, but taking over the Casa Grande Breakers wasn't high on my to-do list. Invading Mexico would be less of a pain in the ass and way less work to clean up.

"You want me to drive? We're in my country now." I gestured to the miles of rippling sand that our caravan of black cruisers crawled across like a giant centipede. The Voids. Oxygen-depleted and just beyond the government's fingertips, the merciless land was beautiful. Home.

He scoffed. "Nah, I've gotten used to it, and my CO would have my head if he knew I surrendered a vehicle to a runner before Dome processing. Don't get greedy—at least we won the fight to let you guys hang onto weapons during supply runs."

After millions in cargo kept getting stolen in raids, the government finally agreed to issue lasers to the Voids runners. It made missions much more fun. I loved new toys, especially ones that went kaboom.

"Thanks for the weapons upgrade. I haven't gotten my hands on one of these babies yet." I patted the shiny white laser on my hip. "Bet this thing can smoke someone halfway across the desert."

"Hell yeah it can. No idea how we can afford these upgraded lasers when we can't afford oxygen, but I'll take it."

I held up my bandaged hands. "No idea how you can afford new weaponry when you can't afford decent antibiotics either. I better not fucking die of flesh rot before we get to the Domes." I'd done my best to scrub both of my hands, and I finally had real bandages wadded around my palms, but it wasn't enough.

"Pentoxamycin is all we're allowed to carry out in the field. Too risky to keep anything better in the Breakers—may as well pass around flyers asking for a raid. Good antibiotics are almost worth more than Zone Passes on the black market," he said.

That's why the government hoarded the most powerful antibiotics at remote locations.

Like Yuma.

I smirked.

"Oh...yeah, not like you need to be updated on black market economics." He rubbed the back of his head. The gas mask straps snapped against his fingers.

"The world's a smorgasbord, if you know where to look," I said. "Which is why wearing this disgusting outfit is unacceptable." I slapped at my ruined skirt. I washed it in a sink on base, but it still looked and smelled horrible.

"You can survive without clean clothes, but good weapons are essential. Just be careful—the lasers have recoil on them, like the old six shooters," he said.

I leaned my head against the window. "Won't be a problem for me. I learned how to shoot with real weapons long before these plastic things existed. Any weapons specialist should know how to handle a gun."

Guns weren't hard to get ahold of. Bullets, on the other hand, were a different story. After the big weapons sanctions, ammunition became extraordinarily expensive. I could get bullets, but it would cost, big time. Lasers worked great, but they were illegal in the Voids. Even though the scanning satellites had been pulled from the sky, and government foot patrols were nearly a thing of the past, getting caught with an illegal laser still carried a death sentence.

Wasn't worth it most of the time. I preferred to do my killing with blades anyway—more personal.

"Damn right," he said. "Any bastard can pull off a half decent shot with these fucking pocket rockets. It takes talent to do it the old fashioned way."

I'd seen his skills with traditional weapons, and he was good. Not as good as me, but still, decent. Good enough to cover my ass in a firefight at least.

"Hope you're right. I'm not thrilled to be piloting this parade of retards, but at least they're well-equipped retards," I said. "Those kids that shot at me back on base didn't even have real uniforms."

"The situation isn't good." He fidgeted in his seat and tugged his collar.

I peered at him. "You heard something."

"Not exactly. Nothing official," he said.

I was a good listener. I'd been a professional listener at one point. I could wait until he came out with it. He shifted in the seat, his heavy gear clattering over the road noise. He looked back and forth between me and the road, waiting for me to restart our usual banter. I kept quiet.

I loved watching people squirm.

He cleared his throat. "Like I said, it's nothing official. It's just. You know. I'm from the Breakers."

"Of course. You can survive the air out here in the Voids for a while. Unlike all the riffraff we've got trailing behind us."

"Wouldn't want to test it, but you're probably right. You know why I'm the only local on this run?"

"Doesn't take a genius to figure out why a bunch of oppressed citizens won't work for their tormentors," I said. "No offense."

"Right. But before, the perks of enlisting outweighed the other issues. Why stay in a prison when you can become a guard? Now no one's taking the bait."

"Not everyone has your steely resolve."

"Cute. Like you're so loyal to the establishment."

"I follow the rules. It just so happens there are different rules for the Voids and the Domes," I said.

"Convenient. I'll remember that when everything blows up."

"You think there's a real revolution starting."

His hands flexed on the steering wheel. "This doesn't leave the car."

"Absolutely." I didn't bother saying anything about trust. Trust didn't exist in the Breakers.

"My little brother...I got him relocated to the Gila Bend Breakers. Nowhere near as awful as Casa Grande, less enforcers around. Last week he told me he's been hearing things."

"They let you talk to your brother?" I said.

"No."

Illegal contact. When a Breakers exile joined the military, the government forced them to sever their old connections. No family. No friends. Part of a loyalty brainwashing program they started five years ago.

Sanchez's secret could get him thrown in jail or even executed. Bold move letting that out, but we had so much dirt on each other that the blackmail was implicit. Sanchez was one of the few Dome drones who knew what I really did for a living.

"If you ever need help getting anything to him—supplies, money—I can take care of it," I said. We didn't traffic in Gila Bend often, but it was on our list of safe zones.

He laughed. "You never miss a business opportunity."

"Sometimes you only get one chance to make a sale."

"Got that right," he said.

"What else did your brother have to say?"

He breathed heavy into the respirator, and it crackled through the mask. "Not much. Don't know if he was scared or excited. Can't talk to him for long without getting busted. All he said was things were happening and there was talk of an uprising."

"There's always talk of uprisings," I said. "It's good for business—people panic and want to stockpile more shit."

"Has business been good lately?"

I clenched my teeth. "No, it hasn't."

"It's not fear mongering."

I tugged at my stained jacket and looked at the floorboards. "We shouldn't be doing this run."

"Government doesn't think anything's wrong. I have to be here. Question is, why are you here?"

"Friend of mine is sick. There's some shit I have to bring back from Yuma to fix her. I have to go."

He waggled a finger at me. "The antibiotics. Now I know why you're so paranoid." I didn't respond to his accusation, and he continued, "You sure there's nothing else? No ears on us right now—bugs don't work out here. We can talk real."

"You sure you're okay knowing cartel business?" If he spilled the beans, I would be the least of his worries. Ignorance was almost always safer.

"It won't be an issue."

I looked up and crossed my legs, nearly ripping the tight skirt. "We made a truce with Las Calacas, the big Nogales cartel. Real assholes. Leader's this crazy chola, Calavera. They were up my ass trying to take over Tucson, so we made a deal. Shit seemed fine. Then last night one of her armored enforcers came after us. Just one guy."

"Anyone with half a brain wouldn't try to take you out with just a single assassin."

"That's what makes it so weird. Couldn't get face time with Calavera before meeting up with you. I left my point man behind to knock some heads together."

"Oh good, I'm sure your one guy can totally prevent the next civil war from breaking out," he said.

Leaving Argon had seemed like my only option, but I was feeling worse about the decision as time went on. I already had one dying crewmember on my hands.

I punched Sanchez's leg. He gripped the steering wheel a little tighter but didn't flinch.

"You've literally got a whole army behind you, and I don't see you doing any revolution squashing. Don't underestimate the power of the little guy." I eyed the radio receiver, tempted to yank it off the hook and try to make contact with Argon, see if he was okay. But I couldn't make that kind of call from a military vehicle. It would have to wait.

He looked at me. "You sure you'd want to stop something like that?" His crushed mustache slowly twitched behind the plastic visor.

I waited, thinking about my answer.

"I don't mean from a business standpoint either. I've read your file. You were kicked out of the Domes. Aren't you angry?" he said and then whispered, "Like the rest of us?"

"I'm done trying to save people. And that includes myself."

"Aren't you trying to save someone right now?"

"That's different. Anyone on my crew is guaranteed full protection. And right now that includes you, so consider yourself fortunate," I said. "Everyone else can go fuck themselves."

I'd moved past the anger long ago. I was comfortable in the Tucson Voids, and it was more fun to exploit the system than it was to fight it. Or so I liked to think.

"Glad to hear that," he said. "You know, there's a lot of eyes on you. People admiring what you've done with Tucson. Made it a real city again. That's the kind of thing they want for the Breakers."

I crossed my arms. "That chat with your brother doesn't sound like it was all that short."

More eyes on me wasn't what I needed. I couldn't completely hide what a figurehead I'd become in Tucson, but the Arizona government was willing to look the other way. I was their best runner. They needed me, and I wanted the Dome access. When someone didn't look the other way, they had a funny way of disappearing in the desert. Saguaro cacti make beautiful headstones, but I wasn't in the mood to dig any more holes in the sand.

"Just don't be surprised if you're suddenly popular," he said.

"Shit, Sanchez. I don't have time for crap like this. Let's just focus on the mission."

"You got it, Xero."

I raised an eyebrow, and we turned our attention back to the road, but I kept glancing at Sanchez—too bad the gas mask hid most of his face. I was good at reading body language, but his eyes would tell me everything. I'd never thought of him as the revolutionary type. Then again, I hadn't known about the secret brother trapped in the Breakers. He oozed guilt, and guilt was a powerful motivator. Maybe Sanchez was more than just a sharpshooter and an ass-grabber after all.

The wind picked up, and dust billowed in great clouds around us. The powerful cars struggled against the gusts, and we swiveled through the dunes, heavy tires fighting for traction in the deep sand. Even through the insulated walls and tinted windows, fingers of desert heat caressed my skin. I smiled. It looked barren, but it was alive. Desert creatures were survivors.

"You look pretty happy for someone with two crew members circling the drain," he said.

"I'm happy anywhere I feel free. And if you make anymore jokes about my crew dying, I'll make sure you reach the grave before they do."

"I wasn't trying to be a dick. You know how long I've been out here in the trenches. I'm just saying to be careful. We've got a serious situation on our hands."

"I'm always on guard," I said and went back to scanning the terrain for obstacles.

I kept my gaze wandering over the sand and my ears open for any sign of trouble from the radio. Nothing but silence and blowing sand. Just the way I liked it.

I was staring at a lone saguaro when the cruiser's back wheels reared up and threw us at the windshield.

"Fuck!" I yelled.

The vehicle teetered on its nose for a second before giving way and lurching forward. The cruiser flipped over, the metal slapping the sand with a hollow thump.

We dangled upside down like failed trapeze artists, and the seat belt crushed my boobs. Sometimes it paid not to have enormous tits. I released the belt and toppled onto the gearshift. My hip took most of the blow, and I stifled a grunt. That would leave a bruise. Sanchez plopped down next to me, landing on the driver's seat in an awkward position that put me eyelevel with his crotch.

He raised his eyebrows.

"Not now you pervert," I said. I kicked at the door, but the cruiser was sinking into the sand, sealing it shut.

"Watch your eyes." Sanchez fired a shot into the windshield. Safety glass exploded into the cabin, and I shielded my face, but a few chunks flew in my mouth. The taste of blood flipped an internal switch.

Ready for a fight.

Sanchez started to move, and I stopped him. "Wait. Tell me this isn't you. Tell me you didn't know this was going to happen," I said.

"I promise you, on my brother's life, I have no idea what's going on," he said with more sincerity than I'd ever heard from him.

I spat out glass. "Okay. Let's do this."

We scrambled through the new opening in the window and assumed tactical positions on either side of the vehicle. At least Sanchez was with me instead of one of those idiot recruits. Next best thing to being with one of my Grease Weasels.

Another cruiser was wedged behind our disabled vehicle. The plates and government markings said it was from the original convoy, but a Skeleton exited the driver's door. Hot sand seeped into my useless business shoes. I kicked off the pumps and left them in the dust.

I aimed between the Skeleton's eyes and squeezed the trigger, bracing for the recoil.

The Skeleton's head exploded.

Combat veteran or not, the decapitation surprised me. Never

seen that kind of firepower from such a small laser. The body flopped into the sand, but the head never hit ground. Mincemeat. Sanchez wasn't kidding about the new equipment.

Blasts rocked the sand, and I dove for cover at the front of the vehicle. Sanchez had the same idea, and I slammed into him, my shoulder colliding with his ribcage. The stupid pencil skirt and disgusting jacket were slowing me down, so I tore them off, leaving me with nothing but the stained white blouse and a pair of pink panties.

I gave Sanchez a look. "Don't even start."

"Wouldn't dream of it."

"These are the Skeletons from Nogales. Even if Calavera broke our treaty, she has no reason to attack a government convoy. You were right. Something big is happening." I gripped the laser. "Pro tip—these are strong enough to bust open their helmets, but their chest armor is tougher. Aim carefully, and you can hit a gap at the center of the throat. Or, if you've got the leverage and a sharp enough blade, you should be able to pierce it with a knife."

"Got it," he said. "Headshots it is."

Another explosion jolted the earth. Greasy smoke plumes mushroomed like storm clouds in the clear desert air. Burning tar fumes filled my nose. From the smell alone, I knew they were using quality explosives, the kind that went off big and burned until there was nothing left. No one in the cruisers would survive. The recruits paid for their incompetence with their lives, and I wasn't ready to pay with mine.

"Hey—got anything else on you?" I asked.

He handed me two large KA-BAR style knives on a belt holster.

"Thanks, man." I secured the holster while he attempted to use his cracked communicator to radio a message into HQ.

I peeked around the corner. Jesus. Had to be two dozen Skeletons crawling through the convoy wreckage. Where the hell had they come from?

"Shit," Sanchez said. "We've got company."

"We're in a bad position, and they're not short on ballistics. We need to sweep the field. Kill what you can, then snag the last cruiser and make a run for the Dome."

Five Skeletons stood between us and the vehicle, but he nodded without hesitation. Escape was still our best bet.

"Agreed. On three," he said and counted.

We sprang into action. I dive-rolled to the left as the two

Skeletons on my side took pot shots. I was a pro at fighting in sand, and I rolled straight back onto my feet, ready to go.

I squeezed off two quick rounds of laser fire. The first nailed a headshot, and I was rewarded with another skull splattered across the desert like a ruined jack-o-lantern. The second shot went low and landed in another Skeleton's chest. It fell to its knees but didn't die. Coughing and gagging, it still waved its laser. Closing the distance, I jammed a KA-BAR into the Skeleton's throat.

Perfect shot. Instant death.

Withdrawing the knife, I turned to face the next one. Sanchez had taken down two Skeletons on his side, leaving one more for me to waste. The Skeleton dashed, its laser raised to melt my face. No room to retreat, so I took the next best option.

I bent my knees and sprang forward, tackling it into the sand and knocking the laser out of its hands. I rammed the knife through the vulnerable spot, and it ripped through its larynx. The knife kept going, slicing up through its chin and jamming into its hard palate. It never had a chance to scream.

More Skeletons advanced from the rear, and Sanchez jumped into the empty cruiser.

"Get in here!" he yelled.

I dashed for the open door, but a sick thunk in my gut made me stop, took me off balance. Pain blasted through my side. A Skeleton had a knife blade stabbed up to the hilt, down through the bottom of my ribs, deep into my belly.

I turned to deal with the attacker, but it raised a laser and fired a shot past my head. The beam missed my face and landed with a small zap in Sanchez's chest. He grunted, and I didn't know if the hit was critical. Laser damage could be deceiving.

I bent back into an agonizing pose that twisted the knife deeper into my ribs. Breathing hard, I shot at the Skeleton's neck, but the pain cost me accuracy, and I missed. I didn't have the right leverage to pierce its Calaca suit with my knife. Then I remembered my emergency defense.

I leaned forward and more blood squirted from the knife wound. Ignoring the bleeding, I grabbed the Skeleton by the head and pulled it toward my face. Through the facemask, its lips were exposed, and from their plump shape, I knew it was a woman. I planted a wet smooch right on her mouth. Within seconds the Skeleton was gagging and choking. I shoved her out of the car. I always said fashion was murder.

I looked back and found Sanchez slumped in the driver's seat, gushing blood. He wasn't moving.

"Motherfucker," I said. No time to get Sanchez's body out of the driver's seat. I hopped in the passenger seat. In the rearview mirror, I saw more Skeletons advancing on the vehicle.

Without closing the doors, I stomped on the gas and steered the damned thing from the passenger seat. The cruiser surged through tall mounds of sand, open doors flapping as it swerved and threatened to roll, but I kept my foot bolted to the gas pedal. We had a decent chance of living through a rollover, but there was little chance of surviving if the Skeletons caught up. The clumsy speed paid off, and the smoke from the ruined convoy receded into the distance.

I didn't see any Skeletons on our tail, but that didn't mean much. Vision blurry, I squinted through the curtains of dust shooting up in our wake, not trusting my eyes. The roaring wind and hot sand that splashed through the open doors seemed muted and faraway. I caught my reflection in the mirror. Pale lips. I'd lost way too much blood.

With one hand, I ripped off chunks of my blouse and tried to stabilize the knife. It burned in my chest, but I couldn't pull it out— the knife was keeping pressure on the veins and arteries it had severed on its journey through my abdomen. Removing it would mean death.

Hot winds gusted through the cabin, but a hard chill traveled through my body. Darkness tugged at the corners of my vision. I shivered. My eyelids closed.

I forced my eyes open again. Someone else needed to drive, but Sanchez was limp. He was alive, his chest still rising, but I couldn't tell where he was hit—was it a heart strike? All I saw was a tangled mess of charred shirt and flesh. Our blood mixed and soaked the seats. Who had lost more?

Who would croak first?

The Dome appeared on the horizon. Close, so close but my fingers slid off the wheel. The pain faded. I didn't want it to. Shock was pulling me under. The world started swirling, and I couldn't tell if it was real or just my brain tripping out.

Nausea.

Spinning.

A kaleidoscope of sand.
My bare foot slipped off the accelerator.
Unlike a real cowboy, I would die with my boots off.

CHAPTER SEVEN

COLD. THE cold was back, inching up my toes and crawling through my veins until my joints creaked with invisible frost. A red light blinked on the thick stainless steel door—locked. I had a private suite. Swanky, but a fancy prison was still a prison.

I rolled to my side and stared at the rows of monitors and pumps beeping and pulsing around me. The small movement sent pain snaking through my stomach. I blinked. Breathed. Tried to figure out if I was still dying.

My hands were swathed in thick white cotton, but my fingertips peeked through the bandages. The nails were a dark, dusky purple, like the end of twilight. Shit. Either the bandages were cutting off my circulation, or I was right about the flesh rot. I couldn't live without my fingers. I had to know.

I pried at the wrappings with my numb fingertips, but I couldn't peel off the industrial tape that held the dressings in place. Too cold. And there was no call button. No way to contact anyone. No way to ask for help. I glanced at my dying fingers and squashed a wave of panic. Panic never helped anything.

Metal vents perforated by hundreds of tiny holes ran around the top of the room, blasting polar wind in all directions. The thermostat was just behind me, its cruel red digital lights blinking, creeping lower by fractions of a degree with every passing second. I had to kill it.

I reached hard, stretching until my fingers flailed in the air, inches from the controls. Not enough. I jerked forward, but cried out and curled into a ball when a sharp pain stabbed through my gut, leaving me gasping and shivering. So much for good hospital service.

Breathe. Regroup.

My mind was taking a vacation in an imaginary pile of warm sand when the door whirred and clicked open.

"Please state your name and Zone Status."

I opened my eyes to a nurse in dark blue scrubs dragging a stylus across a chrome-plated tablet.

"Anastasia Petrovna. Special Supply Agent, senior. Maximum Zone Status in effect until the termination of an A-Level classified mission," I said automatically, my voice hoarse. Just as well. The other things I had to say weren't quite so polite.

"How are you feeling?" the nurse continued as though I hadn't responded. Her eyes never moved from the tablet and a tight bun bounced over the top of her head when she scribbled.

I coughed and knew I'd been intubated. My throat was raw even over whatever meds they had me on. "I feel like I was stabbed, left to die, pumped full of drugs, and then frozen like cheap sushi."

The nurse gave a terse nod. "You were treated for a fully penetrating stab wound with associated blood loss and shock trauma. Surgery was performed to explore damage to the abdominal cavity and to clean and close the wound."

Wasn't the worst thing I'd survived.

I squinted under the bright fluorescent lights and forced myself to orient to the space and think more clearly so I could get the information I needed. Shiny chrome equipment and the pristine white furnishings told me I was at the main hospital in the Phoenix Dome. Spared no expense. A quick retinal scan would have revealed my identity. At least they knew the value of a top runner and hadn't let me die. I moved billions of dollars in cargo every year.

"I'm freezing. And I can't feel my hands," I said.

The nurse finally looked at me with small, round brown eyes. "You shouldn't be lying on your side like that."

She had a valid point, yet she made no move to help me roll over.

"I need you to answer me. Why is it so cold? Why don't I have a call button, and what is wrong with my fingers?" I held up a ghoulish hand in her direction. I'd seen plenty of corpses, and it looked like I should start sending out funeral invitations for my fingers.

"Now that your mental status has been assessed, you will be sedated for rapid healing protocols," she said.

Of course. They didn't want any dirty Voids people stinking up their pretty hospital. I touched my head. My wig was gone. Even without my chart, hospital staff would know I was an exile.

"That doesn't answer any of my questions," I said.

"Your cancer status remains low," she added, her eyes returning to the tablet. "Signs point toward being a good rapid healing candidate. Your recovery should be swift and have minimal repercussions."

I had that going for me. Out in the Voids we were all slowly dying of cancer, but repeated exams said I would stay clear of the big C for a long time—I was an investment that would stay viable for several years. They needed me alive. Hopefully they also thought I needed my fingers.

"That's fantastic. Now. My hands. Answer me," I said.

"You're going to be fine. You need to be cooled for the rapid healing. It helps prevent cardiac arrest."

"This is painful. It's inhumane. You're breaking protocols. You have to give me a call button, I need a full medical report so I can give informed consent, and you can't make me dangerously cold without sedating me first. I'm injured and adapted to a much hotter climate. I breathe different air than you. This hurts."

The raw sting of filtered Dome air burned my throat. For some, the shock of moving between the two environments was dangerous, and Voids dwellers often died entering a highly oxygenated Dome for the first time. As a runner, I could transition without much risk, but it was still uncomfortable. By law they should have helped me with the air and temperature flux.

"You are receiving a higher standard of care than people like you are entitled to," she said.

I went cold in a completely different way. The nurse was lucky my hands were as numb as my psyche.

"I need to know what doctor is assigned to this case," I asked smoothly. I even kept my teeth from chattering. Patience. Resolve. I would have my vengeance, one way or another.

"I'm sorry, I can't divulge that information," she said without lifting her gaze.

I exhaled through my nose and clenched my toes underneath the white hospital blanket. "Can you please tell me what happened to Commander Raul Sanchez?" I said. "You're required to provide me with that information per sector regulations. This is a military law. Violations carry a federal prison sentence."

The nurse raised her head and gave one curt shake. "I don't have that information."

We stared each other down like pit bulls in a prizefight.

"I see," I replied, ever so politely. Everything in this room was being recorded. "Please use your clearance to access his status for me. It should be available on your tablet."

"Try to relax," she said. "You'll be sedated later this afternoon."

Translation: don't cause trouble. An actual cyborg would be warmer, but those were outlawed long ago. The nurse sauntered out and slammed the door, the locking mechanism whirring shut a moment later.

At least I wasn't cuffed to the bed. I didn't know how much time I had. If they were planning on amputating my hands, I had to get out of there before I was sedated. If I could make it back to Tucson, Milo would save me and my hands. I had to push past this.

The vents were still pumping out cold air, but I couldn't let that stop me. I took a breath and ripped off the thin hospital sheets. An icy gust kissed my bare legs, and I resisted the urge to put the covers back on. This had to be done.

I must have crashed and rolled the vehicle when I passed out because cuts and bruises painted my body. A network of bandages crisscrossed from my collarbone down to my waist. Part of me hoped I could stay for the rapid protocol—healing naturally would take months, but rapid healing sequences also came with big risks. Like organ failure.

With the sheets off, I could see past my toes. From the foot of the bed, a shiny new tablet blinked at me from its charging dock. The nurse was trying to fuck me over, but I wasn't totally screwed. That tablet was my ticket to salvation. I thought of my skewered organs and the swath of bandages across my abdomen. This would not feel good.

I sat up, and pain sliced right through the drugs. I bit my tongue to stifle screams. Plastic cording whipped against my wrist and pulled at my hand. Multiple IV lines. They had me juiced to the max with antibiotics and pain meds, and my gut still hurt. Lucky to be alive at all.

If I had my way, I'd be alive and still keep my fingers. I visualized my safe place again, sent my mind into that hot desert nirvana where I couldn't feel pain. With that image in my head, I lurched forward and tried to use my forearms to snag the tablet—missed it, but I refused to give up. I went again, this time ignoring the pain and internal warning flares.

It worked—I got the momentum to push myself down far enough to scoop up the slim device. I thanked modern engineering for crafting such light, compact technology.

Then something crunched in my belly.

I clutched the tablet, flopped back against the hard pillows, and spent a minute breathing heavily through the throb in my stomach. Red spots leaked through the white bandages. Probably ripped some stitches, but it was worth it. Living was pointless if I lost my hands—I couldn't protect anyone without them.

When the pain subsided, I pulled the sheets back over my legs and set to work on the tablet. My fingers were heavier than dead tree stumps, but all I needed was gravity to mash the interface. Hacking was one of my weaker skills, but it only took a few minutes of noodling before the mainframe opened to my touch. Assholes never updated their network security.

Vengeance first. Just in case I died, I left a nice surprise for my nurse friend. Evan was dead, but she taught me a thing or two about hacking before leaving this world. Thanks to her, I knew some handy computer tricks, and that nurse would be sorry she ever fucked with me.

Using another one of Evan's hacks, my medical record popped right up. Just a glance and I was relieved. There was some other garbage in there about a punctured lung and having my gallbladder and a foot of intestines removed, but I didn't really care. What I cared about was flesh rot.

And there was none. My hands had poor circulation from the all trauma and blood I lost during the Skeleton fights. As long as I lived through the rapid healing protocol, they would be back to normal. Sweet relief. If I wasn't missing a foot of intestines, I would have done a happy dance.

Few things are more important than my hands, but I pursed my lips and poked at the screen until I found the next file. I smiled. That bastard Sanchez had made it after all. The laser blast had tagged him in the chest, nicking his heart and destroying his shoulder joint on the way out. A bad wound, but the shot missed totally creaming his heart, and the strike was clean. Good thing lasers didn't leave shrapnel. I'd been hit with real bullets, and it wasn't an experience I wanted to relive.

I gripped the device, so tempted to contact my team back in Tucson. Maybe they'd heard from Argon. The urge was strong, but I couldn't: too risky. Better to die than destroy the whole organization.

With that option off the table, I moved on to the next priority. After digging through layers of search engine filters, I tapped into taboo websites for riot news stories. I'd just found an article about the attacks when the same nurse marched back in. The heavy steel door whammed shut behind her. High security room.

I kept pecking at the screen and didn't bother to look up. "My clearance level gives me legal access to this tablet and associated hospital files," I said. No lie. I was that good.

The nurse's spotless white shoes clacked against the shiny floors as she stomped her way to the bed. "You've violated no less than ten hospital policies."

"I just told you that I wasn't breaking any laws."

"Like Void trash would know anything about our laws." Her hair was pulled back so tightly that it yanked at her scalp, stretching her face.

I set the tablet on my lap and squinted at her nametag. "Amelia. You're wrong. Read your hospital handbook. Read the Phoenix Dome laws. And just for your information, everything you have in the Domes is possible because of Void trash like me. We suffer so you can live the good life. You're welcome."

She smoothed down her scrubs, her beady eyes squinted into brown specks. "There will be consequences for this."

I smirked and pointed to the tablet. "You're right. I've already reported your inappropriate behavior, poor bedside manner, and policy violations to the hospital system. Tonight should be fun for you. At the very least you'll lose your job. If you're really lucky, you'll go to jail. That is, unless you feel like changing your mind. Follow the rules. Bring me a military commander, and I'll consider erasing the report I just submitted."

She ran a clawed hand through her hair, ruining the tight updo. A strand of hair fell across her pale forehead. "You're clearly delusional and violent. No one will believe you." She grabbed a capped syringe out of her scrub pockets. A pale yellow liquid glowed under the fluorescent lights.

"Right, so delusional and violent that I hacked into the hospital record system and filed a perfectly coherent performance note. Oh, and I already uploaded the security footage from this room onto an auxiliary server, in case you were thinking of deleting it." I gestured at the small cameras mounted to the stainless steel ceilings. Checkmate.

Her face flushed. Another strand of hair fell out of the bun. "Why are you doing this?"

"All I wanted was information, but you refused. You treated me like shit for no reason. You're like a spoiled child. You want something to cry about? Come to my playground in the Voids. Take a fieldtrip to the Breakers. I'll show you real sadness. Here, all you have to do is follow the rules. Do your job. But you can't even manage that."

I reached for the tablet, but the nurse grabbed it first. She slammed it back into the cradle. The soft tinkling of shattered glass echoed in the empty room.

"I won't add that to the report—the damaged equipment will end up in your shift summary anyway. But if you bring me another tablet and let me talk to a military commander, I can undo the other submission. Clear your record," I said.

Her bangs escaped the hair tie and flopped over her pinhole eyes. She huffed and tore at the bun. Hair tumbled around her shoulders—it was wavy and longer than I had imagined. She almost looked human.

I laughed. "Good job. Let it all out. Life isn't fair. This is just a taste of the future."

"Enough. Lights out for you." She stuck the syringe into an IV line and pushed the contents in too fast, burning my veins.

A warm euphoria dripped over me as more blood soaked through the bandages and bloomed across the white sheets

"Hey. I'm bleeding again. You might want to do something about that. It'd be a bummer if I died on your watch. For both of us," I said, annunciating my words to keep from slurring.

She pounded the empty syringe into the orange sharps container on the wall.

Monitors flashed and squawked around me. "My blood pressure is falling. Something important ruptured," I said.

"Next shift begins in two hours. Have fun." She pulled her hair back into a ponytail and plodded out of the room.

I won. I broke her mind and destroyed her little world. The

administration would fire her, and I'd have my revenge. Preferably before I died. I hear revenge tastes less sweet when you're dead.

Now it was a race between me and the sedatives. How fast could I make a tourniquet out of a hospital sheet?

Good thing I used to be a doctor.

And a drug addict.

I go down hard.

Chapter Eight

THE NIAGARA Hotel was supposed to be the zenith of modern comfort, but there was a stale sadness about it. The facade was all shiny metal and soft baby blue neon tubes that flowed across picture windows like running water. Everything about it promised some bright future where nature and technology would fuse into symbiotic harmony.

Right.

The whole place was one big lie, a propaganda beacon for the Domes. They couldn't afford luxury. Their resources were dwindling. Their days were numbered. They lived the high life while everything crumbled around them. Soon they would be buried under the same dirt and despair that us exiles had suffered in for the last twenty years.

But until then, I would enjoy their spiffy hotel.

The Dome system pumped pollution directly into the Voids, but the process wasn't perfect, even though the government claimed it was. I breathed in dry filtered air and subtle whiffs of industrial waste. Silver cars glided down the wide streets. Herds of people in pressed suits walked across clean sidewalks. Downtown Phoenix churned with activity, but the air was cool and silent. No wind. Only soft voices and quiet electric engines hummed through the busy financial district.

I looked up at the blue sky hologram and squinted until I saw the Dome shell twinkling beneath the illusion. Phoenix in the summer should blister skin, but it was a perfect seventy-five degrees.

The creepy Phoenix Dome wasn't my favorite place, but I felt good, almost cheerful. We didn't have rapid healing protocols out in the Voids, and I really wished we did. It didn't work well for infections or chronic problems like cancer and flesh rot, but it was a goddamned miracle for wound healing. The bandages on my abdomen were gone, and I could bend down to touch my toes without pain. The slashes on my hands already looked several years old instead of several days.

Back in business.

A detail of ten fresh military recruits escorted me to the lobby. Totally excessive. The government knew how dangerous I was, but they didn't have enough trained personnel for the assignment. It was the American way—substitute quantity for quality.

Glass doors slid open and refrigerated air whooshed over the sides of my shaved head. The hotel was designed as one big cylinder of rooms stacked around a hollow center, and the central lobby ceiling soared thirty floors into the air. Frosted blue glass coated the inside of the circular tube, and I watched the outlines of speedy elevators as they zipped up and down inside the glass shell.

The lobby desk was another mass of glowing blue glass and neon tubes, floating in the entryway like a celestial iceberg. The pale desk attendant ignored us, like it was normal for a whole platoon of soldiers to march into the hotel. We zoomed up to the fourteenth floor in the transparent elevator, and I admired the upgraded facilities as each level whipped by.

After reaching the precipice of my designated room, all but one soldier went back downstairs, leaving me alone with a recruit that looked young enough to be my son. Once the hallway was clear, he grabbed my arm and tried to push me into the door.

Pathetic. I easily broke his grip and stepped to the side. I wanted to toss him down the stairs, but cameras were recording everything.

"You just assaulted an officer. An officer on a medical hold. Do we have some kind of a problem here?" I said.

The young man wore a crisp blue dress uniform that looked like it had come right off the assembly line. He was thin, and his blond, buzzed hair was so pale it was almost white. He reminded me of the bland serial killers and mass murderers that popped up in news broadcasts.

"You're the problem."

Again? Maybe it was because of the riots—Dome citizens don't care for exiles, but usually they limited their displeasure to ugly looks and whispered comments. Or maybe this little twat didn't like edgy women. Stripped of my wig and makeup, I obviously didn't belong, despite the military uniform. Straight out of the hospital they stuffed me in a dark blue coat that buttoned up to my chin and a matching skirt that stopped well above the knee. Super practical.

I inhaled, relishing the rich smell of the hotel. I made sure the pleasure showed on my face. "You jealous or something? Sad you don't get to order room service and sleep on expensive sheets? Or do you just get off on smacking women around?"

The recruit's mouth puckered. "I would never be jealous of something like you."

"A simpleton like you can't appreciate luxury like this anyway. There's only one reason Dome brats like you join the military. Got a shit score on your IQ exam, didn't you? And Mommy and Daddy can't buy your way into the state college anymore."

The recruit's fists clenched. "Fuck you. I'll still go to college one day. I'm not Void trash."

Big mistake. My eyes went dead, and the change had an immediate effect on the recruit.

He froze. "I...I didn't mean it like that." His fingers fidgeted inside his fresh white gloves.

I walked toward him, one foot crossed in front of the other like I was going down a catwalk. The high heels sunk into the plush royal blue carpet, but I still towered over his puny frame. He took a hasty step backward, tripped over his own feet, and smacked into the wall.

I leaned my arm against the gilded wallpaper beside his head. "I'm pretty sure you meant it just like that."

He swallowed, scanning the hallway.

"Don't worry, I'm not going to hurt you. Your own life is punishment enough. Sorry, buddy, but you're not long for this world. You'll never survive your first real skirmish in the Breakers." I pulled away and stood a few feet from him, hands on my hips. "So I'll do you a favor—I'll make sure you lose your job. For your own protection."

Then I zoomed in again, my lips close to his. He inhaled, eyes wide, shrinking into the wall.

I grabbed his balls and whispered, "And I better not see you again. Next time, I take these with me."

He cringed and sunk to the floor, curling away from my touch.

Another pawn flicked off the board.

I left the recruit to marinate in his soiled undies as I sauntered into my hotel room, softly closing the door behind me. I leaned my head against the wall and closed my eyes. Privacy at last. Restraint had its rewards.

Full of chrome and gratuitous neon tubes that lit the room with a soft blue glow, the room followed the same eerie style. Even the curtains were made of a blue fabric that had blinking fiber optic cables interwoven into the panels. But if the bed was half as soft as it looked, piled high with feather pillows and fluffy chenille blankets, I would sleep well tonight. A mound of plush blue and white towels, pajamas, and an oversized bathrobe were neatly stacked in rows on a metallic dresser next to a large flat screen television.

It would feel so good to wear something that wasn't a hospital gown or a sexist uniform. I was fantasizing about hot water and clean towels when someone knocked. I don't give second chances. I put my eye to the peephole and hoped for his sake it wasn't the blond recruit.

The boy was gone, but a pair of older, higher ranking soldiers stood at attention in the hallway. About time they sent someone of an appropriate rank.

After opening the door, I had a good feeling about the officers just from their expressions. I saw battle experience in their hard eyes, and they wore fatigues instead of the obnoxious dress uniforms all the Dome military staff paraded around in.

"Agent Petrovna?" the taller one said. His uniform was dirty, like he'd just come back from the field. Stubble dotted his dark skin, and when he removed his cap, thick black hair curled at his temples. Stripes told me he was a few ranks higher than his partner.

"The one and only."

He extended his hand. "Captain Stone. Pleased to meet you, ma'am. We heard about what you did for Sanchez."

I gave his hand a firm shake.

The younger one was tanned, and with his light blue eyes and overgrown sun bleached hair, he looked more like a surfer than a soldier.

"Lieutenant Avery." He stepped forward and shook my hand. "Sorry to disturb you, ma'am. Can't thank you enough for what you did. Sanchez is like a father to me."

"Sanchez is a good man. I'm glad he'll pull through. We really had our asses handed to us," I said.

They nodded, and I was grateful neither wanted to rehash the details of the ambush. A tall piece of black luggage sat behind them. Stone wheeled it forward and gave me the handle. I raised an eyebrow.

"Everything you need should be in there. Things are happening—it's getting hot. Once you go back inside, we'll reactivate the hall security cameras for safety purposes," Stone said.

"I'll be supervising all the patrols this evening, ma'am. We were delayed getting here because of the problems at the border," Avery said.

"We'll see to it you're not disturbed the rest of the evening. As I understand it, you were also gravely injured and could use some sleep," Stone said.

I gave them a genuine smile. "Thank you. When this has blown over, I'll have to buy us all a round of drinks. Good luck dealing with these new recruits. They're quite a handful," I said.

"You're telling me." Avery rolled his eyes.

Stone kicked Avery's foot.

"Sorry, sir," Avery whispered to Stone, and I swallowed a laugh.

Avery turned to me and said, "It's been very challenging, ma'am."

"There was an incident, just a minute ago," I said.

"We are aware of the situation," Avery said. "Rest assured, it's been handled."

"Are you a genie? Because I think you just made all my wishes come true," I said.

He tousled his sandy hair. "I'm not quite that magical, ma'am."

I still wanted to rub him to make sure. Avery and Stone would both be fun under different circumstances. I resolved to keep my promise about that drink.

Stone cleared his throat. "We've got this hotel monitored—important business and political figures are taking asylum here, so keep your ears open, Agent Petrovna."

Interesting. That explained why I was here and not in the usual dingy military bunker on the outskirts of the Dome. Someone thought I was extra important. Curious. Were these Sanchez's military buddies or were they secret revolutionaries? At that point, it didn't matter. Allies were allies.

"Always do," I said.

With a quick salute and a cursory goodbye, they shook my hand again and left. They had business to attend to, and so did I.

After wheeling in the suitcase and securing the door, I stripped down to my underwear. I tossed the suitcase onto the tall bed, jumped after it, and rolled around in the frothy white blankets and pillows. Sleeping on this thing was going to be better than sex.

But all that would have to wait. I stopped dicking around and opened the suitcase. Clothes, useful things like a pair of camo pants and other casual clothing, were stacked on top along with some toiletries. The case was a treasure chest, and the most important stuff was underneath the clothes. Beneath the padding was a small computer, and I recognized it as one of the newer models we shipped from Dome to Dome. With squirrelly electricity and no true Internet, computers were useless in the Voids, but it was exactly what I needed in here.

There was also a small toolkit that had miniature screwdrivers, wire cutters, and connectors. I found the final major gift tucked in a corner at the bottom of the suitcase—a new communicator with a scrambling unit on it. Perfect. Avery and Stone won the prize for being my new best friends.

Now I could secure the area. I searched the room and located the main cameras and microphones that monitored the sleeping quarters. They were mainly hidden in the glowing decorations, but thanks to Neptune's training, I was good at finding and disabling surveillance equipment. Within a few minutes, I had the system rewired to display another nearby room instead.

After disarming all the obvious devices, I went through the suite and used the communicator's scrambling unit as a makeshift scanner for other hidden bugs. I was right. One remained—a sneaky camera stashed inside the shower. Perverts.

The fancy lighted curtains were glued to the window, making it impossible to see outside. That wasn't an accident, but it was six in the evening, and it would be dark soon anyway. Someone would retrieve me early in the morning, and there should still be plenty of time to gather intel and also get some sleep. Not taking care of yourself after a rapid healing treatment had unpleasant side effects. Like kidney failure.

I slipped on a pair of jeans and a comfortable black tank top, plugged in the computer, and set it on the big executive desk, ready to rock. I should have tried for Milo first, but I couldn't help it. I'd avoided thinking about what might have happened to Argon, and I couldn't ignore it any longer. I tuned the device and hit the red transmit button.

The communicator crackled and hissed. I listened to the soft sputtering and moved the little black box around, trying to find a signal.

Nothing.

I fiddled with knobs and tried other frequencies, but all I ever got was more static. No Argon. It didn't necessarily mean anything. His transmitter could have been lost or damaged. He might be just fine.

Still. Not what I was hoping for. I took a deep breath. Milo. Milo might know.

I adjusted the call frequency, and for several minutes I got nothing but more annoying static and screeching. Then I heard a faint voice.

"Milo, is that you? This is Xero," I said quietly in a codified version of Tohono O'odham. I required all of the Grease Weasels to learn it, but no one else, not even our support teams, could understand it. That plus the scrambled encryption would make decoding the conversation very difficult.

"Xero! You're alive!" Milo said and whooped. He yelled away from the communicator. "Hey, Neptune, it's the boss!"

Neptune was incomprehensible, but hearing her voice was enough. Home base was still secure.

"You're alive!" Milo said again into the transmitter. He cleared his voice and continued, "Um, not that I expected anything less, but I don't know if you've noticed—it's getting crazy out here."

"Oh, I've noticed all right. I noticed it with ten inches of steel in my ribs." I gave him a quick update.

"Holy shit. You make it through rapid healing okay?" he said.

As our doctor, he was responsible for sewing me back together, and he'd seen me almost die from a bad healing sequence. If it wasn't done correctly, organs could explode.

"Right as rain," I said. "All ten fingers and all ten toes, so far." I joked, but the fear of flesh rot still haunted me.

"When it comes to you, that's all I can really ask for these days." He paused. "Unfortunately, there's no trace of Argon. No messages, no bodies. No news."

"What about Calavera?"

"We got one convo with her. It was cut short—like she dropped the handset and ran. Said the riots weren't her doing and that she had to go into hiding. She sounded majorly stressed out. Personally, I don't think she's behind it."

"You think someone's got the screws to her?" I asked. Milo always had a good sense about these things.

"Sounded like it. The whole situation is strange. We haven't gone down to Nogales to check it out in person—wanted to find you first. The last time we had to barge into Mexico it wasn't pretty."

"We're in a compromised position. Stay away from Nogales. If we go to Mexico, I need to be there," I said. "How's Trina doing?"

Not having the Ketacillin for Trina was the worst part of this mess. Risking it all—my life, Argon's life, and not saving her? Unacceptable.

He sighed, and I heard it even over the communicator's static. "Not good. I'm trying everything, but the Zaps have her real bad. It's that drug resistant strain from Russia. I know it. If we can't get her some Ketacillin soon, I'll to have to experiment with stuff cooked up in the lab. Might be even worse than just letting the Zaps take her."

"I'll do everything I can to push for the Yuma run. That's the only place we can safely get to the antibiotics."

"I'm counting on you."

"Look, this channel is scrambled, but we've already said too much. This communicator line should be open until morning, but after that I can't guarantee anything. If I'm lucky, they'll immediately re-issue all of my field gear and launch the mission. Keep doing what you're doing, and I'll be in contact with you again as soon as possible," I said.

"Roger that. Stay safe out there. And get some rest. I don't want to have to steal you a kidney," he said, and we signed off.

Fuck. No Argon. I can't stand blind spots in my information field. I appreciated that Milo didn't mention Copper, our replacement IT guy. I hated him. I wanted to get rid of the bastard but hadn't been able to find any suitable replacements. Milo kept saying I couldn't stand to see someone take Evan's place.

Still, I didn't trust Copper's skills. We should've had more information by now.

No reason I couldn't try hacking the web myself. But first, something almost as important. My stomach rumbled, and a painful cramp rippled through my gut. I grabbed at my belly and grunted.

No solid food since before the hospital. Whatever liquid

nutrition they'd pumped me full of while my wounds were healing had worn off, leaving my insides twisted in knots. I rummaged through the bag, but there were no nutrition bars or gel packs stashed in there.

Now for the million dollar question.

Could I get room service?

CHAPTER NINE

THE ROOM service gods smiled upon me. Real steak and chocolate cake were on the way, none of that synthprotein crap.

I was going to eat it harder than the hearts of my enemies.

While waiting for my food, I used the time to fix my last issue: weapons. No problem. Anything could be a weapon. Well, almost anything, but this hotel sucked for espionage. Even the lights in the bedroom were welded into the wall sconces, leaving no lamps or other handy projectiles. I had a few screwdrivers from the toolkit, but they were tiny, made for taking apart delicate computer pieces, not for prying off hardware. Such a bitch.

In the huge bathroom, the towel racks felt flimsy. Disco. I loosened the bars so they would be easy to rip down. The hotel left big samples of soap and other toiletries around the sink—I could throw those, but after that nasty slumber party in the Breakers, I didn't want to think about giving up fresh soap. I shoved a bar in my pocket for safekeeping. Guardian of the suds, just in case. Didn't want a repeat of that last night in the Breakers.

I scanned the rest of the bathroom for other weapons—shower rod was welded into the wall, but the shower curtain and the towels could be useful. Wouldn't be the first time I strangled someone with a towel. Hazard of the job: I see murder everywhere.

The enormous whirlpool tub wouldn't be much of a weapon,

but I relished the thought of soaking in it later. It was electronic and fancy, so I pushed the automatic start button. Steaming water gushed into the basin. The tub would fill itself, stop before overflowing, and stay hot until I was ready to climb in. Soft sounds of splashing water filled the suite. Soap, hot water, steak, and chocolate. Amazing. Heaven was on its way.

When someone knocked, I jumped to the door and jammed my eye to the peephole. The man in the hallway didn't seem right. The hotel was staffed by Nordic clones—tall and pale with blond or very light brown hair. The guy at the door was short and Hispanic. He wore the white uniform of an employee and clutched a silver tray with stubby fingers. I opened the door anyway. Danger or not, I wanted that food.

He said something about my order, but I didn't hear any of it. His hand swished toward his back pocket, presumably to get my tab, and warning bells clanged in my head. I reached out to grab the platter, but with a little flick of my wrist, and a lot of regret, I flung it back in his face.

Food and utensils flew everywhere, but the man reacted like a true pro, slapping the tray away from his head like a trained martial artist.

Dinner was trashed, but at least I wasn't wrong.

I snatched a steak knife from a puddle of meat juice and sauce. Damn it. The steak smelled delicious, and I wouldn't get a chance to eat it. Fuck this asshole for ruining my dinner. I stabbed toward the guy's neck hard, but he dodged my clumsy attack and rolled past me into the threshold. Fast. Calavera sometimes hired ex-luchadors, and they were dangerous.

I whirled around and flung a handful of chocolate cake right in his eyes. He wiped off the cake, unfazed, and pulled out a long, fat blade.

My knife was pathetic compared to his, and the guy was quick. One stab wound for the week was enough. I forced myself to be patient. It was a gamble, but I circled until I was in front of the bathroom. Water bubbled and steam licked at my neck from the full Jacuzzi.

"Your move," I said.

He sneered, and the muscles in his neck twitched as he tried to hold back.

But he couldn't wait. He flew at me, both feet leaving the ground as he lunged. Definitely a luchador.

I rolled onto my back, landing just inches from the tub. I flung my legs up straight, catching him in the stomach, which gave me just enough time to grab his shirt collar. Using the shirt as a pivot point, I kicked him over my head.

Violence can be an art. He soared beautifully overhead and slammed into the wall above the tub. Tiles crunched, and he screamed.

The impact didn't knock him out like I'd hoped, and he thrashed and gurgled when he hit the water. I leaped to my feet and sunk my fingernails into his throat, pushing him into the tub, not caring if I strangled him or he drowned first. He flailed like a diver in the jaws of a shark, and I pressed down with all my weight. It wasn't long before his thrashing slowed, then completely stopped. His empty brown eyes stared at me through the water.

Served him right for wrecking my dinner.

Blood dripped down the smashed tile wall and blossomed in the water around his head. Couldn't take a bath in there now—tub was contaminated.

No clean water. No food.

Guy was lucky to be dead. I could get creative with revenge.

Both knives were lost in the struggle, and another hotel employee came in while I was hunting for them. He looked like a twin of the dead guy, and his face exploded with rage when he saw the fate of his comrade.

He produced another combat knife and lunged at me. I dodged to the right, hitting the wall. He grinned, thinking he had me cornered. Big mistake. I grinned back, snatched the loosened towel rack from the wall, and put my weight into a hard stab. He raised the knife to take a swipe, but it was too late. With both hands, I shunted the towel rack into the meat of his throat.

The force rammed him into the wall, and the rod made a wet slurp as it tore through his neck, catching on his trachea before punching into the esophagus. If it had been a sharp weapon, it would have gone clear through, but the dull towel rack stopped somewhere in front of his spinal cord.

Blood poured down the front of his white uniform. His mouth made gasping motions, but no sound came out. No air, no sound. He dropped the knife, and it clattered to the floor by my foot. He clutched at the rod as his eyes went glassy and his body went limp. I let go, and he slid to the floor, slumped in a bloody heap. *Buenas noches, hermanos.*

Voices in the hallway. Could be military or more enemies. I snatched the knife beside my feet and looked around the floor for the first guy's knife. Metal glinted behind the toilet, and I retrieved the other blade. Heads would really roll now.

I caught a glimpse of myself in the mirror, wet, covered in blood, dual blades in hand. Blood lust pulsed in my eyes, and I was ready, hungry to go again.

The remains of my fallen room service order lay scattered at my feet.

No steak. No cake.

No mercy.

CHAPTER TEN

CROUCHED IN the bathroom, I was ready to pounce and shred when another recruit appeared. He trembled in the doorway. A seasoned soldier wouldn't have flinched, but this poor bastard was visibly rattled, and he scrambled for his laser.

"Identify yourself," I said, both knives raised to strike.

"Private Johannes, National Guard. Drop your weapon," he said. He fumbled with his holster but managed to get his laser up and sighted in my direction.

This twerp was not a spy. No way. Calavera's Skeletons were well-trained in combat. If she caught any of them shrinking in the face of battle, she'd kill them herself.

I held up my hands but didn't drop the knives. Hopefully this guy didn't have another nervous trigger finger. Without knowing the rest of the scene outside, surrendering my knives actually might be more dangerous than dodging a laser shot.

"Private, can you verify the hallway is secure?" I said.

"Um," he said, sounding surprised a savage like me could speak in full sentences.

"In case you missed the memo, I'm the one who's supposed to be under protection here, so you can stop pissing your pants. Lower your laser, and tell me if you have the hallway secured or not." I kept my arms raised until he stopped looking so twitchy.

He hesitated. "There's no one in the hallway. It's secure."

I hissed. "You moron—get back out there and secure the hallway. We've got a pile of bodies in here if you hadn't noticed."

He started to say something, then gasped and fell forward.

I expected to see another server dressed in those tacky whites, but it was a Skeleton in a full Calaca suit, plunging a knife deep into the recruit's lower back. Before the Skeleton retrieved its blade, I tossed a knife, aiming for the kill space at its throat.

I missed—too hasty. It hit the Skeleton in the chest and bounced right off. The Skeleton yanked its knife from the recruit and dropped the body, the recruit's limp arm whacking the toilet on the way down. The cheap laser case cracked on the porcelain and ricocheted into the whirlpool tub. Damaged lasers and water didn't mix. A loud pop echoed in the tiled room. The tub lit up with a bright flash of electricity, and the smell of burning meat filled the air. Skeleton soup, anyone?

Most decent lasers were water resistant—wouldn't do to be caught in a rainstorm and end up frying. But if the casing was damaged, all bets were off. Newer models were difficult to break, but apparently the military was outfitting their trial recruits with shitty weapons in addition to shitty training. I'd seen more than one black-market laser blow up in someone's hands, so it wasn't that surprising. Our tax dollars at work.

The sizzling body distracted us both, but I recovered first. Instead of retreating, I took the offensive, leaping over the fallen recruit. Before the Skeleton could prepare a counterstrike, I rushed forward, simultaneously striking and blocking. Its knife sliced across my forearm and into my bicep before I knocked it away with a strong hammer-fist jab.

When we hit the floor, I landed on the Skeleton, straddling its waist. No escape. I slipped the blade through the throat gap and drove it up to the hilt. The Skeleton screamed, and as I twisted the knife, its cries soared in pitch before gurgling into silence. From the tone of the screams, I realized this was another girl. Hard to judge sex under the bulky armor, but I always appreciated worthy female opponents.

More shouting boomed through the hallway. It wasn't over yet. For all I knew, the whole Dome was under siege. Fine by me. I was already bleeding and ready to rip shit up.

Speaking of which, I needed to deal with my newest battle wound. I retrieved my knives and used hand towels to wipe off the

Skeleton blood. Once the blades were clean, I shredded wide strips from the shower curtain.

With my mouth and my other hand, I tied a sloppy bandage around the gashes in my arm. Blood dripped through the fabric, but I would live, and almost as importantly, I could still use both hands. I stripped off the Skeleton's holster and used it to store the extra knife.

From the hallway, someone shouted, "Agent Petrovna!"

It was Stone.

"I'm in here," I called. "Got three rogues and one of your rookies down."

"Are you injured?" He didn't enter the room—smart move. Wasn't safe to leave the hall unguarded.

"Lacerated arm, but it's not critical. I'm armed with three combat knives collected from assailants. What's the status out there?"

"Enemy combatants hit the hotel—they infiltrated staff ranks and used the penetration to move fully armored attackers into the building. We have the outside of the facility locked down so additional enemy soldiers can't enter. We're sweeping the rooms, eliminating the initial wave. Care to give us a hand?" he said.

I finished cleaning myself up and cautiously approached the hallway. Stone and Avery covered both ends of the corridor, lasers drawn and ready.

"You bet your ass. Got a spare piece you can lend me?" I asked.

With his gaze fixed on the doorway, Avery smiled. "If anyone asks, you stole it off a dead guy." He tossed me an extra laser.

Remembering how easily the last one shattered, I made sure to catch it. Silver-plated with a red stripe down the sides: it was a better model than the defective one that was probably still zapping the dead Skeleton in the bathtub.

"You know how to use one of those things?" Stone asked. He turned briefly, just long enough to wink at me.

"Pretty sure I can figure it out," I said. "I've been around the block a time or two."

"We'll start from this floor and clear our way down to the ground level. Can you go the distance with that arm? We could use another pro in this mess, but I don't need you dropping in the middle of a shootout," he said, all seriousness.

"It'll take more than this scratch to drop me."

I gripped the laser with both hands.

No one ruins my dinner and gets away with it.

CHAPTER ELEVEN

A PSYCH consult.

The night had gone to total shit, but of all the places I thought I might end up, a psychiatrist's office wasn't one of them. But it wasn't a graveyard, and I was out of that stinking jail cell, so that was something.

I sat on a soft couch that was covered in rich gray suede. It felt nice to run my hands over its cool surface, but I was bleeding again, leaving ugly stains on the lush leather. Behind me, a big picture window overlooked the heart of downtown Phoenix. In the distance, the Niagara Hotel sparkled, standing out among the mirrored bank towers that crowded the financial district. With the banks failing again, most of those towers sat empty, hollow with the echoes of embezzlement and laundering, but their mirrored sides were still shiny, reflecting the mid-afternoon sun holograms like nothing had changed.

What a great time to be alive.

The fake sunlight fell across my shoulders, highlighting my filthy clothing and the smears of unmentionable grime I was leaving on the soft upholstery.

I smelled even worse than I looked.

"Sorry about your couch," I said, holding up an arm to show the dirty bandages. "I can pay for it, if you like."

A man behind a heavy mahogany desk leaned on his elbows, folding his hands and resting his chin on them. "That's an interesting offer, don't you think?" he said.

I ran a toe over the short industrial carpet that matched the couch in color but not in price point. "You haven't been in this office long, have you? Still need to update the carpet to fit your paycheck."

The man smiled, pushed square rimless glasses farther up his nose, and went back to resting his head against his closed fists. "You're right—I just moved into this office a few weeks ago. Do you like it?"

I looked around and nodded. "Yeah, I do," I said honestly. It was all dark wood, soft gray fabric, suede, and shelves filled with books and brass knick-knacks. The three decorative chess sets and a world globe were a bit snooty for my tastes, but I liked money and these furnishings were expensive.

"Reminds you of your own office, doesn't it, Xero?" he said.

I narrowed my eyes and cocked my head, trying to decide how to play this. No civilian should know my Voids name. He'd been digging.

"We don't really have offices in the Voids," I said.

"I think we both know that's not what I mean." He leaned backward in his suede office chair and tucked his hands behind his head, waiting.

I could play the waiting game, too. It had been a long night, and I wasn't fired up to start another round of political dancing. There'd been just about enough waltzing for one weekend.

After a few minutes of silence with nothing but the clock ticking and my blood dripping slowly onto the leather, he came forward again. He stroked his carefully groomed goatee, opened his mouth to speak, but paused and reached under his desk instead. He came up with a black medical kit in his hands.

"Would you like me to help you clean up your wounds a bit better? I saw in your chart they never sent you to medical after the incident at the Niagara or after the jail assault last night," he said. "Not that I need a chart to see you're injured."

I crossed my arms, smearing blood across the same dark shirt I wore yesterday. At least I wasn't stuck in a white top— slaughterhouse chic didn't go over well in the Domes. "I help stop a major terrorist attack, *twice*, save a bunch of innocent lives, and get tossed in jail for my trouble. Funny how you can be queen for a day and then you're back to dog shit the next."

"You've experienced that a lot, and it makes you angry."

I laughed. "Don't try the psychobabble on me, buddy. You already know we share professional secrets."

I rubbed my face and winced—black eyes were settling in for the long haul. Nothing pissed me off more than getting tagged in the face, but I got off pretty easy, considering. Ten guys in a maximum unit, all overjoyed by the idea of gang raping me. I wasn't quite so thrilled with that plan. I may have gotten a couple more knife slices and a few shiners, but some of those assholes were leaving without their balls.

Or their heads.

He smiled back at me. "Good to know we're on the same page, Dr. Petrovna." He motioned to the medical kit he'd spread out across his desk. "Between the two of us we should be able to keep you from ruining any more couches, don't you think?"

"I think we can probably manage."

He leaned over the kit and made eye contact with me. "That is, unless you'd prefer I sent you back to a proper medical facility."

"No, thank you. Not in this city," I said. "You know, I have this nagging feeling I shouldn't have been released to this office."

"You stirred up some real trouble back in the jail with your...creative defense mechanisms. It took a bit of convincing to have you transferred for a psych eval so soon, but I have a good track record of working with violent offenders. Is there a reason you felt compelled to make your ordeal even harder?"

"You mean why did I taunt the guards until they threw me in a max unit where I had to assault several other prisoners to stay alive?"

"You would have only needed to pass a security investigation about the incidents at the Niagara. Now you need a psych clearance from someone like me," he said.

"It was worth it. They sent me to jail without just cause and then didn't tend to my medical needs. The guards violated policy by tossing a female into a cell full of violent sex offenders, and policy was violated again when I was denied medical attention after fighting them off," I said. "I may have killed a lot of people in the last few days, but it was all in self defense, and I saved the lives of dozens of political figures and military personnel. They owe me."

Avery and Stone were being held for questioning at a military justice facility in another part of the city. Getting caught firing lasers with an unauthorized Voids dweller was enough to crucify them both. I was allowed to carry firearms, but only outside the Domes on official cargo runs. Of course, no one remembered there were legal provisions for unusual situations. Like terrorist attacks. Easier just to toss everyone in jail and let the system sort it out. Slowly. I didn't have time for that shit.

He nodded. "I see. You like it when you're able to make someone break their own rules."

"I find it amusing when people violate their own sacred ethical codes without a second thought. I'm sure you know a little something about that."

He tapped lightly on the desk. "I just might."

"What did you say your name was again?"

"I didn't actually—you interrupted when I tried to introduce myself," he said.

"Golly, where are my manners? You'll have to excuse me. It's been such a hard week," I said in a fake falsetto tone. I'm nothing if not a lady.

He licked his lips, and a look crossed his face. It was gone as quickly as it came, but it was enough to make me pay attention. Then I realized what was bothering me. It was a dance. We were two experienced hunters stalking each other through the jungle.

"You will be most interesting to work with," he said with a hint of that predatory edge, but then he sat straight up again and was back to his soft and caring psychiatrist routine. "My name is Dr. Shepherd. Ezekiel Shepherd."

He straightened a name placard so it was facing me: black background, real gold lettering. Nothing but the best for Mr. Shepherd. The gold matched the color of his ritzy silk tie.

"Zeke, eh? That's a tough name to grow up with."

"You have no idea," he said softly. "I usually stick with Dr. Shepherd. However, you can call me something else, if you'd like, Dr. Petrovna."

I kept my face still, but it was weird hearing a civilian call me that. Really weird. I was too old, meaning I couldn't erase my real name from the hard copy records of Dome census data. Made it difficult to bury my past life. Still, you'd have to do some hardcore snooping to find information about my former career in the Domes. This guy had done his homework.

He'd been waiting for me.

"And what would that be?" I said.

"You can call me Xed. With an X."

I tried to choke back a laugh and failed. I thought about the layout of the outer office, wondering who could hear us. "You've got to be joking."

"Don't worry. This place is sound proof, and there are no bugs. I don't expect you to accept that, but once we clean you up a bit, you can check yourself."

"You may as well keep calling me Xero if you want me to call you Xed."

The guy sitting in front of me with neat rimless spectacles and his preppy blue dress shirt was claiming to be Xed. The Xed. I'd seen stranger things, but not by much.

"Very well. I can tell you doubt me, but I assure you, if nothing else, I do have basic medical training, and I'm not going to harm you in the middle of a government office building. I just want to fix you up so we can have a nice chat." He flashed me a politician's smile.

If he had wanted to kill me, he wouldn't have brought me to his office. I stared him down and let him know I wouldn't think twice about slitting his throat, even inside a Dome. We studied each other and shared a moment of silent agreement.

"Okay," I said. "I'd hate to ruin any more expensive furniture."

I approached the desk, and he pulled up a chair. We spent the next half hour cleaning and stitching up my injuries. A needle in his cold hands took quick, delicate bites across my skin. He grabbed my arm and inspected the rows of meticulous sutures that he'd sewn along my knife wounds. The strength in his grip was surprising, and I noticed he was more muscular underneath his crisp dress shirt than he appeared.

"Well, that's much better, isn't it?" he said when he finished bandaging over the stitches. His medical kit had waterproof dressings—great because you could shower with them and not ruin fresh sutures. I'd sell my soul for a hot bath. One of the greatest tragedies of the week was missing out on that whirlpool hot tub at the Niagara.

He started cleaning up the medical waste. He'd been careful, but blood still splattered the dark wood.

"Got a rag or something?" I said.

He extracted some sterile wipes, dragging one across the desk and leaving it sparkling with a sheen of disinfectant. "Good as new."

"You wouldn't happen to have any antibiotics, would you?"

He leaned back. "What kind?"

"Anything really. These wounds were open in a cesspool all night, and I don't have time to deal with flesh rot. Even old school penicillin would be better than nothing."

He ducked under the desk and came up with a vial and a syringe with a heavy-gauge needle. "I think we can arrange that." He shook the vial and removed the syringe from its packaging, but I stopped him before he drew up the antibiotics.

"Let me do that," I said.

He handed over the vial and the syringe. The bottle was cold, labeled with the appropriate title, and factory sealed. Never hurt to be extra careful.

"You've got a fridge down there? Didn't you just move to this office?" I said.

"Always good to be prepared. These are strange times."

I snickered. "They are indeed." I was starting to like this guy.

I drew up a syringe full of the thick white liquid. "This isn't going to be pleasant. I need a big muscle to shoot this into. Hope you don't mind me getting naked in your office. Wouldn't want anyone to think you're molesting your patients."

He stood up and came around to my side of the desk. "It should really go in the gluteus. Let me help."

Sure. Why not?

I peeled down the right side of my pants, exposing the upper ass cheek. He sterilized a patch of skin and gave me the injection with practiced confidence. I winced with one eye, but it wasn't that uncomfortable, given the size of the shot.

"You have a gentle touch." I rubbed my ass for a second before pulling up my pants.

"I pride myself on having a certain finesse in my job. Can I interest you in any pain medication injections while I'm at it?"

"No. I don't touch that stuff."

"Interesting," he said slowly and disposed of the garbage.

I sat back down, and he resumed his position behind the desk.

"I have a few questions to ask you," he said. "Would that be all right?"

"You just fondled my ass, so you may as well get to know me a little better."

"I'm not usually so forward with strangers, but then again I don't usually provide emergency medical care in my office either," he said.

"Right, because most psychiatrists don't keep refrigerated

antibiotics in a secret cubby under their desk."

He bit the corner of his lip. "Like I said. Never know when disaster might strike."

"I'll show you mine if you show me yours?"

"Don't you want to check for bugs first?"

"You wouldn't air your dirty laundry on tape."

He flexed his knuckles. "You're no amateur."

"But you already knew that," I said. "You did your homework. What do you want from me?"

"I'm pretty sure we're clear about each other's identities, wouldn't you say?"

"I'm willing to go with that hypothesis. For now."

"I just want to offer you help. If you find my performance sufficient, perhaps we can discuss a few business ideas at a later time," he said.

From the way he was looking at me, he had more than business in mind, and that was just fine by me. I never missed a chance to mix business and pleasure.

"Business ideas? You ever been out to the Voids?" I said. He looked like a lifelong Dome dweller, but you never could be certain.

"I'm from the Breakers, but I have a limited resistance to the outside. Not enough to live in the Voids, no, but I can travel there for short periods of time."

Definitely no active surveillance in the room. Not something you could reveal, even jokingly. If anyone figured out you had atmospheric resistance, your days in the Dome were numbered. May as well toss your Zone Pass in the fire and pack your bags for the great outdoors.

"How? How can you get away with working inside the Domes if you're from the Breakers?" I asked with genuine surprise.

"I'm very, very good with computers. I manipulate the government systems for certain purposes, like obscuring my own birth status," he said. "Unfortunately, there's not much I can do for you. I'm a few years younger, which let me escape the paper trail. You were born just before the cut off, and you're also a well-known government contractor. I couldn't erase your history without arousing a great deal of suspicion."

"Not something I need, but still, I'm impressed. Erasing your birth status is no easy feat." I only knew one person who had pulled that off—and she was dead.

"You'll find I'm very capable in a variety of areas if you decide to accept my business proposition. However, as I said, I would like to focus on your needs first." He leaned over the desk again. "So, my question is, what can I do for you?"

"Well, for starters, I could use a fucking hot shower. I don't mind tangling with riffraff, but I'll be damned if I like smelling like one."

"That should be easy enough to arrange. Beyond that, what else can I help you with?" "Since you asked, there are a few things. One, I need information," I said.

"About the attacks," he said as a statement. "I don't know a lot, but I have gathered some news. My reach doesn't extend very far into the Voids, so I'm limited to what I can see in the Domes and the Breakers. Turns out Voids dwellers don't like working with people outside their own...persuasion."

"We're particular like that. Breathing the outside air for too long will make you real surly. Trust me."

"What I do know is that these Skeletons are involved, but they're not working with the gang they're associated with—Las Calacas. I believe you know their leader, Calavera?"

"Don't get me started. She started a turf war with me when she moved into the Nogales territory. Continuous fighting gets expensive, so we called a truce. That goes down, then suddenly there's Skeleton attacks everywhere, and according to my guys, Calavera doesn't know what in the fuck is going on."

"That fits with my intel. We need to handle this. You've already experienced some significant upsets from this crisis, and I don't want them to affect my organization either."

"You want me to help you take down whoever is in charge of this splinter cell?"

"That may be part of the equation, but I'll get to that later. First, tell me what else you want."

Interesting negotiation strategy—figuring out what I needed so he would have more leverage to work with during the bargaining phase. An obvious manipulation, but there were things I wanted, things I might get without giving him anything in return. Best thing about crime—sometimes you actually got a free lunch.

I cleared my throat. "I'm not especially proud of this, but one of my colleagues has gone missing. I don't think he's dead, but he's definitely MIA, possibly kidnapped. I want him back." I gave him a description of Argon.

He clucked his tongue. "Nothing rings a bell. I can't promise anything, but I can put my feelers out into the Domes."

"Finding him is a top priority, but the thing I really want, I already asked you for. I need antibiotics."

"And I've got the same question I had for you earlier—what kind of antibiotics are we talking about here?"

"I need Ketacillin, specifically. It has to be Ketacillin."

He wiped a hand down his face. "Ketacillin. Even I don't have access to that. At least not on hand. It would take some doing."

"If you can't get it, then do the next best thing. Pass my psych exam and help me get through all the political snafus so I can go on my regular run to Yuma."

"Sick crew member?"

Exposing weaknesses wasn't a smart move, but in this case, there wasn't a lot to lose and a hell of a lot to gain.

"Yeah. Lung Zaps. Real bad. Drug resistant—our resident medic says Ketacillin's the only real hope, and that shit is hard as fuck to get your hands on. We can't transport her anywhere else because of all the official and unofficial quarantines." The gangs and cartels were just as serious about enforcing infectious disease protocols as the government. No one wanted to die from a superbug.

"Tough situation, but not impossible. I'll pass your psych eval and grease a few palms to get the supply mission cleared again. The rebel attacks messed up shipment schedules—shouldn't be difficult to convince them to put the run back on the docket. I can also help smooth over the smuggling process in Yuma."

I never would have guessed that one of the largest Dome-based drug dealers in the country was a practicing Phoenix psychiatrist. He was like a male version of me. Fucker even just about stole my moniker. Our profession was living up to its reputation. Knowing how to manipulate minds with chemicals was a lucrative skill. Not surprising that some of us would use it for less than virtuous purposes.

"Sounds too good to be true," I said. "Now you know what I want—all my cards are on the table. I know who you are, you know who I am. Now's the part where you make your unreasonable demands, and we dance around making threats and counter offers."

My leverage sucked. I needed him to pass my psych eval or shit would get gnarly. I could cook up a fake report, but it would take weeks, or even months for all that bullshit to get pushed through the system. Same deal for smuggling Ketacillin directly from the black market.

Trina would be long dead by then.

"I'm disappointed that you think so little of me. In my opinion, a truly successful relationship is built on trust, just like they taught us in school, right? A good businessman always lets the customer taste the milk before buying the cow. I will help you do these things you've asked for. If you're satisfied with my services, then perhaps we can work on some longer term business strategies."

I chuckled and pointed a bruised finger at him. "You're good, I'll give you that. You're good." He really was. This was the only way I would even consider working with him.

"You know as well as I do that making someone work involuntarily is no way to form stable alliances. You catch more flies with honey than with vinegar."

"Says the guy who basically stole my name and tried to take over my business?" I said.

"With all due respect, I've been in business almost as long as you have, albeit on a much smaller scale due to the limitations of working within the Domes. It's taken time to grow my empire, but it's quite impressive now. As for our monikers, we formed those separately. I called myself Xed long before I knew about you. It was a childhood nickname from the Breakers, actually. Perhaps it's fate that we seem to be so similar, and you found me in this time of need."

I pursed my lips and drummed my mangled fingers on the desk. It hurt, but I didn't care. Sometimes a little pain brought clarity, brought you back down to earth.

"I've had my people try to make contact, but I always got the same message—I don't fuck with you, you don't fuck with me, and everyone stays happy. Why do you want to work with me now?" I said.

He shrugged. "I was intimidated, and I didn't want to risk being crushed or overtaken by your Voids enterprise if I revealed too much."

I squinted and continued tapping. "And now you're big and bad enough that you're not threatened by us?"

He took off his glasses, laid them on the desk, and grinned. "Threatened? Not in the slightest—but I don't want to pick a fight. Our organizations are probably equal in destructive force right now. No one would come out a winner in that battle, and I'm not eager to obliterate everything I've worked so hard to build."

I sat quiet, thinking, and then broke out in another ironic

laugh. "The Alphadrine. That's what you want."

He smiled wryly. "Among other things, yes, that is a piece of valuable capital I don't have direct access to. I would like to help you widen your distribution area."

"I don't know why I didn't think of it before—must have gotten hit in the head too many times last night."

He put his glasses back on. "Does that change your mind?"

"No. Now this all makes more sense. That's what I'd want in your position, too. I can't give you Alphadrine, or anything else, without discussing it with my team. But, I will gladly suck on your milk before buying your cow. So, what's next?" I put my hands on the table, palms up.

"Good. I say we put the paperwork in motion to get you out of this situation, then we retire to my place where I can assist you with your first demand: a hot shower."

"I won't argue with this plan." Hey, spending the night at a rival's house was totally worth getting into some literal hot water.

He held out a hand for me to shake. "What a nice name for a partnership," he said. "Xed and Xero—X marks the spot."

Chapter Twelve

A LONG ride past the urban center of Phoenix brought us to the Dome's edge, out to a northern section of old Scottsdale. Before Phoenix had a Dome the area had been filled with ranch houses and golf courses for wealthy Republicans: the Beverly Hills of Arizona. Even with the reduced acreage, the district was essentially the same—a desert playground for the wealthy. Took some serious cash to keep that much land.

Xed had a serious chunk of that community. At night, through tinted limousine windows, I missed the scenery, but I got the effect. We traveled through miles of empty territory before stopping in front of an impressive mansion. Even in the dark, the white structure towered into the sky, dimly lit by a fake quarter moon.

He led me inside a high-ceilinged parlor. Everything was white marble and chandelier crystal, bright and blazing, crying sparkles like an expensive disco ball. Shit hurt my eyes. The place smelled like someone had sprayed down every surface with bleach, and the fumes stung my nose. After the dirty shit holes I'd visited this week, the bleach didn't seem like such a bad idea. Xed kept it clean.

"Nice place you've got here," I said. "Looks like an old coke lord's house."

"It was, but he's extraordinarily dead now. Zero down payment," he said. "And in case you were wondering, this place is packed with security features. If any Skeletons are tracking you, we should have enough armaments to fend them off. The building has a full doomsday switch."

Meaning there was a flawless security measure that would keep everything out. It could also keep everything inside. The emphasis on the doomsday switch wasn't lost on me.

I sat on the arm of a white couch. "Don't worry, I won't run away. And if you were planning on raping and killing me in the comfort of your own home, that's not a problem either. I'll just kill you first."

And it would be fun.

He faced me in the entryway, hands behind his back. "I meant we can capture and interrogate someone if we're attacked," he said. "Besides, I'm pretty handy with a firearm, but I'm not much good with hand to hand combat. I'm more of the man behind the desk, the guy behind the computer. Trying to overpower you physically isn't on my list of smart things to attempt."

"Duly noted," I said. He was probably telling the truth, but I wouldn't trust him until I tested it. The most surprising people ended up being decent fighters.

I looked around at the grandiose furnishings—the white design had probably helped hide all the blow residue. "Isn't all this wealth a bit suspicious?"

He shrugged. "I make a lot of money in my legitimate practice, especially since I have so many active government contracts. If I used my dirty money to buy something, now that would be conspicuous. I could almost purchase this entire Dome."

I nodded slowly. "Not bad. I'll have to spank myself later for not realizing your organization had gotten so prolific."

Balls. If his cartel was that big, he'd been flying under the radar for a long time. Or he was bluffing. Hopefully bluffing. I imagined one of those empty bank towers filled with Xed's money, stacked to the top like a grain silo. My silos were empty. Damn it.

"If you don't believe me, I can show you my bank statements," he said.

I ran a hand through my grungy hair. "Nah, I'll take your word for it. You hold up your end of whatever bargain we make—that's all that matters. Anything else is just dick-jerking and chest-beating."

"We can talk more about that over dinner, perhaps?"

My stomach bunched. Nothing solid in my gut since leaving the Voids. No sleep. My organs were going to start screaming if I didn't get some basic needs taken care of. Soon.

"We can talk about anything you want as long as it's over food," I said.

He folded his arms and leaned against a sculpted column. "Whatever the lady desires."

"You always this formal?"

He blinked and didn't change his position, but his face went blank. "No, no, I am not. But I'm always in the Domes, and there are cameras everywhere. I keep it official. For safety."

"Even in your own house?"

"When I'm in my own house and a stranger is with me, yes."

I smirked. "Well, Xed, maybe you just need to get to know me better."

He stood up and walked closer. "Exactly what type of person are you, then?"

"Thought you already had a pretty good idea of that."

A step closer. "People change. There's a great deal of buzz around your name," he said.

I crossed my legs. "So I've heard."

"Didn't have you pegged as a revolutionary."

"I'm not. I'm just a simple housewife." I winked.

He snickered. "Cute," he said. "So, you're saying you don't want anything to do with this insurgency?"

"Nope, not in the slightest. Why, you thinking of joining up?"

Another step. "Why would I do something like that? All of my power, my whole business, is set up in the Domes. Overthrowing the government would ruin everything I worked so hard for."

I chuckled. "But if everything happens to come crashing down, you wouldn't mind having a partner in crime who could help you navigate the Voids, right? Someone who happens to have a lot of pull with the exiles."

He pushed his glasses up and licked his lips. "Never hurts to have an insurance policy."

"Well, I'm an expensive policy. Not sure you can afford my premiums. Or my grocery bills. I'm about ready to eat my own arm just so my kidneys don't start shutting down."

He touched my face, fingers on my neck, thumb gently caressing my bruised cheekbone. I let him keep his hand there. He smelled like raspberry soap and bleach.

"We can remedy that—I assure you, my bank account and my pantry are more than ample. Would you like to take a shower or a bath and get cleaned up before dinner?" he said.

"You have no idea how much I would pay you for that."

"The first one's always free."

We both smiled, all shark teeth and snake eyes.

I loved second chances. Xed's place made the Niagara look like a flop house in the Breakers, and the enormous bathroom, covered in that same rich white marble and decorated with ornate chrome fixtures, matched the rest of the mansion in extravagance. No wonder Xed smelled like raspberries—all the toiletries in his bathroom had that same scent. Weird.

Eager as I was to get my hands on some hot water and good soap, I wasn't sure how I felt about smelling like my dubious new friend. Thankfully, the expensive soap I'd slipped into my pocket at the Niagara had survived the night somehow. Much better option. I needed to start stashing soap the way Neptune stashed grenades.

After I peeled off the plastic wrapping, the soap filled the bathroom with the pleasant scent of fresh rain, and I spent damned near an hour burning myself in the big shower's endless hot water. My skin went all chapped and pruned, but I scraped the prison grime out from all my naughty bits and blasted the stench out of my hair. The Mohawk was great for that—less hair to absorb nasty odors.

Once I was thoroughly de-skunked, I slipped into a whirlpool tub that swirled with ultrasonic jets. I felt reincarnated, ready to live again. The thick steam still smelled like clean rain, just like after a monsoon. I loved desert storms, as long as they weren't contaminated. Nothing like acid rain to ruin a perfectly good afternoon.

Next to the Jacuzzi, a chessboard with transparent acrylic pieces sat on a marble stand. Of course Xed would have a fucking chessboard in the bathroom. I plucked a clear queen figure from the board and twirled it in my wet fingers.

"Hey, Xed," I called, hoping it was loud enough to hear over the roaring Jacuzzi. Had to be a security camera set up in the bathroom anyway. I knew he was watching, cock hard and crotch hungry, but I didn't care. I'd scrub every bit of that raspberry out of his skin and leave him raw.

Didn't take long before he knocked.

"Get in here," I said.

He cracked the door, glasses steaming up as he poked his head inside. "Everything okay?"

I curled a finger at him. "Over here."

He adjusted his tie and glided to the tub, shiny dress shoes squeaking on the slick floor.

I swam to the edge and held up the chess piece. "Come and get your queen." I dropped the figure into the churning water.

He leaned over, and I snatched his gold tie, pulling him closer, forcing him to brace against the slippery tub.

"Not so fast. Have to pay your premiums first," I said.

He swallowed. "Perhaps I can make a down payment."

I yanked on his tie again, my damp fingers leaving dark streaks on the silk fabric. "Hope you've been saving up. Queens don't come cheap," I said.

He panted, blowing steam around our faces with each breath. "I always. Get. What I want," he said.

That's what I thought. In reality, Xed was no gentleman, and I waited for that monster to break free, for him to snap and try to strangle me, drown me in the bath. Fucking or fighting—I'm always up for either.

I wanted to know what he was made of.

I let go of his tie and floated back to the other edge of the tub, arms outstretched. "Queen's at the bottom. Let's see what you can do," I said.

He stood up, uncurling until his back was totally straight.

With moist hands, he placed his glasses in the center of the chessboard, and slowly, he unbuttoned that crisp, perfect shirt.

CHAPTER THIRTEEN

THE OVERSIZED crawler rumbled over the rocky desert soil, vibrating my bones, making me grip the corrugated steering wheel tighter. Back in charge of the convoy again. Back on my run.

Free again.

An armed accessory vehicle, stuffed with two supply soldiers, churned through the sand behind me. I had Xed to thank for getting the extra manpower approved in time for the run—not my regular staff, but I didn't have a choice. Trina was coughing up blood, and Milo said we were low on plasmasynth. Yuma had plasmasynth. It had Ketacillin.

Everything depended on this run.

We cleared the Dome without incident, making it more than halfway to Yuma with only minor setbacks. But we couldn't relax yet—the most dangerous part of the run was yet to come.

The dead zones loomed—a long stretch of desert that had no settlements and poor communicator reception. Most supply trains wouldn't traffic here. Like the Bermuda Triangle of the desert, nothing good ever happened in the dead zones. Bad weather, bandits, poisonous critters, toxic rain, the list of potential ways to die went on and on. I'd crossed these plains more than any other person on record.

That didn't make it any less dangerous.

My gaze darted across the fried brown and red landscape, searching for trouble. Agitation on the horizon. Sands blew and created a dusky glow in what should have been a clear sky.

I picked up the radio. "Delta, Echo, stay sharp—I think we've got a haboob on the way, looks like a big one. Be ready to dig in and bunker down if it shifts in our direction."

"Roger that," Delta said.

Better not to know the real names of my field operators—anonymity was safer for everyone. Xed assured me they were capable, and this wouldn't be a training run. I adjusted our course so we'd veer around the sandstorm. Haboobs were not something to fuck with. You could choke to death just on the flying sand, and that's if you were lucky.

The radio buzzed. "Agent Petrovna, this is Delta. We've got trouble behind us,"

I scanned the desert. "Oh, just fabulous."

A rogue crosswind was pulling together a supercell, and it loomed behind our caravan. The low pressure sucked it toward us, circling around the crawlers in a horseshoe of angry clouds. It would eat us alive. We only had one option—to steer straight forward, which sent us right back into the haboob.

"All right, I want you to juice it to the max. Follow my lead. We'll try to outrun the lip of the storm and bank west before we hit the haboob. If we don't make it through, drop anchor and shelter in place in the cargo hold. You must make it into the hold. Got it?" I said.

"Roger that," Delta said.

I flicked buttons on the dashboard, ground the gearshift until it clunked into place, and wailed on the gas pedal until it hit the dirty floorboards. We were overloaded, and the crawlers weren't rated for these speeds.

I hadn't checked to see how many desert driving hours Delta and Echo had logged. Hopefully it was enough. Even with my experience, I almost lost control. I clung to the steering wheel, fighting against the wind to keep the crawler upright as we sped around sand banks and jutting rocks.

Faster, damn it, we needed to go faster, but the engines were maxed out. The steering wheel bucked in my hands, and I put some serious muscle into keeping us on course. Not enough, not nearly enough. The crawler couldn't take anymore. We were no match for the environmental calamity heading right for us.

Darkness swallowed our caravan. I smelled rain and ozone as lightning flashed through the black curtain of swirling sand.

Failure.

"We're not going to make it," I said into the radio. "Activate shelter in place protocols. Do not exit the vehicle if the storms approach too fast. Drop the anchors, throw on a gas mask, and don't move till I tell you to. On the count of three, you need to switch off the overdrive, downshift, and slowly come to a stop. Do not rush this process. Got it?"

"Confirmation. Ready for your signal," Delta said.

I counted down and threw the switches. With a trained elegance, I brought the cargo crawler to a graceful stop, the treads softly pushing into the turf. Excellent landing. I dropped anchor and heavy steel mechanisms plunged deep into the sand. Everything went perfectly.

Then the other crawler slammed into me.

The blow threw me against the safety harness. It pinched, but it kept my face from smashing into the windshield. Always wear your seatbelt. That's rule one in the training manual for a reason.

Guess Delta didn't get that manual. He crashed through the windshield and went flying from the vehicle.

I cringed as his head splattered against my crawler's rearview camera, treating me to a close up view of his brain matter. *No bueno.* And no hope for him now. I snatched the gas mask from the seat beside me and crammed it on my head. No time to get into the cargo container, so I let out the straps of the restraint harness and rolled down to the floorboards. I tucked myself as far under the seats as I could get.

Reaching a hand up, I grabbed the radio and tried to contact Echo. "Do not leave the cabin. Repeat. Do not leave the cabin. Fasten your safety harness and take shelter beneath the seats."

No response.

My fingers dug into the radio handset, waiting. Silence. I threw the handset at the dashboard, and it clattered back onto the seats.

A minute went by. I felt the tension in my stomach, bracing for the hammer fall, knowing it was going to be bad. I listened to the swooshing winds, fingers digging into seats, praying for the weather to suddenly change directions, sucked away by good fortune.

Fate was not on my side.

The two storms met.

Winds ripped against the armored sides of the crawler. Thunder shook the ground, vibrating the heavy carapace. Through closed eyelids I saw flashes as lightning struck the metal and grounded itself into the earth. Hard rain banged against the steel like gunshots.

I breathed slowly, forcing full breaths through the old respirator. It would help keep the sand out of my lungs. I was resistant to most of the chemicals floating around the Voids, but even the strongest of lung tissue couldn't handle a pound of sand lancing into bronchi at a hundred miles an hour.

The rain kept blasting, but I smelled a change, even through the gas mask. A corrosive wind blew through the cabin. It was coming.

Acid.

Technically not just acid, but insidious storm clouds that had sucked up and concentrated all the atmospheric toxins from here to the gulf. I was in for a nasty chemical bath. See, there's a reason for policies—I wore one of the uncomfortable, tight, acid-resistant polymer suits. Been a few years since I'd had a really bad chemical burn, and I wasn't looking forward to another.

Not my preferred way to die.

The haboob slammed the crawler, and the vehicle lurched back and forth, steel screeching and cargo thumping in the back of the hold as the winds lashed away. The double paned windows creaked, groaning and heaving under the strain. With a loud pop, glass rained down on me.

Shards ripped through the black polymer suit. The glass left gashes across my arms and back, but that wasn't what I was worried about. My suit was compromised. No time to get into the cargo hold without risking getting blown away or fried by lightning. No escape.

The rain. It poured through the broken windows, filled my nose with acrid fumes. The first drips of the acidic rain touched my skin, and I screamed into the mask. With water gushing into the cabin, I wasn't sure if I would drown or die from chemical burns first.

I hauled myself back onto the bench seats, still in the direct spray of the caustic rain, but at least I wasn't swimming in the footwell. The wind sucked at me through the broken windows, the corrosive rain ate at my flesh, and the crawler's steel shell shuddered against the air pressure.

Sand clogged the respirator, adding suffocation as another path to death. I concentrated on my lungs, desperately trying to breathe slower, get enough air through the mask, but it was a losing battle.

The wind bellowed like a rabid coyote, and a tidal gust shoved at

the crawler. Anchors snapped.
The whole thing flipped.

CHAPTER FOURTEEN

GRAVITY ROLLED me onto the edge of the shattered passenger's side window. Glass shredded my suit. Blistering rain dripped across my torn flesh. Holocaust on my skin. Agony shoved me to the brink of consciousness, but I held on. Passing out would mean death by crushing or drowning, and I didn't want to go that way.

But the burns. Nothing was worse than burns. I wanted to unzip my skin and crawl out of it. Suicide fantasies raced through my mind. I could hang myself with the safety harness. Slit my throat with glass. The laser. There was a laser in the glovebox. Anything to stop the burning. Maybe I'd be reincarnated as a dolphin swimming in clean water. I was almost ready to make that happen.

Then the rain stopped.

The wind stopped.

The lightning and thunder stopped.

It was all just gone. So silent. I thought I had actually died, but the excruciating pain reminded me that was only a fantasy. The desert was a cruel mistress—her storms were as swift and violent as they were brief.

My head felt like a jar with marbles bouncing around in it, and I couldn't figure out which way was up. But the sun was out again, and the rays peeking through the broken glass helped me get my bearings. The driver's side window lay flush against the wet desert sand, and I dangled from the safety harness.

I groaned and hooked my fingers inside the rig's center, pulling apart the release tabs. Falling a few feet, I thumped against the soaked driver's seat. I ripped off the gas mask and lay there, just breathing.

With an embarrassing moan, I summoned my strength and climbed up the seats toward the passenger side windows. It was a sloppy dismount, but I had never been so happy to fall five feet. Smacking face first into the sand seemed like an accomplishment. I was out of the wreckage. I was alive. The storm had moved on. Everything else was just gravy.

Except the burning. That needed to stop.

I got on my hands and knees and tore off the damaged suit. The sun was already evaporating some of the chemicals. Better. Much better without the suit holding in the acid, but my flesh still burned. I needed clean water.

Relief hinged on whether I could get into the hull of a crawler. The crash welded the two vehicles together in a gnarled, metallic embrace. No way to get inside mine. The back door to the second crawler was buried in the sand but cracked open. I scrambled over there, thrusting my hand through the gap.

After a minute of fruitless groping, I stopped. Calm down. Think. I could do this. Dig deep. Literally—I spent a few minutes digging a trench to get better access to the hold. Once I burrowed a foot down, I got an arm inside.

I grabbed all kinds of shit, but nothing felt right. When my fist finally closed around a water jug, I hooted with joy. Dumping the water over my head felt like angels pissing on my face. Fucking heavenly liquid gold.

With the burns soothed, my head cleared enough to do damage control and check for any life-threatening injuries. Despite the holes in my suit, it still did its job, protecting me from the worst of the toxic deluge. My skin was red and raw—mostly first and second degree burns that would feel like shit for a few days, but wouldn't kill me. Small favors.

The other injuries were much more serious. The rain ate through the stitches Xed had sewn through the prison lacerations, and the new slashes from the exploding glass oozed blood and separated plasma. The gaping slices hung ragged, tortured from the acid. At least I wasn't bleeding out—ironically, the chemicals were sealing off some of the vessels. Good enough until I found a first aid kit.

Next priority was trying to radio back to a command base—whether that was the Phoenix or Yuma Domes or my crew in the Voids, it didn't matter. Wouldn't be the first time I'd had to wander the desert on foot, but given my lack of clothes or supplies, the extreme weather risk, and my fucked up body, it wasn't exactly a good idea.

The radio in the rear crawler was toast—the engine wouldn't start, and it looked like the whole head unit was smashed. Wouldn't be radioing for help without some serious electronic surgery. Echo was nowhere to be found, and aside from chunky stains clinging to the back of my crawler, Delta's remains were scattered by the storm. Poor bastards.

After scuttling back inside my flipped crawler, I discovered the electrical system still worked, but the radio was damaged. It turned on, but all I got was static. No sign of any connecting transmissions. Might be fixable, but it would take tools I didn't have on hand.

I found my laser toward the back of the cabin, scraped from being juggled about during the storm, but the shell was intact. Usable. Thinking back to the fried Skeleton at the Niagara, I wouldn't risk firing a cracked laser that also took a dip in an acid bath.

At least I had a weapon. I usually verified and double-checked all shipments before going on a run—that way I knew exactly what was on hand and how the contents could affect the mission. This time, we left too fast, and I had no idea what might be back there. Could be nuclear weapons, could be kitchen appliances. Dangerous oversight.

I climbed out of the cabin and buried my face in my hands, fighting a sudden wave of intense nausea. Get it together. The sun was sinking, and I needed a survival plan. Good thing I had the laser—weird shit came out at night in the dead zones.

Action on the western horizon caught my attention. Hard to tell if it was just steam or if it was actual smoke, but a big cloud plumed up over Yuma. I squinted, trying to get a better read on what it was, and spotted more movement. Must be an illusion. Looked like a group of people trudging across the sands.

I shook my head, wondered if I'd cracked something in my skull, but as minutes went by, I was convinced it really was a band of people trekking toward me. What the fuck? This was not a place you traveled on foot. Not if you enjoyed life above ground.

The people came into focus, and the cloud rising up from Yuma expanded, blackened. Had to be smoke, and a lot of it. Dome fires were unheard of, and nothing else would have enough fuel to burn so hard. Desert storms were violent and short lived, but maybe the supercell had traveled far enough to nail Yuma. Except Yuma's Dome was newer. And new Domes were armored behemoths, impossible to crack. Shit didn't make sense.

The group was definitely headed in my direction, probably hoping to raid the dead crawlers. I had the laser, but I wanted more. Time to go digging.

I dug deeper and wormed my upper half through the opening in the second crawler. No light in there, and I fished around blindly. I hoped we weren't carrying any incendiary devices, or other volatile shit that might explode if I grabbed the wrong thing.

Nothing blew up, and I came out with more water, a long piece of black fabric, and a big stick that looked like the bottom part of some garden tool. Not amazing, considering some of the fantastic items that ended up on my cargo trains, but at least everything was useful. I doused myself with water again and poured the rest down my throat.

I used strips of the fabric to cover my bigger wounds and made a crude toga with the rest. The smoke coming out of Yuma had spread even farther, just in that short time. Something outrageously bad went down.

The group headed toward me looked like refugees, dirty and shambling, traveling with great difficulty, except for one man who walked in front. He had long black hair, and he wore a dusty dark trench coat with a satchel slung over his shoulder. Striding purposefully, he carried a staff in his left hand. He rallied the people, and they began calling and waving their hands, screaming for help.

Great. Just what I needed—a group of stragglers to rescue. Well, I had news for them. There would be no rescue coming from me, not with the radios down. They didn't seem hostile, but desperation quickly took hold in the desert. We're all just thirsty beasts, looking for blood.

"Who goes there?" I called when they were close enough. I raised my own staff, made myself look even bigger than I already was, as though they were animals I needed to intimidate. I must have been quite a sight—a giant, half-naked woman with a floppy neon Mohawk shaking sticks and lasers.

The man held his hand up, signaling for the group to wait while he came just out of easy striking distance.

"I've got survivors here from the Yuma Dome. We're trying to make it to Gila Bend," he said.

Dome people out in the dead zones? Shit. I looked over his shoulder. Ash painted their clothes. They panted, struggled to stand. Some collapsed, lying so still that they may have already surrendered to the cruel air. The man in the trench coat wasn't having any trouble at all. Who the fuck was this guy?

"You're from the Voids," I said.

"Not exactly," he said. "It looks like you've run into trouble yourself. Perhaps we can work together and travel to Gila Bend. There's strength in numbers."

I peered at him, trying to figure out how he was breathing so well. "A haboob and a super storm cell collided and fucked up my crawlers." I hooked a thumb at the wreckage. "Radios are down, and the entrances to the cargo hold are blocked, so I don't know how useful I'd be to your group. You may as well keep trucking."

The man motioned toward my laser with his chin. "I obviously can't force you into letting us join you, but I think I can help you out. These are dangerous times to be wandering the desert alone."

"It's always a dangerous time to be wandering the dead zones. Look, buddy, you want to tell me why the fuck you dragged all these Dome dwellers out here? You get a kick out of watching people's lungs explode?"

"Guess you missed the news. Yuma is gone," he said calmly, but there was sadness in his blue eyes.

My mouth dropped. "What?"

"Can't you see the smoke spreading out behind us? There was an attack on the Yuma Dome this afternoon. I'm guessing there were multiple charges set around the perimeter—it went up so fast. Total chaos. I gathered these survivors who decided it was better to strike out for Gila Bend. I didn't force anyone to come with me, if that's what you're wondering—not many will make it out of there alive."

I stood there for another minute or two, processing what he had said, staring at the billowing smoke that had engulfed the western sky. "Jesus Christ."

Something like this hadn't happened since the early riots, back when everything was chaos and anger and security around the Domes hadn't been very stable.

If it was the same person or organization behind the Skeleton attacks, then this was more serious than some minor acts of civil disobedience. This could be the beginning of a true war.

Even though this had colossal implications, I ultimately focused on one thing: Trina. If Yuma was in ruins, then there was no way to get the Ketacillin she needed to survive.

"This really fucks up my plans," I said.

He ran a gloved hand through his long hair. "I'm assuming you're a cargo runner from the Voids."

"Yeah, you probably know me. I'm Xero."

He squinted at me, and recognition flashed in his eyes. "Ah, Xero. Tucson's territory boss. We've never met, but yes, I've heard of you and seen you in various transmissions before. Your reputation precedes you."

I nodded, satisfied I wouldn't need to intimidate him. "Good. If you partner with me, you should know what to expect. I don't tolerate bullshit, and I don't fuck around."

"I also know you don't give help freely, but I assure you, I can give as good as I get. In fact, I think I can get us back up and on the road again, if you don't mind."

It was a nice way of saying I was quid pro quo regardless of the circumstances. He wasn't wrong. You didn't get to where I was by doing thankless favors.

I glanced at the dead crawlers and then back at the ragtag stragglers who had all fallen into the sands behind him. "You think we can get the crawlers back on the road? You know how many tons each of these things weighs?"

"Trust me, I have a plan." He grinned.

What a weird motherfucker. I kind of liked him—there was a sharp intelligence and wit behind his eyes, and he wasn't bad looking either. He had the weathered, confident look of a person who had survived things most people couldn't even dream of. I saw that look every day in the mirror.

"You got a name?" I said.

"You can call me Radar."

I thought awhile, scanning my memory for anyone matching his name and description, but came up empty.

He chuckled. "I wouldn't expect you to know me. I'm discreet."

Meaning he was an independent mercenary or smuggler. No one else would have such an easygoing confidence in the middle of a literal disaster.

"Are you working for Xed?" I said.

"No. I'm a free agent," he said, tacitly confirming my suspicion.

In some ways it made me trust his abilities even more, given it was not an easy time to be an independent operator. It was nearly impossible to get anything done without being connected to one of the major cartels.

I cocked a hip, looking him up and down with a new appreciation. Guy was more dangerous than he looked.

He smiled as he watched me processing the information. "Don't worry, I'm not foolish enough mess with the likes of Xero, injured or not."

"Good choice. I'm hurting, but that just makes me even more vicious."

We locked eyes. Professional agreement.

"Good. At least we understand each other." I extended a hand. "Partners until we get out of this mess."

He thrust out his hand, and we gave each other a good shake. The dirty, worn leather of his gloves scraped against my palm.

"Partners," he said.

In the Voids, shaking hands was a contract in blood. We could trust each other, at least for the moment.

I walked past him and got closer to the fallen survivors. Twenty or more lay on their backs, choking and gasping. Some only wheezed softly, giving weak coughs as they sucked in too much sand. Dead weight.

I aimed my laser and rapidly shot half of them in the head.

Sloppy flecks of brain and skull sprayed the other victims. They tried to scream but couldn't get enough air into their lungs. Sounded like a group of mewling kittens. Sad.

Something cold pressed against my leg, and a second later electricity sparked through my body, bringing me to my knees. Not enough to kill me, but it was like pissing lightning. Radar loomed over me, his metal staff poking into my leg.

"What the fuck!" I scrambled to my feet, pointing the laser at his head.

"That was uncalled for," he said.

I scanned his equipment. The staff looked like it was just a chunk of plumbing pipe. Threads wound up the ends of it, but I saw no electronics to explain the shock.

"If you're going to make a decision like that, I'd appreciate it if you discussed it with me first," he said.

He had something of a point, since we'd just declared a partnership.

"You're right. I'm not used to needing permission for anything. I'm used to being the boss-lady."

"I understand. For the duration of this mission, I think we should reach a consensus before making any major tactical movements."

Professional. He had fighting skills and manners. If my crotch wasn't on fire, it would be wet.

"How in the hell did you do that?" I said.

He dug the pipe into the ground and put a hand on his hip. "There's more to me than meets the eye. I'll explain later, but for the moment, just know I'm an engineer by trade. I'm good at putting things together."

"I wouldn't mind seeing what's under that coat. I'll strip search you later."

He laughed. "You're an optimistic thinker."

"Optimism or death. Anyway, sorry about killing your buddies, but you know they wouldn't live. They were too far gone. They would only be suffering and holding us back. I've watched too many Dome dwellers slowly suffocate to death in the Voids, and it's not a pretty way to go. This was merciful. You know I'm right."

He got a faraway look in his eyes, and he cast his gaze downward, that same sadness falling over his features. "You're right, but I think there's still hope for these people if we can get them to Gila Bend in time."

They were rough looking, but they might recover if we got them into an oxygenated environment before dawn rose on a new day.

"I'm not exactly thrilled with the idea of spending the night out in the dead zones, so if you've got another idea, I'm all ears," I said.

He smiled and patted the dark leather satchel. "I think I can arrange something."

CHAPTER FIFTEEN

I DIDN'T believe in magic, but this guy was a goddamned wizard.

"I'll be a son of a bitch," I said as the crawler thumped back onto its treads. The ground shook. Sand licked my ankles. Radar grinned.

Using some magical winch he'd rigged from parts in his satchel, he'd managed to yank the crawler upright again. Unbelievable. The thin ropes and little black motor didn't seem strong enough to lift me, let alone an enormous cargo vehicle.

"I can build my way out of anything," he said.

"You're hired."

"Who said I'm for sale?"

"Mercs are always for sale. Everyone has a price."

He whacked my bare arm. "Don't think you can afford me. Heard Albuquerque cleaned your clock."

I clenched my teeth. Mustn't kill my pet merc.

He gripped his staff but kept smiling. Asshole knew I couldn't waste him.

I cleared my throat, blinked a few times. Smiled back. Politely. "You heard wrong. You know how much cash Alphadrine pulls in? More than you can dream of." And it did. If you had the staff and the time to fucking peddle that shit right. Fuck me.

"We can talk payment later," he said.

Maybe he wanted into the Alphadrine racket too. Everyone wanted their piece of our stash. Couldn't blame them—being out of the market for a few months meant the demand for Alphadrine had skyrocketed. Once I got us back out there, Xed could kiss his empire goodbye.

"Consider this cargo a down payment. Mutual funds. Let's get that shit," I said.

With the crawler out of the sand trap, we opened the doors to the supply hull, and it was like peeling back the gates to heaven. Water, food, clothing, and medicals supplies lay scattered around the steel capsule.

At the very back, packed carefully amongst layers of egg crates and Styrofoam, were grenades. Big, expensive grenades. No wonder they were so eager to push this supply run—these were serious munitions. Would have been an interesting way to go, but the packaging had obviously done its job, since nothing went kaboom. Neptune would have creamed herself.

Radar dragged a hand across his face. "Dodged a real bullet here, didn't you?"

"You aren't kidding. Normally I'd say we dump them, but that's some extra fancy weaponry. What say you?"

"Valuable enough to risk it. At least someone packed them correctly. If they were going to explode that would have happened already."

"I'm into it. If the government writes off this shipment, we'll get to keep these."

"After what happened in Yuma, I'd hang onto them anyway. No telling what might go down next," he said.

I rummaged through more boxes. "Whoa, check this out. There's a bunch of albuterol and atropine back here," I said. "I can shoot your guys up with a little cocktail—it'll make them feel like shit, but it should help them breathe until we get back into a Dome. No oxygen tanks, but there's some filter masks back here. Maybe a few will live through this."

He clearly cared about the survivors. Couldn't understand why, but it was a decent trade for getting the crawler out of the sand, and generosity now might help avoid extortion later.

"You have medical training?" he said. A brow twitched.

I could have sucked the hope right out of his eyes, like eggs from the shell.

"I'm actually a psychiatrist, but yeah, I went to medical school. I know what I'm doing. Mostly."

"Wonderful. Please. Do it."

Delicious. Quid pro quo. We could eat each other's sins.

The black cloud of Yuma shimmered in the distance. Still on fire. I shuddered, awed and jealous—where could you get those extraordinary explosives? I wanted them. The grenades in the cargo paled in comparison to whatever had wrought such fantastic destruction.

Radar gathered the survivors and crammed them into the supply hull before the last sunrays disappeared. After shooting everyone up with a rescue cocktail, I made sure none of them died from the bolus, then gathered a kit of goods for the cabin.

Radar brushed the glass from our seats and systematically took apart the dashboard, trying to repair the radio.

"I've got the wiring fixed, but the mechanics were soaked in the storm. Should work again once it's dried out, but that will take time," he said. "Would be nice to let someone in the Breakers know about our situation."

"Right. Gila Bend's Dome is dusted."

Back in the day, Gila Bend had been a nice small Dome, another crossroads like Yuma, but its population was too small to justify the resources needed to keep it running. Officials decided keeping Yuma as a border crossing was a better decision.

"Been dead for years now," he said. "But it should have enough oxygen left to keep these guys alive, at least until communications are restored and we can figure out a way get them back into a Dome."

Such stupid hope. Might be weeks before a rescue mission, and they would be long dead before that, even in a partially controlled Dome. But we all had crusades, and this was clearly his, doomed or not. Darwin was a total pain in the ass.

We chugged water and scarfed emergency rations I'd dug out of the cargo. The dry protein bar tasted like caviar, and I grunted with pleasure as I slugged down the tasteless slop. Nothing like a disaster to make you enjoy life's small pleasures.

"If you don't mind, I'll drive. I know the way to Gila Bend, and you can tend your injuries while we travel," he said.

I raised an eyebrow. "Sure you can handle this thing?"

He laughed. "I can rebuild one of these things from the ground up. Pretty sure I can drive one."

I shrugged. "Point taken. Get us there."

He fired up the crawler. The gurgling engine sounded like motherfucking angel trumpets.

"I found a case of morphine back there—brought some of it up in that first aid kit. You should take a shot. Let yourself relax and heal. With a small enough dose, you should be clear before we reach Gila Bend," he said.

I stared at him.

"There's no reason to kill each other. We're both professionals. Shooting your partner before the payoff is sloppy. Give yourself a dose of painkillers so you can clean those wounds better, maybe sew up some of those bigger cuts. You're chewed up bad."

I opened my mouth to say no, but stopped. He was right. Everything hurt. All the burns, all the lacerations, throbbed relentlessly. With the adrenaline washing away, the pain was creeping back. I hated burns more than anything else—I'd take bullets, lasers, and knives over burns.

Just one hit wouldn't hurt.

"Can't argue with that logic," I said, eager to do it before I changed my mind.

With zeal, I pulled up a fat syringe of morphine, watching the chamber fill with the viscous fluid. Even though the drug was ancient, outdated, each cc looked delicious, and I flicked the tube quickly, clearing any bubbles before I jabbed it into my upper thigh. I let out a big sigh and melted into the seat.

So. Good.

"Better?" he said.

"Definitely."

"Take care of yourself. Just leave the driving to me." He turned his attention back to the dunes rolling past our cracked headlights.

Already feeling the euphoria settling in, I wanted to clean myself before I was too drowsy to function. I'd given myself a deep intramuscular injection, so I had time before the full drug load made its way into my bloodstream.

"Sorry, have to strip so I can bandage this shit," I said.

"On my honor—eyes on the road."

"I don't know, peeling skin and crusty stab wounds are pretty fucking irresistible. You might not be able to control yourself."

We both laughed hard. He'd fit right in with the Grease Weasels if I could dream up a contract tasty enough to tempt him. If I moved enough product, got enough capital to lure him in, he'd be mine.

"Not a problem. I'll watch the road. Fix yourself," he said.

I untied the toga—I'd found army fatigues in the cargo but wouldn't change into them until after scrubbing my wounds. Now I could disinfect the chemical burns without wanting to shoot myself in the face, but even with the morphine, it wasn't pleasant.

"You okay over there?" he said, listening to me grunting and huffing.

"I can think of better ways to spend an evening, but I'll live," I said.

After covering myself in burn salve and layering sterile bandages on the larger cuts, I put my clothes back on and cleaned up the medical supplies.

"Put your head on my lap and take a nap. You need the rest," he said.

I raised both eyebrows.

"Merc's honor—I promise to be a gentleman," he said.

No energy to argue—the morphine dose settled in, dulled the pain, and made me dizzy. I mumbled something and laid my head on his pants. They were soft, smelled like wood smoke, sand, and metal, like burning aluminum. He switched off the overhead lights. In the rumbling darkness, I listened to the crawler's treads rolling across the uneven desert sands.

"I'll keep a look out for rabid coyotes," he said.

Not sure what was scarier—the packs of mutant coyotes wandering the dead zones or just how damned good the morphine felt swimming through my veins.

CHAPTER SIXTEEN

GILA BEND had seen better days.

But it didn't smell like shit, and I liked that.

We drove through deserted neighborhoods and down a main street, the crawler's treads grinding over uneven pavement as we passed abandoned businesses, their broken signs hanging from the battered facades. Domed or not, the Old West never really let go of this town.

Gila Bend was so small and off the main grid that the military didn't even bother patrolling the place anymore. Immigration was totally closed, and Radar insisted on rolling right through the center of town, kicking up huge clouds of dust as we pulled the crawler up to the front of an old diner. He left it there—said it would add to our intimidation factor and make rebels think twice about ambushing us.

"You're going to love this place," he said as we exited the crawler, walked past a faded plastic figure of the planet Saturn, and pushed through a cracked glass door framed by rusty metal.

The Saturn Disco was over 100 years old, and somehow it hadn't been absorbed back into the dusty crossroads that lay beneath Gila Bend. Remodeling kept it alive, but slivers of other decades peeked through its pores. Inside, everything was blue and white and covered in cheesy planetary decorations—bad models of spaceships and planets with chipped paint jobs hung from the ceilings, and retro space ornaments plastered every wall.

The joint was dirty, its blue Formica tables cracked and peeling, the white booth seats torn and smeared with decades of grease and ass stains. Tables were packed with pissed off citizens, cops, and wannabe military types arguing about Yuma. Not the best place for a clandestine meeting, if you asked me.

Radar put his back to the wall and stretched a leg along the booth. I sat across from him, feet straight forward, arms crossed.

"You seem to be enjoying yourself," I said.

"It's good to see Gila Bend so alive—check out the community spirit. They're ready to band together and fight. Don't see that in the Breakers very often," he said. "And, this is a perfect place to gather information. It's all here. Just have to wait and listen."

I unfolded my arms and twiddled a grimy half-full saltshaker. "Point taken."

A middle-aged waitress with a stained white apron and poorly dyed red hair shuffled to our table.

"Hey, Radar. What are you having today?" she said evenly, as though the place wasn't bubbling with turmoil, and it was just like any other day at work. Maybe it was. Her eyes flicked to me. "Who's the lady?"

"Trudy, this is Xero—we crossed paths while I was evacuating Yuma," he said.

She tapped her foot. "Good for you. You want the usual?"

Should I be offended she didn't give a shit about a major territory boss chilling out in her restaurant?

He nodded and handed an old laminated menu back to Trudy. His fingers left streaks on the greasy plastic.

"How about your lady friend?" she said.

I stifled a laugh—couldn't remember the last time I'd been called someone's fucking lady friend.

"I'll have the same," I said. Whatever came out would be better than the dehydrated shit we ate yesterday.

The waitress strutted off without another word, and I turned back to Radar. The first rays of morning sun sliced through the window and fell across half his face. His tanned skin was marked with a network of old, faded scars. This wasn't his first rodeo.

He noticed me staring, but I didn't break eye contact. "So you're a regular here," I said.

He shifted so his face was out of the sunlight. "You could say that. Gila Bend is on many of my routes."

Made sense—I didn't have much penetration out here. Made it prime territory for independent operators.

I gestured at the crowd. "I can't hear shit. Not trying to be ungrateful here, but we're kind of pressed for time."

He swung his leg onto the floor and straightened his posture. "Patience is a virtue. Trust me—I've got great hearing, we'll catch some information. And I think you'll be very happy with our meal."

"You have some fucked up priorities," I said.

He grinned and looked around at the pandemonium. "No one has ever accused me of being normal."

I scrunched my mouth into a hard line. "Speaking of which, there's a big fucking elephant in the room I'd like to address. Looks like we're going to be working together awhile longer, and I'm not a fan of secrets biting me in the ass."

He slumped into the corner, nails digging into the seat.

"Don't need gory details. Just want the essentials," I said.

He looked around and jerked forward, tearing out a chunk of the vinyl as he came to a stop close to my face.

"What do you want to know?" His breath was warm on my skin. Violence waiting beneath the surface.

"Just two things. I want to know how you shocked me. And, your lungs. How are you getting around the zones breathing better than a professional runner?" I said.

"It's actually one answer for both questions. I'm part robot," he said.

I laughed, slapping my hands against the table hard enough to make spilled salt bounce into the air. "That's a good one, buddy. I'll give it to you for creativity."

I met his gaze, expecting him to start laughing with me, but his face froze like a weathered statue.

I cleared my throat and lowered my voice. "No way."

Rising paranoia about sentient machines forced the government to make a series of mandates that limited implantable cyborg technology. Penalties were so severe that we still didn't mess with that shit in the Voids. Anyone caught with implantable cybernetics would be executed immediately.

He tipped his head forward and kept his voice low. "More than one reason why I prefer to be an independent contractor." He paused, gray eyes drilling into mine. "We have intel on each other. Are we clear—mutual data will remain discreet?"

I smirked and lowered my head to the same level. "Absolutely discreet." I shook my head. "Man, that is seriously crazy. Motherfucking robot mercenary."

He exhaled and ran a hand through his hair. "That's one way to put it. Since it may come up at some point, I'm like the ultimate runner because I have artificial lungs, and a few other modifications that give me certain...advantages."

Illegal cybernetics or not, I wanted him even more for the Grease Weasels. Bad.

"Like turning yourself into a human taser," I said.

He turned his palms up. "Amongst other things."

"I'm liking you more and more as time goes by," I said. "One day you'll to have to tell me how that went down. I'm sure it's a great story."

He sat up straighter and stopped mad-dogging me. "So I take it you'd like to keep me around for awhile longer."

"You're a cool cat, Radar. I wouldn't be sad if you stuck around—figure we could both use an ally right about now." I closed my eyes, listening to the mob getting louder.

As the sun rose higher, the restaurant bulged with bodies. Despite the growing crowd, our booth in the back had a protective bubble. Smart people. Mercenaries and cartel bosses make for dangerous breakfast buddies.

Trudy tromped back to our table, carrying two huge plates of meat, two pieces of lemon meringue pie, and two big mugs of coffee. She managed not to spill anything as she bounced her way around the rowdy throb of customers. She slung the plates and mugs across the table, everything staying where it was supposed to. Trudy had skills. With a grunt and a nod, but no words, she waded back into the fray.

Real. Fucking. Coffee. For some reason even that loser Xed didn't have any at his swanky casa, and the real deal smelled amazing. I sucked half of it down in one go, not giving a shit that it burned my tongue. Rest of my body was already torched—may as well finish the job for a good cause. The big plates were overloaded with turkey and mashed potatoes smothered in gravy. Didn't look or smell great—had to be synthmeat—but it was genuine enough. Better than packaged rations.

I slid a plate over the uneven Formica table, and it snagged on what I thought was a big crack in the table. When I tugged on it, a tiny manila envelope slid out from under the plate.

Gave the envelope a shake—it jingled. "This what I think it is?"

He laced his fingers together. "Would I ever let you down?"

I poked his chest. "You, sir, are a stranger to me, but you have an honest face." I grinned. "Wanna tell me where to stick these?"

He pointed to a back storeroom. "Where the sun don't shine, of course."

Jackpot. After traversing a creepy labyrinth of hallways, I hit the motherlode: a giant bank of com devices. Rusted steel converter boxes covered with lumpy solder and multicolored wires lined the walls of the small storeroom from floor to ceiling. We needed these in the Casa Grande Breakers. Would almost be worth expanding our distribution network out here just to have this kind of communication set up. Radar could help us do that.

I was almost excited enough to forget it smelled like decades of old grease and rat shit. And that's who I had to call first. The greasy rat.

I picked up the handset and punched in codes.

"Xero. Where are you?" Xed said. The concern in his voice surprised me. Boys. You fuck 'em once, and they get all attached.

"I take it you got wind of the Yuma fiasco," I said.

"It's absolute chaos on the back channel, but the military and media are doing their best to keep that info out of Phoenix. I'm not pleased. I have operatives out there I've lost contact with, and I can't get anyone else on the ground to check it out. Do you have any intel you can share with me?"

"Not much, unfortunately." I brought him up to speed but left Radar out of the story. In these circles, you couldn't be too careful. Your friend could be someone else's mortal enemy, and loose lips could do way more than just sink the damned ship.

"I'm glad you survived," he said.

"Barely, but I'll take it. If I'd gotten to Yuma a few hours earlier, that's it. I'd be toast."

"Now what will you do?" he said calmly like a good little sociopath.

"I was hoping you might have some suggestions. I can get back to the Tucson Voids, but I'm shit out of luck for Ketacillin."

Silence on the line. I waited.

He cleared his throat. "Not to be judgmental here, but perhaps you aren't seeing the forest for the trees? We just experienced one of the biggest terrorist acts of the century."

I scoffed. "Look, the world might be burning down around us, but there's not much I can do about it. One of my comrades is dying. That's what I know. And that's what's important to me."

"You're quite the admirable leader."

"I don't think anyone's ever called me admirable, but I like compliments. So. You got any bright ideas?"

"If you're game, I think we might be able to do a little business. I want to figure out why cities are blowing up, and you want to save your associate. I'll help you get to some Ketacillin, if you agree to help me find your buddy, Calavera. Her Skeletons are involved, and she hasn't been seen in over a week," he said.

"I'm listening."

And he told me.

That Xed. Xed had a plan.

CHAPTER SEVENTEEN

A HOTEL room. In the Breakers. I had no fucking idea such a thing still existed.

The bank of single-story rooms was connected to the back of the restaurant and shared the same cheesy space decor. Nostalgic—all space programs had ceased decades ago, but this place held on to its astral dreams. Peeling planet and star decals clung desperately to the walls and ceiling, falling like our satellites had come tumbling out of the sky.

Radar and I lay next to each other, and I dragged a ragged fingernail along the smooth line of scar tissue that ran all the way down his ribcage.

"Damn, that's a really big scar," I said.

"Side effect of having my lungs ripped out of my chest a few times."

He propped himself up in the surprisingly clean hotel bed, his elbows digging into a stack of yellowed but fresh pillows. The faded blue sheets were tucked up to his belly button, and sweat coated his tan skin. He looked timeless, like he could have been wandering the desert for decades without aging.

I flipped on top of him, straddling his waist, my figure casting a shadow across him, the naked lamp bulb outlining my sagging Mohawk next to a blue Saturn decal. Leaning down, I followed the scar with my tongue, licking back up the slick indentation and ending with a wet smooch on his mouth.

"Tell me about how it happened," I said.

He folded his arms over his head, the grooves in his biceps highlighted by deep shadows. "You want to hear how I was sliced open and my lungs were cut out of my body?"

I bared my teeth and wiggled playfully, like a coyote pup waiting for meat. "Yeah, tell me the tale of your suffering. Hearing about someone's greatest misery tells me more about them than anything else."

"You're a twisted fuck, aren't you?" He grabbed my wrists.

I used gravity to trap his hands against the headboard. He still held my wrists, but I had his arms pinned.

"I've been accused of worse things," I said.

He smirked. "My parents were exiled to the Breakers, but I couldn't breathe the air. I was meant for the Domes."

I released his hands, and he let go of my wrists.

"Ah, one of the lucky children," I said.

"Cursed is more like it. But yes, according to Dome propaganda I would be one of the lucky ones," he said. "So lucky that they couldn't get my Zone Pass cleared for Dome adoption. No foster families available for me there, so I was exiled with my parents. I was going to die in the Breakers."

When the big deportations went down, no one stopped to make a policy for offspring with different lung capacities. Took a while to sort that out—meanwhile, everyone got screwed. If one person was marked for the Breakers or the Voids, the rest of the family was sent packing too. Kids who couldn't breathe unfiltered air got kicked out to die, and parents who couldn't survive outside the Domes got booted along with their exiled children. Lot of ruined families and exploding lungs. Supposedly that didn't happen anymore. *Supposedly.*

"That's sad, man," I said. "But you look like you came out okay in the end."

He shook his head. "It's not that simple. My parents were engineers, brilliant engineers. They helped build the cybernetic technologies that got the Domes going in the first place. But when the mandates happened, they were tossed out of the Domes and their inventions were destroyed."

"Typical government bullshit."

"They knew how to build me artificial lungs, but they would

have been executed if they were caught," he said.

"Too much surveillance in the Breakers." Strands of black hair fell across his eyes, and I brushed them away from his forehead. "So they moved it all out to the Voids, right?"

He smiled, but it was all dead sadness. "They sacrificed a lot for me," he said simply. "This was before you cleaned up Tucson, but I heard your early regime gave us shelter. I suppose you can consider this a belated thank you."

"You're making me feel old, but you're welcome."

"I've always liked Tucson, but we didn't spend much time there. The air in the Voids wasn't quite as bad back then, but it was still hard to buy enough oxygen to keep us all alive. So they got it done and got out, came back to Gila Bend. Tucson was deadly before you established some order."

"You're going to make me blush." I clucked my tongue. "So Gila Bend is your real hometown."

"In a manner of speaking. I guess this is basically where I grew up, and I've spent a lot of time here working. It's not as crowded as Yuma. People here are friendly but discreet. It's a good place, but my parents had to keep moving, camping out in the Voids when sweeps came through."

I poked at his nose. "What's the end of the story? I want all the gritty details."

"Jesus, you're merciless. You can guess."

"Come on. You're a big boy, you can handle it. I like to get to know the people I work with. Intimately." I ground my crotch into his hips.

He rolled his eyes, but I knew he'd give in. I liked a guy who did what I told him to do.

"My parents put me through hell, and I almost died many times while they tried to get the cybernetics working."

"There's something you're leaving out," I said. "You didn't get that final pair of lungs from your parents, and you didn't get those additional modifications from them either, did you?"

"A man's got to keep some secrets. You're right, though. I'll give you that. They died when I was still young."

"That doesn't make any sense. If they figured out how to replace your lungs, why not do it for themselves?" I said.

"Who said they didn't?"

It took a moment, but I got it. "Ah, so they were caught."

Mucking around with cybernetics was no joke.

His face hardened. "They were already under suspicion. So there you go. I think that's more than enough information for one night."

I wanted to keep pressing him, milking him for the truth. Where did he get those adult-sized lungs? How did he escape extermination? But I had a good sense for how far I could push someone, and sucker punching Radar over the brink wouldn't be helpful.

I tapped a finger on his chest, between the clavicles. "That'll do for now."

"Not sure what I signed up for if the people on your crew are anything like you."

I shifted around on top of him. "Don't worry, I'm probably the worst of the bunch, and I promise to make it worth your while." Neptune might actually be worse than me, but he would find that out for himself if everything went right.

He grunted and rolled, landing on top and pinning my waist.

"If we're not all dead before that." He stared down at me.

I tickled his belly button. He giggled, caught off guard, and it was bizarre to hear such a childish sound coming from such a serious face.

"Well, now we've got a pile of premium explosives and a semi-illegal laser to protect us. Got ahold of central command earlier, and they're striking the cargo from the record, releasing the gear as a casualty. As long as I submit documentation for the losses, we're golden. Free toys," I said.

And free Morphine. Mine. All of it. Not as nice as a load of Vinicodone, but the long trek back to Tucson was going to feel a hell of a lot better now. That bumpy crawler ride would be just like gliding across the desert on a magic carpet.

"Smooth work," he said. "You know your shit."

"We could all die tomorrow, but until then, may as well gather as much money and power as we can. Even better if we can take that money and power from clueless Dome drones," I said. "And you know, also save innocent people when you can. Looks like you were right—some of your refugees might make it after all."

Gila Bend still had something of a functional hospital, and Radar managed to make them accept the survivors as patients. Whether he paid in money or charisma, I didn't know, but a rich man is a rich man. I liked all sorts of deep pockets.

He smirked, leaned down, and kissed me. "I think we'll get along just fine." He ran his rough thumb across my forehead, rubbing off a thick smudge of dirt.

"Careful there, chief. You'll skin me alive," I said. "I'd trade my laser for a hot shower right now." My face probably looked like a molting lizard, but I was still riding easy on that old school smack. No pain.

"Sorry, shower's busted. Bad plumbing in this half the building," he said.

My eye twitched. "I should have guessed."

He shrugged. "Such is life."

I stared him down.

If I couldn't get clean, then I wanted it extra dirty.

Chapter Eighteen

A WARM breeze, hot sand licking my ankles, and a cloudless afternoon sky that looked ready for a spectacular sunset—I was back in Tucson. Back where I belonged.

Tall saguaro cacti flanked an imposing steel door, guarding our stronghold. I waved to the security camera mounted above the porch and banged on the door. It swung open, and we stepped inside.

"Honey, I'm home!" I called.

"Boss!" Milo yelled and came running to the threshold. His shaggy, naturally red hair came down past his chin, and a sprinkling of freckles made him look much younger than he really was. Dark circles hinted at the heavy burden he carried as the territory's medical director. Glad it was his job and not mine.

I inhaled the scent of freshly waxed bowling alleys. The Golden Lanes—home. Right next to the old freeway and chock full of extra structure from all the electronics in the walls. Perfect for both drug strongholds and kids' birthday parties, it was the best place in town for our headquarters.

Milo flung his arms out to hug me but stopped when he saw my skin. "Ah jeez, Xero, you didn't tell me how fucked up you were," he said.

"It's been a rough week."

He shook his head. "I've got one Grease Weasel MIA, Trina's down hard with the Zaps, and you're out there playing rodeo clown," he said. "Have to drag you down to the infirmary for the night, make sure you didn't pick up any nasty infections—some of those wounds aren't looking so good."

"You're making me paranoid," I said.

"I aim to please." He stuck his hands in his pockets. A pair of ripped jeans and a faded green and red flannel shirt made him seem more like a teenage groupie than an important medical professional.

Looking past me, he strolled forward and thrust a hand at Radar. "Sorry for the bad manners. Name's Milo—hear you saved Xero's hide out there. Welcome to the Grease Weasels."

Radar shook his hand. "Interesting name."

"We started out as a humble punk band, and the name stuck," Milo said.

Radar leaned on his staff. "Well, there are cartels with stranger names out there. Names aside, I'm glad to be of service. You guys have some impressive security here."

"We don't fuck around," a short woman said as she emerged from a backroom.

"Indeed," Radar said, unfazed.

"Thanks. I run a tight ship." She ruffled bright blue hair cropped into a pixie cut.

He held out a hand. "Name's Radar."

"Neptune. I handle security around here," she said.

She was half Radar's height, but that didn't stop her. When she gripped his hand, she yanked him off balance, pulling him closer. "I hear you're an engineer."

"Correct. Pleased to meet you." His gaze wandered to the shiny bowling lanes. "Do those things still work?"

"Absolutely," Neptune said.

Neptune kept those lanes going like they were new. Kept everything else clean and updated too—most of the wood and vinyl surfaces had been restored, and the main room was painted all in tones of shiny red and gold lacquer. The immaculate remodeling was nicer than anything in the Domes—few would guess we were actually in the middle of an exile's wasteland.

Radar nodded his approval. "Nice restoration. I don't remember the last time I saw a working lane."

"We don't fuck around when it comes to recreation either," she said.

With Neptune still gripping his hand, he leaned forward and said, "I don't fuck around when it comes to anything."

Neptune smiled and released him. "I think you'll do. Remind me to show you some of my toys once you've proved your salt."

"I'm always up for anything that involves tools," he said.

Milo stamped his foot. Old, polished wood squeaked under his boot heel. "You guys are such assholes. He already proved his salt by pulling Xero out of the dead zones."

"He's got a point," I said.

Neptune crossed her arms and said nothing.

"Hey, Neptune," I said. "Radar also helped me bring back some fun stuff. He pulled a gadget out of that trench coat of his and hauled my crawler out of the sand, got it rolling again. Government signed off on that cargo, so the whole shipment is ours. I've got this." I held up the laser. "And grenades. The good kind."

She flashed her teeth. "All grenades are the good kind.'

"Brought some medical supplies too. Little something for everyone," I said to Milo.

"Excellent. We're low on some important provisions. We can unload the cargo later tonight," Milo said. "Neptune, why don't you find Radar a room, let him clean up, and then see if you can find him some food. Xero needs some real clinic time."

"Seriously? You want to drag me all the way down to the university clinic?" I said.

Milo just stared at me.

I threw up my hands. "Oh fine, I know you won't stop nagging me until I go, and I'll never get any peace and quiet." Bastard knew my fear of germs would outweigh my dislike of hospitals.

Milo nodded. "Trust me, disinfecting those wounds will be a lot less uncomfortable in an actual clinic. Once you're cleared and everyone is clean and fed, we can powwow about our next move."

I leaned back and raised both eyebrows. "Look at you stepping up and being a leader."

Milo blushed but then straightened up and took a proud breath. "Well, someone had to run this place while you were off gallivanting through the desert."

"And you're shorthanded," I said and glanced into the dark control room. "Ugh, I purposefully forgot about that idiot. Where is Copper?" Ice ages formed around my heart when I thought of him.

Neptune and Milo stared at each other, both almost saying something before stopping short.

"He's down at the university, trying to see if we can get a sideline to the under web, maybe pick up some contra news," Neptune said.

"Like he could pull off something that complicated," I said.

"Look, I don't have time to go hunting for an IT person you *don't* despise. For now, you're stuck with Copper," Milo said.

I clenched my teeth but put a hand on his shoulder. "You're right. You done good, Milo, you done good. You're picking up my slack."

"Give yourself a break—have you taken a peek in the mirror? You look like death," he said.

Neptune nodded and rocked back onto the heels of her studded black combat boots. "Sorry to say this, boss, but you look like mutant coyote shit."

"I get it, I get it. I'll go to the clinic. And please, someone tell me our shower facilities are working."

Neptune gave me a thumbs up. "All systems are operational."

"I could kiss you," I said.

Neptune scoffed. "Not with those lips." She turned to Milo. "Might want to hit her with an STD blaster while you're at it—she's looking crusty."

I glared at her. "You're lucky we don't have time for another machete fight."

Neptune raised her eyebrows and showed her teeth. "There's always time for that, but I wouldn't touch you with a ten foot blade. I'm not getting squirted with whatever nasty shit is swimming in your bloodstream."

"Yup, get a move on. I'll fire up a Jeep," Milo said.

He might look like a freckled teenager, but he was a good doctor, and he wouldn't stop until every inch of me was disinfected. He loved his job. Too much.

He grinned.

I sighed. I had an ugly date with pain.

And I was out of morphine.

Chapter Nineteen

A HALOGEN light blinded me while the steel stable froze my bare ass. Medical instruments clanged into a pan, echoing in the empty clinic. Pungent with disinfecting chemicals, it smelled like I was huffing mothballs.

"Enough! I'm cleaner than a prostitute's asshole." My head flopped against the exam table. My feet hung off the edge—place wasn't built for Amazons like me.

"Sorry," Milo said. "The last time you picked up a skin infection from the Breakers, you spread it to other people. Like me. If I'm out of commission, we're all fucked. Can't take chances."

He pulled a bigass needle out of my stomach—hopefully the last of what seemed like an endless line of injections, some which left burning sensations crawling and creeping over my skin and through my veins. Add in some Machiavellian scrubbing to remove the peeling burns and damaged tissue, and it felt like I'd been soaked in gasoline and lit on fire like a Molotov cocktail. A long IV needle throbbed in the crook of an elbow—Milo insisted I needed to hydrate, replace lost blood volume, and speed up the healing.

I winced as the needle pinched on the way out. Blood pooled in my navel. "Point taken." Not like I wanted another month long battle with flesh-eating microbes.

He held a piece of gauze over the puncture until it stopped

bleeding. "You sure you don't want any pain medication?"

I put my hands over my eyes, his doctor's headlamp searing through my palms. "I can't. You know how I am."

An ache in my gut, deeper than the needle stick, crept into my chest, made my heart beat faster. I'm a good actress—I know this. But Milo, Milo was smart.

How could he not know I was already high as a kite?

With any luck, he wouldn't inventory his supply cabinet any time soon.

"Yeah, I do, you're a fucking eternal pain in the ass, Xero, the queen of the desert," he said and laughed. I heard him cleaning up—needles, gauze, and sutures squishing and clanking into the sink.

"The one and only," I said, laughing along with him. I sat up again, stifling more than one groan. Still not enough drugs. "Seriously. Thanks for watching shit down here. Couldn't have done a better job myself."

He stopped the cleanup, his smile fading. "I'm doing the best I can."

"But it's not enough," I said. "I know. I'm sorry we failed, but I wasn't expecting a major terrorist event to fuck our shit over. When we get back to base, we'll figure out our next move. It's not over yet."

He turned his back and washed his hands. "Do you want to see her?" he said softly.

"I was going to ask if I could, but I don't want to make things worse."

He dropped his head and shook it back and forth, still facing the sink. "It doesn't matter. She's intubated and unconscious."

Maybe I should have taken more drugs.

I followed him down the hallway, dragging an IV pole. The corridors were dark until we triggered dim lights, which flashed on and turned off again once we passed—limited resources. We had worked really hard to become energy independent. Thanks to me, Tucson had one of the largest solar arrays in the country. No waiting for the government to tell us when we could have power. I agreed with the old dark sky laws that limited outdoor light usage—a holdover from when Tucson was a hub for astronomy research and satellite launches that required pitch-black night skies—but unprovoked power outages were a thing of the past. Now we had the control.

I had the control.

"It's awfully quiet," I said as we loped along the eerie hallway. I didn't believe in ghosts, but I did believe in assassins. Might need to squander some energy for safety.

"I have this whole wing roped off as a private section for security purposes. And because I'm selfish, I want this sector ready to go for injured Grease Weasels. It needs to be empty and easy to secure, and I also just wanted Trina to have privacy," he said. "I have alarms triggered to ring other staff immediately if anything changes."

Our shadows flickered like an old reel-to-reel movie under the dancing lights.

"Well, you did a good job of making it creepy and menacing. It's got that whole murder carnival thing going for it."

Milo shot me a look, and I gave him a shrug. Place needed flowers or some shit.

At the end of the hallway, brighter light shone out through the doorway, and I heard the rhythmic whoosh of a respirator pumping in and out. A stab of anger shredded its way through my heart. Trina lay motionless in the hospital bed, connected to tubes and wires, her chest rising and falling with a steady, even pulse.

The room smelled like death.

With her bleached blond hair spread out around her pillow, she looked like Sleeping Beauty or Snow White. She had been sick long enough that several inches of her dark roots were showing. Her almond shaped eyes moved beneath her closed lids, but her pale lips were deathly motionless where they pursed around the gray ventilator tube.

"She's not contagious like that—the spores are deep in her lungs and it's all being processed by the ventilator,' he said, perhaps noticing my hesitation to get closer.

I wasn't afraid of death or contagion. I was afraid of boiling over with anger. My best friend was dying because some asshole decided to blow up a whole goddamn Dome.

I took several deep breaths and approached the bedside, put my hand around Trina's cold fingers. "We won't let you go out like this."

A twitch. A response from her eyes? I was probably imagining it, but I liked the thought she might be still in there, awake and fighting.

I turned to Milo who was fixed in place, quiet tears tumbling down his freckled cheeks. She was my best friend, but she was the love of Milo's life. Even though he'd watched hundreds, thousands of people die in his lifetime, he looked like a terrified child seeing the ugly face of death for the first time. He wasn't a warrior by nature, but when backed into a corner, Milo would fight and kill with the best of them. Beneath the tears, rage lurked.

I put a hand on his shoulder. "Take this thing out of my arm so we can get back to base. Time's wasting."

CHAPTER TWENTY

HOT. AMAZING. Water. The shower burned my raw skin, but I didn't care. I was too high to care. And disinfected or not, nothing made me feel cleaner than a scalding shower.

I strutted back into the main bowling alley, my heavy black boots clanging on the hollow wood floors. I stopped, planted my feet—whack, whack.

Neptune whistled. "Looking good, boss."

Back in my usual threads—shit-kicking combat boots, black fishnet shirt covered by a hot pink leather vest, and a ripped pair of black jeans. I ran some quick color through my hair in the shower, and the Mohawk was finally gelled right, the bright neon green strands fanning out in a semicircle around my head. Like a puffed up lizard, the boots and 'hawk let me soar until the tips of my hair brushed the ceiling. I always felt more powerful when the Mohawk was toxic green and at full mast.

I grinned, feeling invincible. "Gotta make nice for our guest. Wouldn't want him to think we're a bunch of slobs."

Radar sauntered into the room, in clean clothes and finally without his gloves and trench coat—bastard never seemed to take them off.

"I'm easy to please," he said.

Milo was already sitting at a big table in front of our old shoe rental stand. Instead of shoes, weapons festooned the shelves—never a bad idea to caucus within reach of some heavy artillery. Plates of food covered a white and red-checkered tablecloth.

"Sit down and eat before this shit gets cold," Neptune said.

I plopped down next to Milo and motioned for Radar to take a seat next to me. He started to sit, but Neptune put a hand in his face.

"Xero gave you the okay, but you're on my turf. Policy says no outsiders get weapons around the negotiation table," she said.

Radar still carried the pipe he shocked me with in the desert. Couldn't blame the guy for hanging onto his weapons in the middle of a cartel den.

"If you would just surrender it for the moment, that would be great," she said when Radar didn't respond. Way diplomatic for her—I was proud. Neptune's conflict resolution skills usually involved knives and explosives.

Radar stared her in the eye and said calmly, "No."

She cleared her throat and looked at me. I said nothing, gauging the situation. Who would win in a fight? I had to squash my morbid curiosity for the sake of peacekeeping. If circumstances had been different, watching them duke it out would be fun, but this wasn't the time.

"I trust him—he could have killed me days ago. It's just a pipe," I said.

Neptune stood up, her face turning red. She was glammed out too, wearing black cargo pants and a hot pink tank top that matched my vest. Her blue hair was spiked high and smears of purple eye shadow ringed her eyes, making them look even bigger than they already were.

I put a hand up to stop her, knowing she was ready to blow, and turned to Radar. "Dude, I don't like being unarmed either, but do you think you could do me a solid and just give Neptune the fucking stick?" I said.

He met my eyes, his gaze soft and composed. "No," he said. "Sorry."

Neptune stepped around the table. "I don't know who you think you are, but we don't tolerate bullshit. I'll give you to the count of three to hand over that fucking pipe peacefully."

I thought about trying to stop them, but Neptune was such a hardass, and nothing would make her cool off. Some things just had to play out.

Neptune counted to three and made a grab for Radar's pipe. He didn't move it out of her reach.

"Neptune, don't," I said, but she was too fast.

Crackle. Sizzle. Scream. Neptune's hand made contact with the metal, and she fell flat on the floor. Radar backed away.

"Neptune!" Milo yelled and ran to her side.

She was already sitting back up again, shaking her head and blinking.

"Fuck, I should have warned you about that." I fiddled with a spiked dog collar around my neck.

Milo pulled a stethoscope out of somewhere and was trying to listen to Neptune's heart, but she brushed him off.

"I'm all right," she said and unsuccessfully attempted to get up on her own. Milo helped her back into one of the white plastic bucket chairs.

Radar leaned on the pipe, shifting all his weight onto his right leg. "Sorry about that—didn't mean to give you quite so much juice." He turned to me. "Hard to control when I'm being attacked. Self defense instincts."

I rolled my eyes. "Can't you kids play nice?"

Radar shrugged in response.

Neptune was still out of it, but she slowly came around. "What in the fuck just happened?"

"Play with fire, and you get burned," I said. "I told you Radar would be a good addition to the team."

Neptune showed her teeth and sat up so fast that the chair went backward and smacked into Milo's knees. "How did he do that?" She pointed a finger at Radar's chest.

I looked at Radar, inviting him to explain.

"I've got a few aftermarket parts," he said.

I watched as the information percolated through Neptune's brain. Blinking slowly, her purple-smeared eyes looked like a poisonous butterfly flapping in the sun. "No. No, you fucking didn't." She whirled to me.

I slammed my palm on the plastic table hard enough that it cracked. Plates and beverages bounced in the air. "That's enough. We're a team, and I trust you with your job as security chief, but I am the fucking leader of this crew, and you need to calm the fuck down."

Neptune's face stayed fixed in a snarl, but with an angry grunt, she sat her ass back in a chair. I motioned to Radar who hesitated but cautiously sat down.

Neptune looked like she was literally biting her tongue, and before I could get in another word, she slammed her palms against the table, making another earthquake rattle through our dinner. "You brought a fucking cyborg into our territory? Are you out of your mind?"

I stomped my feet. "I understand where you're coming from, but think about it. The government's falling apart—when's the last time you saw someone get caught for a cybernetics violation? We just had a major terrorist attack—they've got bigger fish to fry."

"Won't that make them even more likely to scan the Voids?" she said in a childish singsong.

"In a perfect world, sure, but let's get serious—they can't even cover security on the Domes. They don't have the resources to do a major Voids sweep."

I gave her a rundown on the military staffing issues that caused so many of the adventures on the last run.

"Fine. Maybe the game's changed," she said.

"Right," I said. "I think that makes a good case for looking at Radar's...hardware in a different light. Besides, he's been doing this awhile, and he hasn't gotten caught yet."

Radar gave one quick nod. "I learned the hard way—I know what will get you iced, and what will keep you safe. I've modded everything so it's nearly impossible to detect any electronics. You'd need to chop me up and start pulling things out to find illegal pieces." He looked away. "And most people who get a taste of my electricity don't see the light of day again."

So the taser thing wasn't a cheap parlor trick after all.

Milo ogled Radar. "I've always wanted to examine a cyborg."

Radar shifted and swallowed audibly. "I'm not really a cyborg—I just have a few extra parts is all."

Milo blushed. "I don't mean any offense or anything, but as our crew medic, I need to have an understanding of any conditions or unique physiology that could come into play. You know, in case you're injured and require medical attention."

Awkward. I cleared my throat. "Okay, so you guys can go over that stuff later or something, but first things first—are we cool here?"

"No," Neptune said coldly but with less anger. "You always trust your instincts on these things, but I'm not kosher with some human cattle prod won't respect my rules. Meanwhile, we don't even know who the fuck he is or what he wants."

"I promise, I'm here as an ally. Attacking Xero in her stronghold would be suicide," he said.

Neptune rolled her eyes. "Oh, yeah, so that's why you come in here and piss me off? You got a death wish?"

"No. I just have my own codes that I live by. I'm sorry our conflicting policies have caused friction, but I hope we can come to an understanding. I think we could be mutually beneficial to each other."

Milo crossed his legs and put his hands palm up on the table. "There's one simple solution to this mess. Well, not simple, but it's standard if you're talking about letting him into the Grease Weasels."

I grimaced. "The A-Plus? Do you really want to deal with that mess right now?"

He ruffled his hair. "No, but if it will pacify Neptune and keep the peace, it might be worth it. To be honest, it will make me feel safer too."

Radar looked back and forth across the table. "What are we talking about here?"

"You know we manufacture Alphadrine—our big cash cow. In the process of synthesizing it, we came across a lot of other compounds, some more useful than others. Alphadrine does a lot of things—induces euphoria, amps you up, helps lung function. Good shit," I said.

Milo coughed. "But one of the compounds we produced on accident was a super-powered truth serum related to the Alphadrine formula. And it has side effects. Bad ones. Makes you trip hard, and instead of euphoria, some people, okay most people, become hypersensitive to pain. It can also fuck up your breathing. In short, it's really effective as a truth serum, but it can be damned unpleasant."

Neptune glared at Radar. "Milo's never let anyone kick the bucket. It's damned nasty shit, but it's a requirement for joining the inner circle. Hasn't failed us yet." She raised an eyebrow. "So, you in?"

The process was so horrific we never subjected anyone to it unless they wanted access to very sensitive information. I shivered just thinking about it.

Radar ignored Neptune and looked directly at Milo. "Pain I can deal with, but if you kill me, I'd be pretty displeased. You sure you can keep that from happening?"

"Absolutely. No one has ever passed away during an A-Plus screening. I'm good at what I do. Really good," he said.

Radar slapped his thigh a few times. "Against my better judgment, I'll agree to this. A team that doesn't trust each other is a disaster waiting to happen—one of the reasons why I prefer to work alone." He shot another look at Milo. "Looks like you're going to get your wish after all."

Milo tried to wipe the eagerness off his face but only partially succeeded. "I assure you, I'll be nothing but professional."

Neptune grinned and tapped her fingers together. "Excellent. Milo can administer the drug and monitor his vitals, and I'll take care of the interrogation part."

"Rein it in Neptune, you're looking like more of a sadist than me, and that's a fucking scary thing," I said.

Radar looked around and groaned. "What have I gotten myself into?"

CHAPTER TWENTY-ONE

I MARCHED into a tiny back room and plunked down in a rickety office chair. Every inch of the soundproof closet blinked with equipment—half of it didn't work. After the satellite harvests, communication became a serious problem. Neptune hunted for tech scraps on our runs, and she brought anything and everything back to the command room for rigging broadcasting devices. One time I suggested Neptune was an engineering packrat—she didn't care for my comment, and the rest of the day was lost to a machete fight.

Neptune and Milo were down at the clinic, interrogating Radar. Maybe I should have gone with them to keep Neptune in check, but I trusted Milo to keep Radar alive. I had business to conduct.

I pulled on a pair of battered headphones and bent a foam-covered microphone up to my mouth. Copper should have fixed our major com lines by now, but since he was absolutely worthless, I was stuck fiddling with Neptune's voodoo gadgets. It took a few tries, but after accidentally snapping off some antennas that Neptune would have a fit about later, I made contact with Xed.

"Glad to hear you made it back safely," he said.

"Glad to hear you haven't died in a giant explosion."

He was silent, then said, "Yes, I think we're all on edge after Yuma. No further reports about the motives for the attack. I assume you have no news about Calavera?"

"We just reached our main base a few hours ago, and we're working through some...technical difficulties. I got torn to shreds out there—can't go hunting until our medical dude lets me off the hook."

"Fair enough."

"Which leads me to the next part of the equation—I'm more than happy to help you track down that cow. After we get the Ketacillin."

He licked his lips before replying. "I did some investigating while you were away. I have a plan, but it's a little unorthodox."

"Hell, I've never done shit by the book anyway. Lay it on me," I said.

"While I was looking into your organization, I came across a few interesting tidbits. Although titillating, most of this information was worthless. Your middle name doesn't interest me.   However, some of it was useful. Like the fact you were originally a punk band."

I scoffed—of course Xed couldn't resist digging in deep, rifling through my metaphorical underwear drawer for the tasty nuggets. "It's not exactly a secret. After the government booted me from the Dome, figured I'd make some shitty music screaming about how they fucked us all over. And so, the Grease Weasels were born. But you know, starving musicians and all, we needed an actual way to make some cash."

"So you started selling drugs?"

I clicked my tongue. "That's one way to put it. Spent so many years in the Dome pumping psychiatric meds into people, I figured it was basically the same thing. But you wouldn't know anything about that, would you?"

He chuckled. "No, not a thing."

"Turns out money equals power. Alphadrine spread. Tucson became mine."

"But your band, it's still popular," he said.

What was he getting at? Pretty sure he wanted to get his hands on our Alphadrine and not our sweet anarchist guitar riffs. "Sure, people around here dig us. Makes a great cover for certain activities. Mild mannered punk band—works like a charm every time."

It was true. We still played gigs regularly between our other activities. The old strip club across the street was a favorite venue. Great stress relief.

"Excellent. I'd like to offer my services as your manager," he said.

"Beg your pardon?"

"You heard me right. I'd like to help you orchestrate your first trans-Dome tour. Starting with a grand debut in the magnificent city on the bayou—New Orleans, the only city north of Argentina still known to have a Ketacillin reservoir."

At first I stifled a laugh. Our regular Zone Passes for New Orleans had been revoked years before—it would take something extraordinary to get us back in there. Not many unlicensed exiles got approval, but sometimes very popular Voids bands were given full Dome access for shows. Music helped keep the bored masses happy, made the government's job easier.

It just might work.

"You clever son of a bitch," I said.

We wrapped up the deal, and I flung the microphone back at the wall of electronics. It hit with a clang and knocked down more bits of junk from Neptune's hoard. I swiveled in the broken office chair and put my feet up on the counter, my heavy boots bending the old wood. Digging into my pockets, I fished out an ampule of Alphadrine, broke it in half, and snorted the whole damned thing.

My eyes bulged. My lungs expanded, and I gasped, head filled with the sudden rush. I shook my head and clenched my fists, holding on as the huge hit swam from my lungs and into my bloodstream.

Pumped up.

Ready to go.

Before they got deep into it, I'd radio Neptune and Milo with the new plan, give them the new timeline. A new ultimatum—no wasn't an answer I'd accept. While they were finishing torturing Radar, I had another errand to run before we hit the road. I cracked my knuckles, one at a time.

Copper needed to prove his worth.

CHAPTER TWENTY-TWO

THE SUN wasn't gone yet, but a full moon blazed over the mountains, pulsing like a neon bar sign about to burn out. A twilight wedge hung low under the last flare of a bright red sunset, fat tips of saguaro cacti silhouetted on the horizon.

My country. My territory. My throne.

And I was burning just as hard as the moon—Vinicodone in my veins and Alphadrine in my lungs. My favorite combo. I ground my teeth, back molars crunching in my jawbone.

"Copper," I called. "Hurry the fuck up."

I stood at the top of the ridge—the Alphadrine rush had shot me up the sandy hillside like cheap Mexican fireworks.

Copper stumbled his way up behind me.

"Chill out," he said. "I'm coming." Each word was slow, ambling out his slack lips.

"Not fast enough." I put my hands on my hips and imagined my body projected larger than life against the moonlight. Invincible.

"Just relax. Don't want to walk into a cactus," he said.

"You're high."

He stopped and looked up at me. "So? Like you're not? You want to share my stash or something?"

My toes curled inside my boots. "Share your stash? You mean give back the drugs you stole from me?"

"I don't steal company drugs."

"Nice try, buddy. I'm not perfect, but there's one thing I don't tolerate, and that's other suppliers on my turf."

He stopped. The sunset was fizzling out, and full evening slithered into the desert. His sweaty face with its pale eyebrows glowed in the moonlight.

He tugged at the sleeves of a dirty blue flannel shirt. "Look, man, you don't have to like me, I get that, but you didn't have to come out here. Let's just fix this line and get out of the canyon."

"Shooting smack is a big no no. I already gave you a chance to get straight. This is it."

He pulled at his long dirty blond hair and swallowed hard. "Man, you're so super high. You riding on Alphadrine? Think no one will notice that?"

"No idea what you're talking about."

"You're something else. I've seen a lot of hypocrites in my day, but you just might be the queen."

I closed the gap, got in his face, and looked in his ugly brown eyes. "I am the queen. Glad you remembered that."

He stepped back with his hands up. "Just hit the lights so we can fix the line and split."

I mashed a dirty red button on a cracked halogen hand lamp and held it up so my face glowed like a Jack-O-Lantern. "Boo."

His feet slipped on the loose gravel. "Jesus." No air, no movement, no sound for a second, and then he said, "All right, I'm scared straight, I got it. You want me to fix this line or not?"

I pointed the light down the ridge. "Lead the way, cowboy."

He let out a shaky breath and trudged down the hill ahead of me. Stupid—no one should ever give me their back.

But I was a good sport. I was fair and just.

I was a patient god.

And we needed our com lines back. We needed to get on the road. I needed reliable contact with Xed. I needed eyes on Albuquerque and Juarez.

I needed to know someone wasn't going to blow up my pueblo.

I couldn't wave a magic wand and get Evan back. With no education system out in the Voids, it was hard to find technicians. Copper was it. That meant letting him live, no matter how much I wanted to snap that fragile little spinal column and plant that ugly head of his on the tallest cactus in the desert.

"Copper," I said, my voice rising and falling like I was calling a dog.

He didn't answer.

With a swift whack, I kicked him in the shin. He let out a surprised cry and lost his footing, tumbling down the hill. I skipped down behind him, jumping to a stop next to his head.

He groaned and rubbed his back. "What the hell did you do that for?"

"You don't want to play by the rules, you get punished. That's how it works."

I shined the light in his face, and he was so high his pupils barely shrank. He pulled up his baggy ripped jeans and got back on his feet. His greasy straight blond hair hung limp around his shoulders, almost long enough for me to strangle him with. Wouldn't be the first time I killed someone with their own hair.

I shook off the thought—creative, but not efficient. And we really needed those lines fixed.

He put an arm up to shield his eyes. "Knock it off, man. You're going to make me lose my tools." He patted his pockets. Fucker was so unprofessional he didn't even bother to carry a toolbox. Evan never would have tolerated that kind of bullshit.

We were close to the river where our main communication lines fed out through the canyon and across the desert. The faint tinkle of water flowing over rough boulders echoed up the ridge. It had rained recently, and the river would be swollen, heavy and fast with the runoff.

Evan had done everything possible to hide our com lines, using the river and mountains to protect them from our enemies. This was the first time any rivals successfully breached our pipeline. I had no proof, but it had to be Copper's fault. Even if it wasn't, it was his job to protect our systems, and he was doing a shit job of it.

"Stop wasting time. Find the line and fix it. We can't leave Tucson until it's repaired," I said.

Copper wobbled but shook it off and loped onward through the desert. I got into a squat and scanned the ground, looking for anything that may have fallen out of his filthy pants.

Rocks, reddish dirt, a few feathers, tufts of fur, and bits of shed lizard or snakeskin littered the ground. All the signs of death and rebirth in my desert, but nothing man-made. I was standing up, ready to whip Copper into shape, when something caught my eye.

There. Down low, skewered on the spines of a bushy cholla cactus. Pink and shiny with gold lettering, it flapped in the light breeze.

Mexican money.

With my thumb and index finger, I plucked it from the spines.

And with dead eyes and a Cheshire grin spreading across my face, I followed Copper the rest of the way down the hill.

The river would wash him right back to Mexico.

CHAPTER TWENTY-THREE

THE COLD filtered air smelled like rubbing alcohol and formaldehyde. Reeking of death, it was the last place I wanted to be again, but there I was, sucked back to the clinic by the blood on my hands and the haze of drugs evaporating from my veins.

Trina. You'd be so disappointed in me. But I did it for us, for all of us.

For you.

Just hours later and she already looked worse—maybe it was the harsh fluorescent lights, or too much Alphadrine jacking up my eyes, but her pale skin had a greenish cast, like a white potato slowly rotting. I reached out to touch her arm, almost expecting my finger to punch through her fragile flesh.

She was soft, mushy and clammy, my fingers sticking to her skin as I slid my hands down to hold hers. Her fingernails were cracked, brittle and yellow like she'd been lying there for months instead of weeks. I wanted to trust Milo, but it looked like we were just pumping oxygen into a beautiful corpse.

I knelt down beside the hospital bed, her lifeless hands still clutched between mine, and rested my forehead there. Even with the air filtration system going full blast, sand on the floor dug into my knees. Nothing could stop the desert from creeping in, following us into our darkest hours.

I closed my eyes, remembering warmth that wasn't there, pulled back into another time when I knelt in the desert and held someone's hand as they slipped away from me.

"You've got to let her go," Trina said. "She's gone. But you're still here."

Everything had fallen apart.

How long had I been out there, knees in the sand, crying over Evan's dead body, hoping for the desert to absorb me like the powdery skeleton of a dead saguaro?

"Come back with me, and I'll help you bury her," she said.

I wanted her to bury me instead. A syringe full of all the drugs Evan and I had brought for our vacation lay capped and ready on my bent knees. Less than a quarter of it would be enough to do me in, but I wanted to be sure.

Never take chances with doses. I knew that. Evan had known that. We played, but we played safely. Which was what made me so confused. Why did she do it? Why did she take so much? I could have saved her, but I'd been sleeping, nodding in and out on Vinicodone.

Too stoned to notice she'd stopped breathing.

My Evangelina. Gone.

Now Trina was there, sent out to find us when we were gone way too long. It should have been the perfect vacation. We had a week all to ourselves at the abandoned resort in Tubac, south of Tucson, where we'd been married. Not like marriage contracts or anything besides vigilante law existed in the Voids, but the symbolism was important to us.

Then she'd died in the very place where I felt like we'd been reborn, lying on the ground next to a terra cotta bench only a few feet from the adobe chapel where we had our wedding ceremony.

We'd come back to celebrate our one year anniversary, to commemorate the empire we created. The drugs built this sandcastle, and they made it all come crumbling down again. Now she was gone, just gone. I couldn't bring myself to touch her cold body anymore, but I couldn't bring myself to leave either. Following Evan seemed like the only way out.

Sand in my mouth and eyes, probably looking even more horrible than I felt, I stared up at Trina. Behind her, the landscape was patchy with dead grass from the old golf course. To the right, next to the clubhouse, an artificial lake sat dry, empty except for a muddy puddle right in the middle of the clay-lined hole. A shell of what it used to be.

With all the money coming in from the Alphadrine, Evan and I had planned to remodel the resort, make it nice again. We had more enforcers on my payroll, and Tucson was almost a place where you could have a life—keep a day job, take vacations, have a family, go out at night without getting shot in the face.

But all my dreams felt like they were frozen stiffer than Evan's body. We were so foolish—how could a bunch of thugs bring any kind of peace to the ruthless frontier? Stupid ideas, even more stupid than two crime lords getting married and playing house.

With her feet planted, Trina thrust out her hand. "Tucson needs you. The Grease Weasels need you. *I* need you, Xero. You're my best friend, and I won't let you die like this."

She wore a long black Lolita dress with frothy satin ruffles decorating the collar and sleeves. Her bleached-white hair with its shock of purple bangs looked like a cactus flower blooming, an unexpected burst of color in the brown, parched desert.

The noon sun hurt my dry eyes, but a November breeze swept away any warmth and sent a chill right into my bones. Dehydrated and strung out, I couldn't tell if I was freezing or burning to death from the inside out.

I shook my head. "I can't."

A smirk turned up the corner of her maroon-painted lips. "Don't tell me you can't. You can. And you will. You're Xero, queen of the desert."

With the sun backlighting her thin silhouette, her kohl-lined green eyes popped against her porcelain skin, and I felt every inch of her gaze burning into my pathetic body. At the shameful syringe on my lap. At the husk of Evan in front of me.

I had no tears left to cry, maybe no moisture left in my body, drier than the fake pond behind her.

"But I don't want to anymore. I don't want to do this without her. This is my fault. Everything's my fault," I whispered, hoping she wouldn't hear me over the wind.

She stamped the ground, palo verde twigs and sand spraying onto Evan's short red hair. "It is. It is your fault. You let this happen. But you know what? Everything else is your fault too. What you've done for Tucson. What you've done for the Grease Weasels, what you've done for me. That's also your fault. You remember where I was when you found me?"

I did. How could I forget? Nearly as hopeless as I was now, she was a starving prostitute pumped full of drugs and sold into slavery by her parents when she was a teenager. She was barely alive when Evan and I pulled her out, rescued her when we busted the last big ring of rival cartels in south Tucson.

We saw something in her, a tenacity that carried her through years of what most people wouldn't survive for a day. It was a decision we wouldn't regret—we made her one of us, and together we ruled Tucson.

I stared in her eyes and remembered the day I pulled her off that filthy mattress in the back of a warehouse made from rusty corrugated steel. She was right. If she could survive that, I could survive this.

I grabbed her hand, and she wrapped her other arm around my dirty waist, pulling me up on shaky knees. The syringe rolled off my lap and onto the sand beside Evan's head.

I turned away and buried my face in Trina's collarbone. She smelled like lilacs and sun-dried laundry. I smelled like carrion rotting in the sun, and I was disgusted at my own overpowering stench, ashamed at letting myself fall this far.

I lifted my head. "Now what?"

She nodded at the chapel, its solid oak door barred by a thick iron-laced beam. "Detox. And then you never touch that stuff again."

"Xero? Is that you?"

Milo. I thought if I was fast enough I'd make it back to base before he came down here.

I stood up and let go of Trina's hand. A syringe rolled out of my pocket and fell to the ground beside her head. I kicked it under the hospital bed, hoping Milo didn't notice.

He took a step forward. "What are you doing here? Where's Copper?"

I pointed to some blood on my wrist and on my knee. Not all of it was mine, but he didn't have to know that. "Ran into a cactus while we were out there. Was hoping to avoid getting another round of your patented disinfection method."

He shook his head. "Hey, it's your skin, not mine. Don't come crying to me if you end up with another round of flesh rot."

I smiled, hoping it was too dark for him to see my mouth twitching. "Fine. I'll let you do it. I just want another minute alone with Trina first."

He nodded. "Hard for me to think about leaving her like this, but it has to be done," he said. "What happened to Copper?"

"He fixed the line, then said he wanted to go into town and pick up some supplies to fortify the exit tunnels, just in case someone gets at it again," I said without missing a beat.

"He's not coming with us anyway. I suppose he can take as long as he wants."

"I'm not sure he'd survive being locked in a crawler with me for more than an hour."

Milo rubbed his head. "That's the truth. You're the worst, but I think we'd all want to murder him after long enough. Hate to say it, but I can't stand the guy. Can't wait till we find a replacement. We never should have let him in the Grease Weasels in the first place."

"Preaching to the choir." Lying was so easy, even to Milo.

"Come next door when you're ready. You and Radar need to rest so we can be ready to leave at dawn. Hard days for both of you," he said.

Somehow, I got them to agree to this crazy scheme, this impossible ploy for the Ketacillin. I thought it would take days of arguing to push a decision, but Neptune and Milo jumped on board right after I pitched the basic plan. They loved Trina too, maybe even more than I did. We each kept the things she'd done for us locked up deep in our souls, stored without keys.

"Roger that." I glanced down at Trina. "I'd leave tonight, but we need to map a route that will take us safely around Albuquerque. Without Calavera around to back us up, we might have some issues staying out of Roja's clutches."

"We don't have time for problems. Trina doesn't have time." He gazed at the floor.

I held my breath, thinking he'd seen the syringe, but then I nodded and he left the room.

Before he could pop back in again, I knelt down, grabbed the needle, jammed it into my thigh, and tossed it into a biohazard container.

No one would ever know.

Chapter Twenty-Four

RADAR PANTED beside me in the dark, spread out on clean satin sheets in my bedroom. After all that stress, I couldn't resist juicing up another perfect speedball and pouncing on my new favorite cyborg.

Mellow but awake, and finally back in my own bed, everything felt like it was going to be just fine. Even with the tricky mission looming, I mentally fast-forwarded right past that and straight to the part where we got the Ketacillin and Trina woke up from the coma. Then Argon would reappear, Calavera would come back to help us demolish Albuquerque, and it would all be hunky dory.

Money would fill my pockets, rainbows would dance across the sky, and Vinicodone would pour down from the heavens.

Maybe it was the drugs, but all that seemed totally possible.

Now I just needed another shower, and the evening would be perfect.

I poked Radar. "Hey. You lucid yet? Wanna get slippery in the bathtub?"

Radar flopped a hand on my chest, just missing my tits. "Don't know if lucid is the right word for it." He giggled.

"Damn, you're still super fucked up on A-Plus. Now I feel like an asshole."

"No, no, you've got it wrong. *I* felt *your* asshole," he said, still giggling.

I rolled onto my stomach. "This what you're really like?" I asked. "They say when you're on truth serum, you reveal your true self, not just true information."

"You ever get shot up with this shit?" he asked.

I nodded even though he couldn't see it. "We test our products at least once, but that's it. I try to keep my people away from all the drugs, but A-Plus is never an issue. No one wants a taste of that. We could turn a profit selling it, but we won't stoop that low."

"I'm not high on the A-Plus anyway. Had a really bad reaction, and Milo shot me up with a bunch of pain meds. Turns out robot circuitry doesn't play nicely with synthetic drugs."

Yikes. "At least your artificial lungs kept you breathing—that can be a problem. We've made a lot of stuff, and most of it's fantastic. Unfortunately, some of it's just plain nasty," I said.

"I've heard stories about you for years, way back when I was just a wee mercenary," he said, slurring. "Heard you sold junk that rotted skin clear off the bone."

I cringed. My mellow just got a little bit less mellow. "That's not totally wrong. We accidentally made some product that was toxic, but we never pushed it. Someone stole the compound and started selling it. That was back in the early days when we didn't have our security together. Before Neptune."

"Good to know you're not a total piece of shit," he said.

I smacked him in the leg. "That truth serum works a little too well."

"Ouch. Man, watch it. I'm sensitive from the A-Plus." He flopped halfway off the bed, trying to escape me. "How the hell long is the half-life on that crap?"

I leaned over and hauled his leg back onto the bed before he fell down.

"Jeez, be gentle. Didn't I say everything hurts?"

"You weren't saying that when I was riding your dick." I lay back down beside him.

"That's before the stuff Milo gave me for pain started wearing off too."

"You're a big boy—you'll live. For what it's worth, you passed with flying colors. Maybe Neptune and Milo will start trusting my iron-clad character judgments."

He chortled, and it burbled into the dark room, making me sit up on my elbows.

"You say it's wearing off, but you still seem high as hell," I said. Coming from me, that was saying something.

"Lady, I don't know about your iron-clad character judgments if you're shacking up with Xed. He's one twisted fuck."

"You didn't say anything about working with Xed before."

"You didn't ask. And I never said I worked with Xed. I've crossed paths with him before and ran into some of his ..work. It's not pretty. I don't have the cleanest reputation myself, but I go out of my way to avoid him. Real sick bastard."

I shrugged with one shoulder. "I don't know—I always appreciate a little artful sadism."

He groped for me, and his hand flapped against my naked thigh. "You're not really a sadist. You're a pragmatist. Like me."

"You just met me. Trust me, I've still got cans of whoop ass and sadism left to open."

"Xero, you're infamous, and I'm observant. I don't get involved with outfits that don't meet my standards."

"Then how come you've never tried to hook up with us before?"

"No need. You never hire independents, and I never need to go looking for extra work. My services are always needed."

"So why follow me now? Why take this crazy gig?"

He was silent, as though he were trying to fight the lingering honesty effects of the A-Plus. I listened to him breathing before he answered. "It seemed like an interesting job, and you're the best organization to be attached to while this madness is happening. If a real war pops, this is no time to be solo. And...I like you. I'll always respect what you've done for Tucson and what you did for my family."

"You keep flattering me like this, and I'll get a big head."

"I think it's a little late for that." He chuckled and then groaned. "Ah fuck your drugs, it hurts to laugh."

I scooted up to his head and lightly kissed the tip of his nose. "Better haul you to the showers before those pain meds are all gone. Need to get some sleep before tomorrow, and you know how I feel about dirty cuddles."

"Anyone ever tell you that you've got a one-track mind?"

"I'm driven. It's a virtue." I stroked his chest scar. "Hey—you're part robot, right?"

He cleared his throat. "I guess? Why?"

"Think you can learn to play the drums by Tuesday?"

CHAPTER TWENTY-FIVE

THE NEW Garden District smelled like wet tree sap and old grave dirt, and with a fresh hit of Alphadrine ripping open my alveoli, I could almost list the local flora with my eyes closed. Nearly ten years since I'd been let into New Orleans, and nothing seemed different. Our lodgings, a restored plantation house, looked authentic, but the plastic wood paneling and accent trimming gave it away as a knock-off.

With only a few snags, we had dipped low through New Mexico, dodged any action from Albuquerque, and sailed right through the open wastelands of Texas. No bandits. No Skeletons. We made it to New Orleans early with plenty of time to iron things out with immigration. The run was going perfectly. Almost too perfectly, but fate owed me a turn or two. This kamikaze plan might actually work.

A quick jam, then we'd swap some Alphadrine for the Ketacillin, and be back on our way. As long as the territory boss wasn't a pain in the ass, everything would go smoothly. However, knowing what an asshole she could be, I made sure to keep myself good and medicated. Couldn't be too careful.

We sat on purple velvet couches in a downstairs parlor, decked out in show gear, waiting for transport to the concert venue. Ready for a gothic extravaganza, Neptune and I wore dramatic black lace dresses while the men sported tailored long-cut black suits. The sleeves on my gown covered any remaining bandages, and I wore enough makeup to cover most of my fading black eyes and healing skin. Trina would approve—I borrowed the dress and makeup from her closet. The gown would have dragged the floor on her, but it barely kissed the tops of my low-cut dress boots.

"Wow, I haven't been to New Orleans since I joined the Grease Weasels," Milo said. "I wish I could go out and wander the new French Quarter."

I loved Milo to death, but his fake cheerfulness struck a nerve. I thought I'd done a good job of balancing out the Vinicodone and Alphadrine to give myself a level high, but I found myself getting sleepy and irritated anyway. Too much Vinicodone. We made good shit, and it was easy to go overboard. I blinked, eyelids heavy. I needed another hit of Alphadrine to wake up.

I took a breath and tried to ignore Milo—he needed the false optimism. He said he was fine trusting someone else with Trina, but we all knew that was a lie. Everyone was waiting for him to have a total meltdown.

I forced my eyes open. "Xed's kept up his end of the bargain so far, but I have a feeling Voodoo still isn't thrilled about us being here. I wouldn't go wandering out on the town—no reason to tempt fate."

"I'm not scared of that bitch, but I don't want to fuck up our chance to save Trina," Neptune said. "We stay put."

"Keep it simple. We do the gig, make some noise for posterity, then we hotfoot it over to the Café du Fleur for some old world beignets and a meeting with a fucking mystical bitch," I said.

"Mystical bitch?" Radar said.

"Yeah, before she became a dirty government sellout, she was the Voodoo queen of New Orleans, back before the tidal wave washout. I don't give a shit if she's magical or not, but she's definitely still a bitch," I said.

Neptune winked at me. "Takes one to know one."

I tried to come up with a snappy comeback, but my eyelids fluttered again, vision flickering like a broken television set. I swallowed and gave a really fake sounding laugh, hoping Neptune wouldn't notice.

"Everything okay back on base?" Milo said.

"So far so good. Wish that asshole Copper would pick up his communicator though," Neptune said.

How long before Neptune realized Copper wasn't just out on some long supply mission?

"You're still not happy about us all leaving," I said, trying to speak clearly. My lips felt like they were coated in peanut butter.

"Fuck no, I'm not happy about it. We've got a good base crew, but Copper's not exactly the most reliable IT guy. Look at Milo, he's going to wet his pants worrying about Trina, but we don't have much of a choice," she said.

Milo bit his lip and shoved his hands in his pockets. "Hey, now, I'm doing just fine."

Ignoring Milo, Neptune waved a hand in my face. "Dude, you look fucked up too. You okay?"

Radar inched forward to look at me. "What's the deal? You sick?"

Milo shoved them both aside, and my heart raced. He put a hand on my forehead and pulled up on an eyelid to look at my pupils.

Shit.

"I'm fine," I said. Nope, no one was believing that. Not even me.

"How long have you been feeling like this?" he said. "Your pulse is all over the place, and you're diaphoretic. Does your chest hurt?"

The Zaps. He thought I was coming down with them. Well, that was a relief. I was totally not in the mood to explain my surging drug habit.

"No, but my stomach hurts. Probably shouldn't have eaten those synthmeat tacos down in El Paso," I said. I was going for sarcasm, but the words came out mushy. So, I had that going for me.

"May be a delayed reaction to all the antibiotics I pumped into you before we left base," Milo said. He put his head against my chest and listened to my shallow breathing.

It took a few tries, but I focused enough to find his head and push it off my chest. I held up a hand. "Stomach's really not feeling great here."

Milo frowned. "Think your lungs are clear, but I need a stethoscope. Crap, all my medical supplies are out in the crawler."

The crawler, which was currently in a holding area at the edge of the Dome, waiting to be smuggled in the backdoor.

My stomach seriously felt like I'd eaten a cactus. I tried to stand up, failed, then leaned forward and vomited all down my lacy black dress, right into my boots.

Milo jumped back, narrowly escaping a chunky shower.
I really needed to stop getting puke in my shoes.

CHAPTER TWENTY-SIX

I STILL wore Trina's black dress, and even over the scent of a crowded New Orleans street, I smelled her perfume coming off the damp fabric. The reconstructed Café du Fleur was just like I remembered it, complete with the lingering smell of urine that wafted from the street into the cafe's outdoor tent. Went nicely with the lingering scent of vomit in my hair.

Despite all the restorations, the New Orleans Dome was busted. The weather was my first clue that shit wasn't right: blazing one second, freezing the next, humidity and fog streaking through the streets and then disappearing. I could taste the outside. In a Dome that meant system failure. New Orleans needed cash fast, or it was in trouble.

That's where our Alphadrine came in. Xed knew what he was doing.

We marched through the humid air, its organic gutter stench another omen of failure that made me sad for the city. At the back of the green and white striped tent, a woman sat at a wrought iron table. Dark brown eyes glared at me from a heart-shaped face with perfectly smooth skin. Her spongy dreadlocks were rolled into tight, even sections that fell into a neatly tied ponytail at her shoulders.

Voodoo.

The edge of her long layered white dress flapped in the breeze.

Another bad sign. There shouldn't be any breeze in a functional Dome.

I should have felt bad for the city, bad for Voodoo, but all I could see were dollar signs and power. The city was dying. We had leverage.

Voodoo stood. "Xero, queen of the desert. We meet again."

She walked toward us. I led the group with Neptune and Radar forming the middle and Milo pulling up the rear of a diamond shape.

I held out my hand. "Enchantée," I said. "How have you been, Voodoo?"

Voodoo stared at my hand but didn't shake it. She moved her gaze to the rest of the crew. "Didn't I tell Xed I must speak with you and you alone before I allowed any of this nonsense to happen?" she said.

I put my hands on my hips. "Is that why you changed the concert schedule? This is news to me, and there's an arena packed with angsty teenagers waiting for their first real show. Immigration will have a fit if we don't play the gig."

Voodoo crinkled up her lips into a loose pucker. "I do not like it when my directives are disobeyed, but because I am wise and merciful, I will grant you a compromise. You may keep your crew in this outer tent area, but only you may accompany me inside."

"Fine. They can wait out here," I said evenly. I had my shit together again. I'd be more careful with my drugs in the future.

Neptune grumbled.

I turned around. "Stay here."

"This is bullshit," Neptune whispered. "You're sick. You just tossed your cookies and almost passed out. You can't go solo into a meeting with some bayou psycho."

Voodoo whirled, her dreadlocks and skirt twirling around her lean frame. "Is there a problem?"

Neptune started to say something, but I turned back and cracked a smile.

"No. No problems. So, you wanna dance?" I said.

Her face was still, staring at me like a beautiful mask. "This way." She walked inside with a calm confidence, knowing I'd follow.

"Don't go in there," Neptune said, her body rigid.

"I'm fine. It was just some bad tacos. I've got this."

She exhaled. "Can't let you do this, boss."

"We have to play ball. Trina's life is at stake," I said, peering around Neptune to stare Milo right in the eye, daring him to tell me no.

"Are you sure you're feeling okay now?" he said.

"You still look rough," Radar added.

"Thanks for the confidence booster," I said.

Radar shrugged.

"I could be missing both arms and still beat her in a fight. Trust me," I said.

"Fine. But at the first sign of shit, we're going in guns blazing," Neptune said.

They staged themselves on the porch, ready to be the cavalry. A moist breeze blew hard through the tent canopy, carrying along putrid scents that smelled more like the Breakers than a newly renovated Dome. New Orleans never could catch a break, and in many ways, I sympathized with Voodoo and her shitty situation.

"Good luck," Radar said. "Kick some ass so I don't have to do my electric eel impression in the middle of a Dome."

I clutched an ampule of Alphadrine in my pocket and grinned. "Time to play."

CHAPTER TWENTY-SEVEN

THE INSIDE of the cafe was hot, smelled like boiling fryer grease and fresh chicory coffee, but the place was empty except for Voodoo leaning against the striped wallpaper. Good thing. The kitchen staff didn't need to see what I was about to do to their beloved leader.

My mouth was dry, my pulse thumped in my neck, and I flexed my fingers, full of Alphadrine and ready to harvest some body parts.

Voodoo had pushed the green chairs and wooden tables back to the wall, leaving an open space in the middle of the cramped room.

I strutted inside and stood in front of an open stainless steel counter that revealed part of the kitchen. Voodoo came away from the edge, her spine straight and proud. My gaze darted around, distracted by the old menus and display cases of merchandise tucked into the walls of the small room.

"I always did like this place," I said. "Used to come here all the time when I was in college before the Dome restrictions."

She raised her eyebrows. "A lowlife like you went to college?"

"Yep. I'm a doctor. Means I can patch you up after I poke a few holes in you." I bounced back and forth on my heels, wiggled my fingers, and tried to shake off some of the Alpha jitters.

Her jaw tightened. "That ain't going to happen," she said, briefly slipping into casual speech. Jackpot. I was getting under her skin.

"You don't want to do this," I said. "Remember what happened last time?"

I'd left her alive. Barely.

She composed herself again. "Business out here is not so simple."

"I get that. We roll like this in the Voids, but in the other Domes, daytime fighting isn't exactly encouraged," I said, the words shooting out of my mouth too fast, like little machine gun pellets.

She sneered, her arms darting out to grip the edges of a chair. "New Orleans is not like the Domes you are used to. On paper it's government controlled, but I'm the real the leader of the French Quarter. We're abandoned, just like we've always been abandoned. People here do what I tell them to do."

I cracked my neck and tried to look calm when I was amped up and ready to swashbuckle. "I can understand that feeling of abandonment."

"You are nothing but a monster, a greedy, filthy, lying creature. How could you possibly understand our suffering? How can you possibly understand how we've been used and left to die?"

I laughed in her face. "Lady, you ever been to Tucson? No one would ever put a Dome down there. We always were and always will be on the fringe."

"Yet you poisoned my town. You burned my people's flesh. You do not care about anything other than your precious money."

I shrugged. "Money is power. You know that as well as I do, or I wouldn't be here. You want my shit."

Her hands curled into claws, and she stepped forward. "My people are dying. New Orleans is suffering. The air quality is not good enough to keep everyone alive."

Ah. Now it made sense. That was why they wanted the Alphadrine. Not just for the money, but for what it did to your lungs, opening up all the little air sacs and sucking more oxygen into your bloodstream.

She was right. Alphadrine worked, and it felt great. I was ready to swim Lake Pontchartrain on a single breath.

"So that's why you're pissed. It's a tradeoff. More people will live. Alphadrine will improve their breathing, help with the bad air, but it's addictive as fuck. Once you start this, you can't stop. People will need it to live," I said.

How true that was. My hand touched the other ampules in my pocket. "Still, it's your choice. The Dome has decent security— would be hard to saturate this place with Alphadrine if you didn't want it imported."

Her eyes bulged. "Choice? I have no choice. I can't sit still while my people die."

"And you can't get the government to fix the air filtration and climate control system," I said. Couldn't resist.

Her fingers clenched, and she spat out, "Fuck. You."

I bit my tongue. "Sure, but I don't think we've ever been that close." Might be kind of fun, fucking and trying to kill each other at the same time. Xed had let me down the other day.

"I would never touch someone as filthy as you," she said.

"Go ahead, call me names—drug dealer, dictator, slut, whatever. You can hate me, but we would never sell a drug that eats holes in your skin. That's just bad business. Killing off our client base doesn't make any sense," I said.

Whoever had stolen that failed compound from our labs trafficked it all the way out to New Orleans and probably made a decent profit before all their customers died off. Unfortunate, but we had nothing to do with it. You make one bad drug, and suddenly everyone's up your ass.

"Say what you want, you created that awful chemical. It is still your fault. If you want permission to deal in my territory, you are going to have to earn it. Show me you are more than a coward who deals poison from the shadows," she said.

I jumped up and down twice, shook out my shoulders. I had done what I could to avoid a fight, but she wasn't giving me the option of passing, and I wanted blood. Bad.

"Fair fight? Are you going to have goons come out of the attic and turn this into an old kung fu movie?" I asked.

"Fair fight. Me against you. First blood."

"Weapons?"

From inside the pockets of her dress she extracted two twin knives. Nothing special—just two ordinary blades about the length of a hand. Without a word she threw one directly at my face.

I ducked, and the knife landed in the beige wall a few inches above my head.

"Isn't this a historical landmark?" I said.

"Not the southern side. It was destroyed in the tidal wave. Arrogant beasts like you do not pay attention to history. Pick up your knife."

I put one hand against the wall's sticky paint and pulled at the knife with the other. It came out cleanly in my hand with only a few sprinkles of drywall falling on the baseboards.

"This is completely unnecessary," I said. "Last chance to change your mind." I wanted to fight, but killing her would cause more problems. I wasn't sure if I could stop myself from slitting her throat once we started.

She dropped into a fighting stance, knife clutched in an overhead stab position. Big, telegraphed move—I already felt sorry for her.

I stood still while she launched across the room, straight at my neck. At the last second, she dodged to the side and tried to land a hit in my diaphragm. I saw it coming from a million miles away, the Alphadrine putting my mind into overdrive, making everything run in slow motion.

Her knife sunk into the wall, her weight driving the blade up to the hilt. She lost her balance, surprised the strike missed.

I flipped around and sunk my knife into the back of her thigh with one quick stab. She screamed as red blossomed across her white dress. I missed the femoral artery, but plenty of blood splashed onto the brown tiled floors.

She flailed at her knife with a shaking hand, trying to pull it out of the wall while holding her bleeding thigh wound with the other. Her emotions blinded her. We'd tangled in the past, and she was a dangerous opponent—cold, calculating, and precise, like me when I was in the right mood. We'd traded blows and watched each other's blood drip more than once.

Kind of sad actually, seeing her grow so soft, languishing in the good life of the Domes. I'd been looking forward to a hard fight.

"First blood?" I said calmly, but in my head I saw my knife running through her throat, stabbing through her trachea until I hit spine.

I backed away until I was against another wall, out of range. I trusted myself less than a starving pit bull in a room full of babies. I watched her tense face, her eyes pulsing, her teeth clenched as she gasped air in short bursts that sent strings of saliva cascading over her full lips. She kept breathing heavily, but the fire drained out of her eyes, her face softening.

She stopped yanking at the knife, leaving it lodged in the wall. "First blood."

"Good." I put my knife down on the counter. "You want me to sew that up for you?" Like either of us would trust me to do that.

She shook her head, her dark skin turning a shade paler as

blood continued to run down her leg.

"Suit yourself—you better get some pressure on that soon or you'll pass out." I looked over her shoulder into the kitchen. "Hey, you got any beignets left back there? I've totally got the munchies."

CHAPTER TWENTY-EIGHT

BACK IN the plantation house, we spread ourselves out in the parlor again. Radar shared the purple velvet loveseat with me. I ran my hands back and forth over its soft surface, brushing the fibers this way and that. Least I missed it earlier when I threw up—be a shame to ruin such nice furniture.

The Alphadrine was fading away again, but I couldn't risk doing another big hit of anything, not after how much I'd taken. Just a tiny bit of Vinicodone to take the edge off. I lay horizontally across the couch, my feet hanging over the rim as I leaned against Radar's side.

"That's not exactly a fighting-ready position," Radar said.

"Any position is fighting-ready for me. I'm always ready to go."

He put a hand on my shoulder and gave me a mild zap. "Oh yeah?"

"That feels good. Keep going."

"You're one weird chick." He took his hand off my shoulder.

I ignored him and kept playing with the velvet. "The Dome may be breaking, but they sure have a lot of great stuff. This couch feels real. You hardly ever see actual velvet anymore. Think of all the awesome crap we can get if Voodoo gets over losing that duel. We can put velvet all over the Golden Lanes—it'll be just like the 1960s."

"I see you've still got your priorities in order," Radar said.

I hung my head backward to meet Radar's gaze. "Never underestimate the importance of style. Image is everything."

Milo sat in a high-backed chair that was also upholstered in dark purple velvet. He stared down at his hands, fingers fidgeting while he thumped his foot against the hollow wooden floors. The tapping echoed in the high-ceilinged room.

I swung my feet off the couch and faced forward again. "Milo. Hey."

His head snapped up to meet my gaze, but his eyes were still unfocused and faraway. "What?" he said.

"I'm just fucking around. First priority is getting the Ketacillin. Don't worry, Voodoo is desperate. She put on that show to make herself feel good, and I didn't kill her with that little stab wound. Now she'll let us do the concert, we'll get the Ketacillin, and race right back to Tucson."

Neptune leaned against a column by the front door, waiting for trouble to come knocking. "Can't believe they won't even let us have knives."

"I don't like it either, but it's standard Dome policy unless we're working with the government," I said.

She started pacing around the room, looking for possible weapons. "Yeah, but the other Domes aren't secretly run by a psychotic bayou priestess," she said.

"We can use that to our advantage. New Orleans isn't monitored like the other Domes, judging from your showdown. You couldn't get away with that somewhere else. We'd all be in jail by now," Radar said.

I turned to him again. "Sounds like you have some experience in that arena."

"I've been a merc for a long time. There's not much I haven't tried," he said.

"Sexy," I said.

Radar rolled his eyes.

Someone knocked, and within seconds, Neptune was at the door, demanding to know who it was.

"Voodoo. Open up," she said through the thin door.

Neptune opened it a crack. "You alone?"

The hazy porch light illuminated Voodoo like a fallen angel, wearing another clean white dress identical the one she wore when I had stabbed her. Neptune craned her neck from side to side, looking for guards.

"No. I prefer to do business alone, but I have others waiting. If you make one wrong move, this whole place will go up in flames."

"Pyrotechnics, I like it," I said without getting up. "Let her in."

Voodoo pushed past Neptune and stood in the center of the room, trying to hide her pronounced limp and failing.

I looked at her leg. "Shouldn't you be in the hospital or something?"

Radar and Milo started to get up.

"Stay seated," Voodoo said.

I waved for them to sit, and they settled back down.

Neptune stayed rooted in place with her arms folded. "I'll stay right here, thanks."

Voodoo glared at Neptune then turned back to me. "Your dogs are disobedient."

Neptune showed her teeth. "I bite too, but usually you have to pay extra for that."

"Disgusting," Voodoo said, annunciating each syllable. "I cannot believe I agreed to let scum like you into my territory."

I adjusted myself on the couch. "I get it, you don't like us being here. Stop playing these games, let us do the show, we'll swap drugs, and then be on our way. Love your city, but if you hadn't heard, there's a lot of shit going down out west. Things to do, revolutions to squash. You know how it is."

Voodoo took a step closer and faltered, catching herself before taking a nosedive into the old wood floors.

"Need to sit down?" I motioned to one of the empty chairs near Milo.

Her mouth stiffened. "No. That will not be necessary."

"All righty then. You already know what we want, and you already know what we have. I won our little duel. What more do you need?" I said.

She shifted the weight off the injured leg. "I do not trust you and your dirty drugs. I need proof they are not contaminated."

"We only sell product that's totally pure. Swamp Rat, or whatever you guys called that accidental drug, would never have been mass-produced by our labs. I've told you this so many times—I don't know how else to explain it to you," I said.

"I do not care what you or anyone else says. You must prove your product is real."

"Can you give us access to a lab?" Milo said. "We can give you chemical readouts with purity ratings."

Voodoo shook her head. "We trusted scientists before, and what happens? Our city washes away. No, I do not care what a lab says. I want a live demonstration. I want you to take it and prove it is safe."

"No," I said. "We don't do drugs. It's bad for business." Lies. Hypocrisy. Irony. My best friends.

Voodoo gave a snort. "I see how it is. You will not taste your own poison. Then the deal is off."

"No!" Milo yelled and stood up. "We'll do it."

I stood up too, hoping no one noticed my slight wobbling. "Milo. This isn't something you can decide." Had to put on a good show.

His fingers dug into the fabric of his pants. "I don't care. I'll take it."

Voodoo turned to Milo, a satisfied grin on her face. "I see at least you have some sense."

"I'm a doctor. I promise you it's safe. It's addictive, you can overdose on it like any other drug, but if used correctly, there's very little risk of death or other harm."

He didn't mention the risks of speedballing it with other powerful narcotics, but you know, sensible users would never do such a thing. Totally.

I cleared my throat. "Okay. We'll do a dose of Alphadrine, but someone has to stay sober. We're not all getting stoned—too easy for you to kill us and make off with the drugs for free."

"I'll stay sober," Neptune said. "I'm not letting your thugs take out our crew while I'm tripping balls."

"No. The doctor can stay sober. I want reports on your vital signs, and it is too risky to bring in one of my outside medics. And, if you are lying, the doctor can bring you back to life. I do not want to dispose of your bodies. Too much trouble."

I set my jaw and wrinkled my forehead. "Fine. That's reasonable."

I tried to remember how much Alphadrine I had taken in the last twenty-four hours. Another hit sounded great, but having my heart explode did not. Too bad Voodoo didn't want to buy any Vinicodone—more of that would put me on a cloud.

I turned to Radar. "You ever done Alphadrine?"

"No. Same as you guys, I stay away from the drugs I traffic. Like you said, bad business," he said. "And I don't need the lung enhancing benefits."

"Wait. Shit. Milo, you said he had a bad reaction to the A-Plus?" I said.

Milo frowned. "Er, yeah, he did."

I stepped toward him. "Does that mean he's going to react to the Alphadrine?"

Milo opened his mouth, closed it, and then opened it again. "Not necessarily, but it's not a good sign." His gaze darted between me, Radar, and Voodoo.

"New deal. Radar stays sober, the rest of us get high," I said to Voodoo.

"No deal. I say who tries the Alphadrine," she said.

"Look, he's allergic to a similar compound. That has nothing to do with the safety of the drug itself," I said.

Radar put his hand on my arm. "It's fine. I'll do it. I trust Milo to keep me alive if it comes to that," he said. "I'm pretty hard to kill."

I shuffled forward until I was just a foot from Voodoo. "Business cards on the table now. We're not going to be in any shape to negotiate later if we're dosing Alphadrine. Whatever money you worked out with Xed is fine, but you know what we really want."

Voodoo stared hard into my eyes and smirked. "You want the Ketacillin. I trust Xed updated you on that process?"

"What are you talking about?"

"Your business partner does not seem to be very good at communicating. I do not like him either, but he is more palatable than you horrible creatures."

I swallowed. "We're not close with Xed. Out with it."

"I do not have the Ketacillin."

Milo shot forward and curved around me closer to Voodoo. "What do you mean?"

I put a hand on his chest and moved him back.

Voodoo scoffed. "As I said. Ketacillin is nearly impossible to get your hands on, and I do not have any. But I do have one of the reagents. You are chemists. If you are as skilled as you say you are, you should be able to recreate the full antibiotic."

Point of fact, Trina and Argon were our lead chemists, and they were both out of commission. Doing any heavy chemical work without them would be incredibly difficult. Milo and I were in charge of the design process, the neuropharmacology and physiology aspects, not the actual synthesis parts. Next to Argon and Trina, we were little more than preschoolers in the lab.

Thinking of Argon sent another wave of frustration and anger pounding through my skull. My Grease Weasels. My team. My family. I wanted them all back. Now.

Vinicodone still slowing my thoughts, I briefly lost focus, trying to think of what else we could do to find Argon. In my heart, I knew he was alive. He was too clever to go down that easily. But doubt is an insidious creature.

So is distraction. I should have seen it coming, but it was too late.

All I saw was the flash of Neptune's spiky hair as she made a quick leg sweep that left Voodoo crumpled in a pile of tangled limbs on the ground.

"Stop. This isn't going to help," I said.

I leaned over and caught Neptune's arms as she straddled Voodoo, settling into a ground and pound position.

Neptune snarled.

I was so focused on Neptune that I missed Milo sneaking around my left side. He slid in beside us, landing solid punches in Voodoo's face. Her skull meat made dull thwacks against his knuckles, and her head thumped against the floor. The hard blows rumbled up through my legs.

Restraining Neptune without hurting either of us was no easy task. The Vinicodone bump gave me extra flexibility, calmer thinking, but decreased reflexes. With each flail, she almost escaped my grip. Meanwhile, Milo grabbed Voodoo's hair and flung her head into the ground with a rage I'd never seen from him. No one would survive that kind of a beating for long.

Boots pounded behind me. Radar's shadow appeared above us, and his thick arms came down, yanking Milo off and tossing him to the ground.

Voodoo tried to escape, but failed, her fucked up leg buckling, and she stumbled backward until she toppled again, her upper body landing in the adjacent dining room.

I stood up and snatched Neptune and Milo by their collars with quick grabs, like they were naughty children. High or not, neither was a match for me. I tossed both of them onto the loveseat.

Dropping to one knee, I pushed their heads together so they could hear me whisper.

"Big mistake. We're two seconds from literally going up in flames. Sit down. Shut up. Don't move," I said.

I looked up at Radar. "Keep them still. I don't care if you have to shock them unconscious."

He nodded. All of his mercenary experience was reflected in his face and in his sure, relaxed body movements. He was the perfect partner for a crisis. He would take care of business, regardless of the cost.

I stalked into the dining room where a dazed Voodoo was fishing in her dress for something. Her face was already swelling, one of her eyes puffing up and turning dark. Blood trickled from her nose and mouth.

"You couldn't leave it alone, could you? You had to keep fucking with us," I said and kept walking until I was standing over her waist. Leaning down, I snatched her wrists to keep her from pushing the signaling device in her ruined white dress.

Voodoo was silent, her jaw set in a stubborn clench, her nostrils flaring with each puff of air forced through her nose.

Being an Amazon on a designer drug cocktail had its advantages. With ease, I hauled her another foot across the room and planted her ass in one of the flimsy dining room chairs. The chair creaked and rocked under her weight, and her head accidentally flopped against the table. A lacy white tablecloth was draped over the dining room table, and drops of her blood pooled on its waxed surface.

I held her small wrists together by curling one of my large fists around her delicate skin. With my free hand, I dug through the white dress until I found the communicator. I tossed it across the room. After frisking her for more weapons or transmission devices, I let her go.

"Now. Let's all just calm down, shall we?"

She was silent.

"Glad we can finally talk like adults. Here's the deal. You don't have what we want, but we'll still take the reagent. Someone we care about is dying, and we need that medication very badly. The only things I really want from you are the Ketacillin chemicals and information about where I can get the other part of the formula. I assume you know where it is."

Slowly, Voodoo gave a single nod, her eyeballs still swirling in her head.

"Excellent. That's what I want to hear. I'll make you a deal. I won't kill you right now."

I saw her getting ready to spit in my face, so I crammed a piece of her own white dress into her bloody mouth.

I laughed. "And you call me crass? You going to behave, or do I need to keep you gagged while we finish our little conversation?"

She averted her gaze but shook her head, and I pulled the cloth out of her mouth.

"Good. Now. As much as I'd like to, I won't gut you. And, I'm willing to give you a full load of Alphadrine for free. Xed asked for a big chunk of change for this shipment, and that price is fair, but I don't give a fuck. All I want right now is the reagent. You give me that, I'll let you live, and you can have the whole cargo. If the batch isn't up to your standards, I'll pay you for the Ketacillin. Or, you can come to Tucson and try to take out your debt in blood, whichever you prefer. That's my final offer. You game?"

A selfish little drug-addled part of me wanted her to say no, to give me an excuse to slit her belly and watch her hot intestines spill onto the antique dining room rug.

Voodoo stared at the floor, her pupils dilated and unmoving. "I accept. I hate you. I hate your lying face, and I hate your drugs, but my people are more important than my own morals. The other part of the reagent..." she paused to swallow the blood running into her throat from her busted nose. "...the other part is in Albuquerque."

Of course. Of course the other reagent was in Albuquerque.

My favorite place. Right in the dragon's den.

This wasn't Voodoo's fault. Xed and I needed to have a chat.

I kept my face neutral. "Great. Lovely doing business with you. You want a coffee or something? Not to be an asshole, but you look like shit."

Chapter Twenty-Nine

The Punch Bowl, alive but slowly crumbling, looked like it was held together with superglue and broken dreams. Somewhere beneath us lay the skeleton of the long-dead Superdome.

Nothing lasts forever.

That didn't mean I wouldn't do whatever it took to keep the Grease Weasels alive. We had to go on stage before Voodoo changed her mind and canceled the concert or canceled the deal. Naturally, I had to take more Alphadrine to go on with the show. Even I thought it was a bad idea to suck down that much, but it didn't stop me. Nothing could stop me. Alphadrine made me invincible.

Still in Trina's dress, I fluffed up the skirt ruffles, ran my fingers through the Mohawk, and bit my tongue. I breathed in dust so heavy it felt like I was eating chalk—lungs wide open, I almost tasted the grit in my bloodstream.

Out in the stadium, the crowd was a throbbing sea of flannel shirts, dirty jeans, and bad neon wigs. Alternative hairstyles were a big no no in the Domes, and someone was pulling major strings just to let this crowd wear the ridiculous wigs.

Meanwhile, I got to have the real deal—walking around the Domes with my natural hair flying was a rare treat. Made me wonder what it would be like if we ever took over the Domes. No doubt the Grease Weasels would be covered with all the tattoos and piercings I wouldn't let them have now.

Milo, tricked out in his black suit, walked around the stage, his guitar slung over his shoulder, checking equipment. It just wasn't the same without Argon and Trina. Trina should have been on drums and Argon on lead guitar. But Radar sat on the drum throne, thumping on the bass drum pedal, testing the sound. Neptune stayed on the bass guitar, and Milo upgraded to lead. I usually stuck to vocals, but I grabbed the rhythm guitar slot to fill the gap.

I closed my eyes, thought about what it would be like if we were your average punk band, and I didn't have the fate of the whole region clutched in my sweaty palms.

I pushed those ideas aside and opened my eyes. The lights were bright. The crowd was loud. I was lit up like a dumpster fire and ready to burn some shit to the ground.

I flipped an antique red and white Fender over my back. "Yo, Grease Weasels, you ready?"

I tapped my foot and felt like one giant jugular vein waiting to explode.

Neptune thumbed her bass guitar, but nothing came over the amplifiers. She shook her head. "Sound's jacked, boss."

I stared at Milo. "Doctor, doctor, fix our shit."

Milo shuffled to my side and whispered, "I'm trying, but the equipment is fried. Maybe Neptune can deal with it."

"What?" Neptune said.

"You're the engineer. Get in there and figure it out," I said.

She dropped the bass, the instrument thumping on the hollow stage. "Right now I'm security. I can't deal with wires and bullshit tech problems and protect us at the same time."

"I get that. Which is why Milo is supposed to be the sound guy," I said.

"Exactly how many jobs am I supposed to be doing right now?" Milo said.

"Look. We have to work together to pull this off," I said.

Radar stood up, drumsticks still clutched in his fists. "I can take a look at it."

Neptune showed her teeth. "Stay back there in your playpen, rookie."

He didn't move, but I felt his electric thrum from across the stage. "If I'm such a rookie, then why do you need my help?"

Neptune stomped to his side. "I don't. It's called being part of a team. You do what we need."

Radar stared back. "That's exactly what I offered. To do what we need. You need to relax."

"Both of you calm down. Neptune, you keep running security. Radar, poke at the amps and try not to short anything out," I said.

He left the sticks on top of his snare drum. "Give me five minutes."

Milo and Neptune glared at me.

"Now's not the time to get butt hurt. We have a show to do and lives to save," I said.

"You're stretching us thin," Milo said.

"Gee, you're quick. It's almost like we're in a tight spot."

"That's no excuse for working us to death."

"If you really feel that way, find a new job. I thought you'd give up anything to help Trina."

Milo dropped a bundle of cables onto the dusty wooden stage. "That's not what this is about. We're under a lot of pressure here, and we don't need you being an asshole on top if it."

I laughed. "Pressure? You want to talk about pressure? Buddy, you want to try on my big girl shoes and see how they feel?"

He scoffed. "Really? Who the hell do you think's been running things when you go off the map for days at a time?"

Competing with the roar of the crowd, our voices rose with our tempers. Over the top of Milo's messy red hair, I saw teenagers standing up, screaming at the stage and tossing garbage. They wanted their music, and they wanted it now. Everyone needed to hold their fucking horses.

No one tells me what to do.

I jabbed a finger at Milo's face. "Yeah, because I love getting blasted with acid rain. Having a knife rip up my spleen's what I call a party. I'll try to give you a heads up the next time I get the urge to let someone make sushi out of my intestines. Maybe you can cut up some confetti for the fiesta."

His pale face turned ruddy. "And who sews you back together again? You'd be screwed without me."

I sucked in air and closed my eyes for a second. Patience low, Alphadrine high—not a good combo.

"And your girlfriend would be dead without me," I said.

Milo's eyes could have been ice picks. "Don't go there, Xero."

Loud feedback hummed over the swish of the crowd. Trash hit the stage, cans and crumpled papers pinging against my boot heels.

As the building heated up, I felt like I could smell the sweaty armpit stank of every one of those oily teenagers, and I clenched my fists to keep from hurling bottles back into the bleachers.

The amps popped and buzzed behind me, and I thought I saw sparks twinkling.

"Fixed it," Radar said.

Neptune kicked one of the amps. "You call that fixed? Sounds like shit."

"Better than no sound at all," Radar said.

Too much noise. The crowd was getting louder, restless and angry. Radar and Neptune kept bickering about the sound system, and Milo lobbed more insults my way. I stopped hearing any of the words, everything swirling into one big mosquito drone, going up and up, louder and louder till it felt like my head was going to explode.

All that frustration, all that rage, all that damned Alphadrine eating up my lungs, boiling over until it churned into real heat, prickling across my skin, sweat dripping from my pores and redness swelling all the way from my face to my fingertips.

"Everybody just shut up!" I flipped the guitar back over my shoulder, gripped it with both hands, and whipped it over my head.

Radar and Neptune jumped back as it sailed between them and crashed into the bank of amps. Electricity zinged through my fingertips, the shock waves from the impact rattling up into my eye sockets.

I may have overreacted.

Like clusters of firecrackers exploding, sparks danced across the cables, shooting embers around the stage. It didn't get any more punk than literally burning down the house, but this was over the top, even for us.

Then before anyone could scream, before the crowd could react: flames. Big flames. All those amps. All those wires. All that fuel. The stage, a big bank of dry wood beneath us, caught fire like it had been soaked with gasoline. The fire followed the amp lines down into the audience, crawled along the bottom of the stage and lapped at the base.

An island of fire marooned us on the platform.

Then the screaming started. All those little bodies with their fake punk gear scattered, screaming as the flames surged across the amphitheater.

So much for our Zone Passes to New Orleans.
Worst. Week. Ever.

CHAPTER THIRTY

ALBUQUERQUE. I hated that city. I'd never liked it, even before their territory leader, Roja, started spending every waking hour trying to crawl up my ass. Never liked the whole state of New Mexico for that matter—like Arizona, only with more drugs and less cacti. I liked my cacti.

And I hated competition.

Roja was also responsible for the amazing armor the Skeleton uniforms were made from. I wanted to get my hands on it, bad, but that would mean giving in to Roja's demands for an equal partnership. Not going to happen. At least New Mexico was known for its psychedelics, something we didn't specialize in, or I would have nuked the whole place long ago, fancy armor or not.

No drugs all day, and we were still an hour out of the Albuquerque Dome, flat white sands with scrubby deformed bushes surrounding the crawlers. It was the desert, but it wasn't my desert.

Not yet.

With fine dust blowing everywhere, every single grain felt like it was stuck to my eyeballs, and all I wanted to do was get the hell back to Tucson, take a fucking shower, and mainline a huge hit of narcotics.

My bones hurt. My head hurt. My skin hurt. The little tendons in my hands hurt. If I had a soul, it would probably hurt. If I had remembered what Vinicodone withdrawals felt like, I never would have started shooting it again.

I had to lay off the sauce until we got back into Tucson. I told myself it was the stress, not the drugs that had made me accidentally roast the Punch Bowl, but I wasn't buying it. Yet somehow, the Grease Weasels were buying it, still thinking I was fighting off some superbug.

I slapped my palms on the dashboard. "Running out of patience here. When are we going to get clearance?"

Radar looked at me. "This is your mess. And this is why I usually fly under the radar."

"I see what you did there," I said.

He rolled his eyes. "I'm part of the team, but I'm not used to working with one. When you're ready to go full mercenary, let me know."

Neptune and Milo were in the other crawler in the interest of conflict management. Tension between us was so thick I could feel it across the desert. As beautiful as it was when the Punch Bowl imploded, I wanted to keep any new fires to a minimum.

Static crackled and Milo's voice came over the radio. "Xero. What's your temperature?"

I grabbed the handset. "It's fine, I'm fine."

"I need a number."

"What's worse, high or low?"

He paused. "I give up. Just try to stay alive until we reach the Dome."

Seemed reasonable to me. "Roger that."

Neptune came over the radio. "We're running out of fuel here. Get Xed on the horn and figure this shit out before we die of exposure."

I closed my eyes and tried to forget it all—the pain from the Vinicodone withdrawals, the exhaustion from the Alphadrine withdrawals. Zero patience. Worst of all, I had to ignore the drugs I still had stashed nearby. The bump in the glovebox. The hit in the toolbox. The bit I still had in my boot.

The full load of Alphadrine in the cargo area.

They all sang to me, and I wanted to come out and play with them.

"How much fuel do we have left?" I said.

"Not enough, not for where we are. Skipping El Paso really screwed us," Neptune said.

I sighed. "Get off the line. I'll try to work some magic." But I didn't feel like I was full of magic—my insides felt like a hazardous waste dump.

"Work fast." Neptune clicked off.

I looked over at Radar. "I'll need you to stay at the wheel while I deal with Xed. Thanks for driving again. "

"No thanks needed. I don't like to judge, but you're clearly not okay to drive."

"Excuse me?"

"You can get mad, but you know I'm right. Milo's not paranoid. Something's wrong with you."

"You want to fight me for that?"

He didn't bother making eye contact, hands still on the steering wheel. "No. I never want to fight you. Ever. We'd both end up dead."

Hard to argue with that. "Just keep an eye on the road while I try to figure out how the fuck to get into Albuquerque without getting shot full of holes."

He nodded. I liked that about him, how he was totally okay to just let it go.

I punched in the right codes and listened to static that sounded endless before it cleared. "Where are you?" Xed said.

"Where do you think we are?"

"You're not approaching the border?" His voice was calm, flat as ever.

Keep. It. Cool. I wanted to reach over the airwaves and strangle him. "Your contact was unreliable, and we can't get clearance to approach the Dome. Security's on high after what happened to Yuma, and Roja won't come out to the desert to rumble with us."

"Are you okay? You don't sound well," he said.

"Just fucking peachy, Xed. Sitting out here in the desert getting crispy. Really love how you set us up like that back in New Orleans."

"I honestly didn't know that Voodoo wouldn't have a full vial of Ketacillin. Communication with New Orleans is patchy. I'm sure you can understand after being there."

"Right. I'm sure Voodoo just totally lied to you."

"There was quite a mess to clean up behind you. It took a lot of strings to get you out of there with that stunt. You should be rotting in a jail cell again."

"Subtle. I get it. This is the second time you've bailed us out. Doesn't mean you can wrap me around your soft little fingers all day long. I'll play ball for now, but there'll be a reckoning later."

He laughed. "I look forward to it."

"Don't be so sure about that. Where the hell is Roja?"

"Probably out in the desert. The Silver Jackalope Festival is going on right now."

I coughed. "Excuse me? The what?"

I could almost hear his damned smirk over the line. "Never heard of it? So close to your territory too—it's a music festival held in a sealed mineshaft."

"Of course, the Silver Jackalope Festival. Everyone knows about that." Yeah, I had no idea. I cleared my throat. "What the hell is Roja doing there?"

"Pushing product, what else?"

"Love that smug tone. Believe it or not, there's more to life than pushing smack."

"Roja isn't really a pusher."

I wanted to throw the handset into the desert. "Smack, high end armor, doesn't matter. It's all black-market swag. I deal it all, too."

Oh, but how I wanted that armor. Part of my reason for calling the truce with Calavera was so Roja might sell me that stupid armor, but after I rejected her equal partnership deal, she refused to deliver it. My desert was my desert, and I wasn't sharing with anyone.

"I like how you've diversified," he said.

I smiled, teeth showing, dry air on my tongue. "I'm sure you do. You love money."

Breathing on the line. Dude was probably fingering himself under his nice clean desk. I heard tongue movement then, "Money isn't everything. Otherwise, I'd be more upset about New Orleans."

"Good. But if you don't get us out of this desert, you'll never see a return on investment. Antibiotics or not, if I don't see movement within the hour, we're heading back to Tucson."

"Guess you don't care about your team members as much as you claim to. Maybe we should ask Copper about that."

He knew. That son of a bitch knew. I swallowed, pushing down a sudden tide of bile rising in my throat.

"How I run my territory is none of your business. Just get us out of here or all deals are off."

Silence. Then he said, "Understood. I'll do what I can."

He clicked off before I could respond.

I clutched the handset, the plastic grill digging into my fingertips. With great effort, I put the device gently back into its cradle.

Radar shifted. "That went well."

"I love Trina. I'd give my life for any of the Grease Weasels, but I mean it. If we don't get clearance soon, I'm taking us back to base."

"Two people are missing. No sign of Argon, and Neptune said there's been no contact with Copper either."

Copper. Still not sorry he was dead, but no one needed to know that yet. He didn't count as one of us. No way Radar didn't notice the little jab Xed threw in there.

I opened my mouth to say something about Copper, somehow prep Radar for the eventual news, but closed it. I smelled death and tasted rotting carrion on the back of my tongue.

It was leaking through the air vents.

I sat up. "We have a problem."

He arched forward, scanning. "It's late in the season."

I snatched the handset again. "Neptune. Lock the doors. Grab weapons. Incoming."

"Already on it." She sounded hungry for combat.

Radar seized his pipe, and I pulled my illegal laser from under the seat. I heard them before I saw them come over the ridge. A cackling sound, like a pack of delirious teenagers, echoed through the thick glass windows.

The rabid coyotes. Not really rabid, worse than rabid, but that's still what we called the mutant beasts. They were on us, a brown flood of mottled fur, flowing around the crawler like dirty water. The noise, their horrible shrieking, rang in my ears like they were right there in the cabin with us.

So many of them, more than I'd ever seen, all that blood, fur, and scabby flesh jumping and swirling around our crawler until there was no sun.

A foul darkness engulfed the cabin.

They clawed at the vehicle, ripped at the treads and tore at all the seams. We couldn't stay there, but running wouldn't do any good.

Radar flipped the crawler into gear.

"No. They'll get sucked in the engine, and we'll be screwed. We can't move till they're gone. Trust me," I said.

"How long till they give up?"

I thought back to the last time this had happened. "Sometime this week."

"Not an option."

"New options are welcome at any time."

He gripped the gearshift but didn't move. "Thinking."

Nothing from Neptune over the radio, but I knew she was busy guarding the crawler and waiting for my directions.

Flashes of light burst through the smear of fur that covered the windshield, and coyote shrieks boomed through the cabin. Blood streaked the windshield and bodies fell away from the glass. Sunlight leaked back inside through the crimson haze, projecting a bloody kaleidoscope pattern onto the seats. I clutched the laser, tense, finger ready to squeeze off rounds. Radar didn't move, sitting calmly as though nothing had happened.

Fwap. A hand slapped against my passenger window, wiping aside a thick sheet of blood and fur. A full gas mask pressed up against the glass, the bulky air filter clicking on the slick surface.

"Welcome to Albuquerque," a female voice said as an armored fist motioned for me to open the door. "Come on out. And try not to die."

Chapter Thirty-One

I COULDN'T believe I didn't know about the Silver Jackalope Festival, and that smug tone in Xed's voice still rang in my ears. He was right—I should have known about this. I was slipping. Or maybe I'd just been trying to ignore Roja and her whole territory for too long. Rookie mistakes, but she had that effect on me.

Roja stopped and jumped off her black mototractor, letting it flop into the crispy white sand. A bold move, riding around in the desert in such an unprotected vehicle when you needed a respirator, but Roja always had been a daredevil.

We shut off our engines, and even Radar looked tense. With nothing but two crawlers and Xed's word that Roja wouldn't waste us, I can't say any of us thought it was a great idea to follow a known enemy out into the middle of the desert. I wanted a whole army with me, just in case. I wanted not to be shaking and sweating from withdrawals. I wanted a lot of things.

Like a fat dose of Alphadrine.

That same dull landscape surrounded us, smothering us with all that hard white sand covered by bland rocks, sun-bleached weeds, and dead lizards. It looked like a setup, but I knew an execution ground when I saw one, and this wasn't it.

Roja stood in her shiny black combat suit, hands on her tiny waist, motorcycle boots dug into the sand, gas mask glued to her face. I was glad her head was still hidden under an armored helmet. The thought of her red hair made my stomach turn.

I picked up the handset. "Neptune. Hold your bombs."

She laughed. "How did you know?"

"I hardly ever let you play with explosives."

"Exactly, and this is a perfect time to use them. We're about to get jumped."

"Nope. Look around. Too many places to run, too many vistas for counterspies. Roja's not that stupid," I said.

Radar leaned over. "And I know Xed. He won't let us die yet—we're too valuable still. Roja wouldn't risk pissing him off."

Neptune scoffed. "Fine. But I'm bringing a flash grenade down with me."

Radar grabbed his pipe and slipped on a pair of black sunglasses. "Let's get this over with. Raves give me headaches."

"You knew about this thing too?"

He smiled, the corners of his mouth turning up just a bit. "Sorry, I'm just surprised. It's the biggest festival in the Southwest. All the super-rich Dome kids from the Western states pay big for the event. Tons of drugs and other black-market goods—rich kid's playground. I've made epic cash taking up contracts here, but I'm too old to deal with that shit anymore."

"Great. Well, we've been at war with Albuquerque since I got into this game. I stay out of this area."

His smile spread.

"What? Out with it, or at least wipe that grin off your face."

He coughed. "War isn't what I heard. More like...lover's quarrel."

I flopped back in my seat. "You're lucky I feel too shitty to get into it with you."

Radar shrugged.

Outside, Roja waved her arms and hit the button on her mask's intercom. "I thought you guys said you were on a tight schedule. What's the holdup?"

She kicked the ground at her feet in wide sweeps, spraying waves of sand and weeds until a big rusty metal circle appeared beneath it all. She pointed down at the plate, and somehow, even though I couldn't see her face, I knew that petite mouth of hers was blowing me a kiss.

No way to avoid it anymore. I had to follow her down there.

Into the abyss.

Chapter Thirty-Two

INSIDE THE mine, deep into a pit over a hundred years old, everything smelled wrong. The cool musk of deep earth and mold mixed with the pulsing, live scent of fresh human sweat and blood—bodies sucking in the artificially purified air and pumping out waste. Keeping that big space oxygenated would cost a fortune. The government couldn't even afford that kind of thing anymore. These kids really did have some serious money.

We stood in the dark at the bottom of the elevator shaft, in a holding chamber behind a thick metal door. Rainbow lights leaked around the frame, casting bright smears of neon across our faces. Guess it wasn't meant to be a second air seal after all.

Roja, her gas mask still on, popped latches and spun at the door's portal hatch before she yanked on it, trying to pull the heavy thing open.

Even before the door gave way, I smelled drugs, tasted them at the back of my throat, bitter, but sweet and smoky. The place was swimming with them, an ocean of smack waiting for me to drink it all in.

I rubbed my sweaty palms together, nausea swirling in my gut like a nest of angry rats. My heart thumped too quickly, too hard, and saliva pooled in my mouth almost faster than I could swallow.

Withdrawal.

It sucked bad, and the cure was literally floating in the air around me, just on the other side of that rusty door.

Then it swung open, and light blasted my eyes.

Bodies. So many bodies all jammed together, half-naked and smeared with paint that glowed in the black lights. With the strobes, the techno music thumping, the writhing mass of flesh all high as fuck and dancing, it was hard to focus. Radar was right—my head hurt.

Roja left her gas mask on and motioned to follow her through the crowd. Just the little whiffs of whatever junk was aerosolized felt wonderful, took a bit of the edge off, and made me want to eat the fucking air like pudding.

Even with the rooms stuffed to the brim, people stepped aside for Roja, leaving a trail for us to follow her. She had complete control, and everyone respected her.

I missed that feeling.

We traveled through rooms of heaving bodies, each little chamber another sect of debauchery separated by a thick door and guarded by security—probably helped keep the population in each colony regulated and made security manageable.

In the chaos, it was difficult to see anything, but I finally realized everyone was wearing the same shiny headwear—silver antlers. Right. Guess it was called the Silver Jackalope Festival for a reason. Had to give some respect for using our local myth, the jackalope: a jackrabbit with deer antlers. I'd been high and hallucinated them myself more than once.

So many painted bodies and shiny antlers, I couldn't process what was going on in each quarter. I put my hands in my pockets and did my best to not reach out and grab a handful of pills from one of the silver trays scattered about each room. With so many drugs, I had no idea how people weren't overdosing left and right.

Maybe they were, and I just couldn't see the dead beneath all the gyrating bodies.

After what seemed like forever, we came to a cavern set off from the main party—it was quieter, drastically less crowded, and farther back in the mineshaft. A handful of people sat on plush red couches or toured the floor, chitchatting with the other guests. At the back wall there was a buffet full of steaming dishes and very few people taking advantage of them.

Roja stopped and turned around to face us. "Everyone else can stay here, have a bite and sit down in one of the comfortable chairs.

This is the VIP lounge—you should have fun." She pointed a finger at me. "But you, you come with me to the beyond."

"That where the Ketacillin is?" I said. I couldn't decide if I wanted to get out of the mine immediately or stay until I shoved my guts so full of drugs that I exploded.

"That's where everything is," she said.

I rubbed my eyes and tried to ignore all the pulsing music and obnoxious lights sneaking into the lounge from the main party rooms. A cool, oxygen-heavy wind went across my forehead; it felt good, evaporated some of the sweat. Each purified breeze was like a wad of cash blowing away. Hard to deny—the decadence was sexy.

I shifted to face my crew, wondering why any of them were following me on this ludicrous quest. Domes were blowing up, people were missing, enemies were coming out of the woodwork, but there we were, chasing a dream at the bottom of an ancient mineshaft filled with drugs and naked rich kids slathered in glowing paint.

Radar stood still, gripping his pipe, sunglasses still glued to his eyes. I wondered where his mind was, what was he thinking about. Milo was next to him, bunching up his flannel shirt in his pale fists. His freckles glowed in the blacklights, and he looked so very young.

Neptune's eyes were so big I thought she might have taken a hit of something, but then I saw the look on her face—she was just hungry for action, sensing things could go sideways at any second.

We were in an electric powder keg.

Neptune lifted an eyebrow at me. "I'll allow it. Anything coming through the hatch would have to get through us first anyway." She jerked a thumb at Roja. "And sick or not, I'm pretty sure you can take this broad. Give a holler if you need backup."

Milo grabbed my hand, and I winced at how sweaty my palms felt on his dry skin. "Be careful."

I smiled, and it was real. "Thanks."

He might be furious with me, but we were still a team. A family.

"Hurry back," Radar said.

I couldn't tell if he was worried about me too, or if he just wanted to get the fuck out of raver hell.

"I only have until sundown to get back into the Dome before my Zone Pass gets pinged," Roja said. "Do you want to talk business or not?"

"Let's move," I said. "But I'm snagging some food first. If I don't, we'll all regret it."

"Quickly."

Food, though I probably needed it badly, was the last thing on my mind. Nerves got the better of me—I couldn't face Roja like this, trembling and sweating like a pimply teenager on a first date.

I dashed over to the buffet, snagged a pastry with one hand, and dug my fingers into a basket of pills with the other. No idea what it was, but I didn't care. All my neurons were screaming for chemicals to fill their aching, empty slots, and I needed something.

Like a pro, I palmed a handful of red capsules, slipped them into my mouth, and washed the bitter things down with a gulp of some sweet juice out of a silver chalice. The mixture tingled my tongue, felt so good going down my throat. I crammed the pastry in afterward to keep up appearances.

I swallowed hard and turned around. "I'm ready."

Had anyone noticed? I didn't think so. I tried to look confident as I waved to my crew and trudged after Roja.

I followed her through another series of guarded rooms, and after several minutes, we came to the end of the line. The final chamber.

This time, the door actually sealed, and the airlock hissed as it closed behind us. A safe room. In case the air supply ran out, this place probably had its own separate hookup. I tasted the extra oxygen, felt it clearing my head.

No guards followed us in, and we were left alone in the suddenly quiet chamber. The party noise was completely blocked out, but the walls, ceiling, and floor were plated with pure silver, and our footsteps clanged in the small room.

Roja finally peeled the gas mask off her face and shook her head. She wore deep cherry lipstick, and her long eyelashes, coated in dark mascara, fluttered in front of lids painted with sparkly gold eye shadow. And her hair. Seeing her red hair was like a punch in the throat. Drugs needed to work faster.

"Much better. I don't know about you, but I just hate wearing those things all day," she said.

"I hardly ever use one," I said.

"Ah, well you always were blessed with great lungs, amongst other things." She scanned me, and it felt like her gaze was touching me in all the soft hidden spots. I shivered.

The far back wall was occupied by glass cabinets packed with sealed foods and medical supplies. Silver couches topped with white vinyl cushions filled up the rest of the space. Couldn't be certain, but it looked like there were panels that could be pulled out of the wall joints—probably for more storage, a refrigerator, a toilet, and perhaps a bed. I bet Roja was planning on using this as a hideout if things went to shit.

"I hear you're not well," she said.

"Just too much time on the road. I'm fine." How many times had I said that this week?

She nodded at the couches. "Why don't you have a seat, and we'll talk."

I hated letting people tell me what to do. but sitting sounded more than good. I kept waiting for whatever I'd swallowed out in the anteroom to hit me, but it had one hell of a loading time. Obviously not up to our quality, which made me smile a bit. I'm all about the instant delivery.

I flopped down on a white vinyl couch and couldn't hold back a sigh. The room with its cool air and sudden silence was just so good. Now I needed that junk to make a landing in my bloodstream.

Roja sat next to me, and I didn't say anything. I should have said something. Why wasn't I saying something? You don't let enemies snuggle you on the couch.

Not even if they looked exactly like your dead wife.

She ran a hand through her short, bright red hair, blinked those big hazel eyes, and pursed her tiny soft pink lips. God. She looked just like Evan. Butterflies in my spleen.

"Better?" she said.

I smiled, felt it get big and sloppy. "Yeah. Much." There was almost a purr in my voice. Oh. Maybe the drugs were hitting after all. I should have guessed what everyone at a rave would be eating like candy. Shit.

Now I had to deal with being locked in a sealed chamber, rolling on euphorics with someone who probably wanted to kill me. Someone who also happened to look like my beloved dead wife.

I looked at her eyes again; her pupils were enormous.

Fuck.

We were both high on DISC.

Nothing good could come of this.

Roja loved to sample products, another reason why we never struck a truce. I wouldn't work with dealers who used their own exports. Because, you know, shit like this happens.

I should have stood up, gotten out of the damned death trap, but all I wanted to do was wrap my fingers around her slim waist and pretend like Evan wasn't dead.

She put a hand on my thigh. I didn't move it. "So, having a change of heart? Thinking of working with me after all?"

I tried to center myself, get my shit together, shake off the rising tide of DISC. Now I was thankful for the slow high. There was still time to salvage the situation.

"I still can't trust you. That's been the problem all along. You made a deal with Calavera, but you didn't call it off with Juarez."

She licked her lips. "Calavera. Our mutual liaison."

"I'm still pissed you gave her that armor, but you won't give me dick."

She raised an eyebrow. "Oh, I'll give you better than dick, baby."

I made a face.

She tapped her chest. "Check this out—new batch of stuff, even better than what Calavera's Skeletons are rolling in. Lighter weight, harder to pierce, resistant to explosives. Can't beat it."

"So what do you want from me?"

She got closer, her nose right in nuzzling distance. "You know what I want from you."

I had to fight the swirl of chemicals in my brain telling me I should put my hands on her face and touch every inch of that soft skin. The fluorescent lights in the room were hazy, the reflections on the silver-plated walls leaving trails across my vision. Tracers. The drugs were moving.

I leaned back. "Stay on topic. Look. There's complicated shit going on. I want to know where we stand."

"You're right about that. Show me your cards, and I'll show you mine."

I felt like all my cards were on fire and burning in my hands.

"What do you want to know?" I said.

"Calavera. Xed. Yuma. The Alphadrine. The Ketacillin. What's the real story?"

I blinked, trying to organize it all in my head. When I had it as straight as I could, I told her everything. At least as much as was safe.

"So there you go," I said. "Dicks, pussies, and cards all on the table."

"Damn. I was hoping you knew what happened to Calavera."

"You don't?"

"Bitch is missing for real. And I don't like that you're working with Xed."

"That makes two of us. And I don't like that you're still working with Juarez. That can't ride. It's me and Calavera's new alliance, or Juarez, not both."

"Juarez has great cash flow, and you weren't playing ball. By the way, you have rats." She smiled.

It took me a second, and then I laughed. "Copper."

"Right. Sorry for the trouble, but I can't help playing with you every now and then. Copper's not with me, though. I'm not that crude."

"I know. He was with Juarez. Well, that makes me feel better at least."

"Oh?"

I just looked at her.

She laughed. "I see. You always were good at pest control."

"Of my many faults, mercy is not one of them."

She touched my arm. "Right now your biggest fault is working with Xed and not with me. I work with some dirty mofos, but Xed's in another league of bad."

"Xed's not in my long-term plans, but until my crew is back in one piece, I have to do whatever needs to be done. He has more leverage than I realized."

"There's a reason for that. I'm telling you, get out now," she said.

Her hand crept along my shoulder until it tickled my collarbone. Surprised, I inhaled and tried to fight off how much I liked it. Couldn't blame it all on the drugs.

I avoided her eyes. "So you'll help me."

She pursed her lips. "The Ketacillin reagent's yours. I don't care for Xed, but the Alphadrine trade he arranged will be a nice little boost for us."

I should have just left it at that. "What about the armor? And Juarez?"

Her hand slipped under my shirt. "I think you know that still requires some negotiation."

Her fingers were warm and soft, and I as collapsed into her touch, a wave of color crashed over me. The drugs, coming home, taking roost. I had never been into euphorics for a reason, and now I was powerless against a rising tide of intense light, colors that had no names, and lust I couldn't control. Her fingers could have been angel feathers or the devil's tongue, and I wanted all that sin and salvation.

I closed my eyes, but the nameless colors didn't go away.

"Stay right here," she said.

Wasn't sure if I could have gone anywhere if I wanted to, but I felt her get up off the couch and come back a minute later. I opened my eyes, blinked, and tried see real life again.

She was smiling, looking even more like Evan than before, holding two champagne glasses that glowed with some sparkling beverage.

"Better stay hydrated," she said.

She lifted the glass to my lips, and I was so thirsty. I took big gulps of the effervescent liquid. It was light, a little sweet, and so fizzy it felt like electric zaps on my tongue.

"Drink up. There you go. This will make you feel great."

It took a second, but even through the rainbow fog of the DISC, I realized what she'd just given me, smelled the earthy aftertaste lingering on my palate.

Chupacabra.

I tried to sit up, but she pushed me back down.

"Just relax. It'll hit in a minute. It's pure. You'll love it."

Made from a glowing cave fungus, Chupacabra was a powerful hallucinogen.

And it did not mix well with large doses of DISC. A little was fine, but a little was not what I'd taken.

I wanted to articulate that, but all that came out was, "Oh, no."

"Don't worry, the half life is short, you'll be fine to leave tonight, I promise. Enjoy the ride with me. This is the good stuff."

I shook my head, floppy like a dead kitten. "DISC. I took a lot. In the foyer."

"Shit."

Shit was right. DISC was unpredictable, especially the cheap kind—mixed up and tweaked from the remains of scavenged prescription drugs, anything was possible.

We didn't make either drug for a reason.

But then I didn't care. All the euphoria from both drugs was on me, and I felt like I was floating in space, watching the rebirth of the universe, one with everything. I'd never experienced anything like it before, and I thought I'd burst with a joy I didn't know was possible, like a flower blooming so hard it exploded.

Hands shook my shoulders.

"How much did you take? How much?" she said.

I smiled but didn't answer. Hard to be worried when everything just felt so damned good.

In the background, a radio squawked, and the chamber doors slid open. The hallucinations and reality blurred into one, but part of me knew the screams were real. Over the shrieks, I heard my crewmembers yelling, heard Neptune's voice barking out orders.

Then the intense flashing started, blotting out everything else. These were no party decorations. Someone had set off a flash grenade.

In my brain, something broke. I knew it instantly, like watching a fragile light bulb implode, I was shattered. My body went rigid, then numb, pins and needles crawling up and down my arms and legs.

All the voices, all the colors real and imaginary, it all faded away into that silent pulsing light that was so very loud.

CHAPTER THIRTY-THREE

A DEEP night sky filled with star clusters whooshed overhead. Cool air and bits of sand brushed across my skin. I was alive, alive and traveling somewhere. With a brain full of mud, I tried to remember what happened.

It came back to me in pieces, but then I had it.

The Silver Jackalope. The drugs. The blackout.

Where was I being taken? Injured or not, I wasn't going down without a fight. I blinked, my vision not quite clear, but I didn't care where I was. I had to get out. No one takes me prisoner.

I sat up with all my strength, planning on springing to my feet, but a sharp jerk pulled me back down. My arms were stretched out, handcuffed to either side of a black cargo Jeep.

Trapped.

Crucified.

"Sorry about the handcuffs. You've been having a lot of seizures...and delusions. Almost ate my face off a few times," Radar said. He turned around in the driver's seat, and I saw the outline of his sharp jaw backlit by the headlights.

I relaxed and let my arms go limp again. "Scared the shit out of me. Why do you have me strapped down in the back of an open Jeep?"

He turned back to the road. "Neptune wants everyone back at

main base. Activity on the border—probably Juarez. Milo gave the go ahead to transport you, but all the other vehicles are out on patrol. Didn't want you accidentally jumping off, or you know, ripping out my eyeballs while I was driving."

I had the good sense to feel sheepish. "Oops. My bad."

"Glad to have you back." It sounded sincere.

I wanted to rub my eyes but couldn't reach my face.

"You feel safe?" he said. I knew what he meant.

"Yeah. Drugs are out of my system. Head feels like a sack of manure."

"Not surprising."

"Arms hurt too."

I sat up and looked at my wrists—they were bruised and scraped from what I guessed was at least a few days of thrashing around. Probably ripped out a few IV lines too, from the look of it—several big ones were still stuck in my arms, practically welded down by some thick adhesive bandages. The IV bags dangled from the Jeep's roll cage, sloshing and spinning as we bounced over rough terrain.

"Sorry, it's not safe to stop now. We're almost there. Hang tight."

I sat back again. A clean hospital johnny covered my torso, and that was it—wind blew right up the bottom and reminded me I was alive.

"What gives? Trying to let the whole town have a free show?"

"Sorry, Neptune wanted us out of there pronto. You can change at headquarters."

Even cuffed like some cheap thug, the dark open sky and dry scent of the desert made me feel at home. If I was going to be tied down, there were worse scenarios. Better scenarios too, but Radar was busy driving.

I shifted in my restraints. "What happened?"

"Where do you want me to start?"

I sighed. "You knew."

"All along."

I'm not really the blushing type, but my face was suddenly hot. "Why didn't you say something?"

"Wasn't my place. Everyone else was blinded, thought it was impossible you'd be shooting smack again. I don't know you so well, but I do know druggies."

Druggie. I deserved that, but I didn't have to like it. "So why are you still here, carting my stupid ass around?"

"You want to kick me out of the club?"

I laughed. "Are you kidding? I'd cuff you to this Jeep if I could."

He laughed back. "If you hadn't zombie attacked me a few hours ago, I might consider the offer."

"You didn't answer the question."

"I told you before. I'm an old school merc. Far as I'm concerned, this is a long-standing contract, and the current mission isn't even done." He swallowed. "Plus, I like you. You're better than you think you are."

I definitely might have been blushing. Chalk it up to a rough week. I cleared my throat. "I'll take it." I'm not the mushy type either—had to cut that shit off.

I looked around, trying to figure out what part of town we were in. Streaks of old neon signs rushed by. Miracle Mile, a shitty boulevard lined with broken down sketchy motels, dead palm trees, and roachy strip clubs. Close to home.

"I'm afraid to ask, but how's Milo?" I said.

"Milo...is not happy. Neither is Neptune."

"What happened down in the mine?"

"Some little skirmishes broke out in the other chambers, nothing too major, but Neptune tossed a flash grenade just for fun."

"Right. Might have been more fun for me if I hadn't made some poor mixing decisions."

"Hallucinogens are unpredictable. Especially that DISC. Nasty stuff."

"I may have accidentally washed it down with Chupacabra."

He coughed, a hitch of shock in his voice as he said, "That'll do it. You started seizing, probably triggered by the grenade pulses, and Milo couldn't get it to stop. Your temp skyrocketed, and you stopped breathing a few times. Wasn't good. Your girlfriend was really upset."

"She's not my girlfriend."

He shrugged. "She felt bad—once we got you stable enough to move, she gave us the Ketacillin reagent and sent us on our merry way."

I let out a breath big enough to cause a sandstorm. "We got it. We got it." What I didn't add was *I didn't ruin everything after all.*

"Milo's down in the lab, trying to synthesize it."

Milo wasn't our lead lab tech. Argon was, and Argon was still missing. Emphasis on the missing. I refused to believe he was dead. In my sweet little fantasyland, I'd imagined we'd get the reagents, make it back to Tucson, and Argon would appear from his hidey-hole so he could work his chemical magic on the Ketacillin. Whipping up exotic antibiotics wasn't exactly something we did regularly out here. Would Milo be able to make it work by himself?

I said nothing, and that question hung between us.

The Jeep shifted as we took a big turn and Radar continued, "There's always your buddy Xed."

"I don't want anything else to do with Xed if I can help it. Trying to yank all the weeds from my yard, you know?"

"You must be a natural pesticide." He paused and then said, "They know about Copper."

I closed my eyes for a second—extra long blink. "Let me guess, and you knew all along."

"Nobody likes a know it all."

"Copper was a snitch for Juarez. Had to be done."

Silence.

"Oh for fuck's sake, you knew about that, too?"

"I keep my ear to the ground."

"Well, Jesus fucking hell, speak up the next time you just so happen to know a key piece of information."

"Ask and you shall receive."

Seemed like all my dirty laundry was hanging out there in my front yard for the entire desert to see. The drugs. The murders. All my nasty little secrets, exposed. Radar didn't seem to have a problem with me nixing Copper, but I could almost be certain Milo and Neptune wouldn't be quite so accepting.

"You always this mysterious? We're going to need to see a little more team spirit in the future," I said.

"I told you. I work alone."

"Welcome to the big leagues. Time to learn how to play nice with others," I said.

He turned and looked at me again. Okay, so I hadn't exactly been doing the best job of role modeling, what with the drug problems and lies and all. Speaking of which.

"How long has it been?" I said.

"Few days. Milo decided to rapid detox you."

Well, that might also help explain why my head burned like a Casa Grande garbage dump, but I wasn't having any cravings.

I clenched my sore fists hard, fragile veins feeling like they would rupture. "You let him do that?"

Rapid detox is dangerous, and although it's quick like it says in the name, you're just as likely to croak getting through it. He should have let me wake up and asked me if I wanted to risk it.

"It was the right thing to do. Milo's good, he knows what he's doing. You'll feel like shit for a few more days then be ready to roll again. As a professional, I thought you'd understand that," he said.

He was right, which made me even crankier. I wanted to get lit up again just out of spite.

"Tell that to my head. Skull feels like it was put through an uncalibrated decon wash," I said.

He reached out and touched the top of my head. "No rest for the wicked."

I sighed and tried to accept what Milo had done to my body. Only I had a right to destroy myself. I'd deal with Milo later. "What about...everything else?"

He shook his head. "Juarez is on the move. No sign of Argon. No Calavera. Xed seemed to know about your...problem as well. Said to contact him when you woke up."

"He's going to have to take a number. I'll call him when I feel like it." More like I'd call him if anything else blew up. I wanted to think we could handle Juarez on our own but couldn't quite convince myself.

From the corner of my eye, the bowling alley came into view. A ten-foot tall cobblestone wall surrounded the building, big letter blocks, yellowed from years of exposure, spelling out B-O-W-L across the top. An oversized cement bowling pin and chipped red ball jutted out from in between the O and W letters. Barbed wire spiraled through the ornaments and over the cobblestones, gun turrets peeking over the edge every few feet.

Headquarters. Hot water and freedom from these stupid cuffs. It was going to take an hour just to wash the sand out of my ass crack.

"Once we get you settled, I'll check in with Milo, see how things are going with the Ketacillin, let him know you're awake. Neptune was pissed, but Milo said he wouldn't leave the lab until he had some results."

"Tell him I died, just to fuck with him."

He braked hard, sand flying up into the back of the Jeep and splashing across my bare legs. He flipped around to look me directly in the eye.

"It was too close to joke about."

Chapter Thirty-Four

Still in my hospital gown, I lay sprawled across the cool slippery wood of the farthest bowling lane in our headquarters, fluttering my arms and legs like I was making snow angels, trying to keep my shit together. I figured communing with the great bowling spirits would bring some clarity.

Radar told me to leave my IVs in until Milo came back to hang something new, but I'm not always good at following directions. I ripped them out and threw the lines behind me. Got some blood on the lanes too—Neptune would yell at me for that later.

I wanted to jump right in the shower, but Radar reminded me Neptune would probably waltz in and ram a blade up my *culo* if I didn't wait for briefing first. Sand would have to stay up my ass awhile longer since a machete enema wasn't a preferred removal method. I wanted to put on better clothes too, but at least the hospital gown was breezy.

A door opened at the front of the building and slammed shut, vibrating the greased planks beneath me.

"Fuck! Fuck this organization, fuck Xed, fuck that Cajun bitch, fuck Albuquerque, and fuck this goddamn bowling alley!"

Milo.

The ground shook, wood cracking like cannonballs landing all around me.

I sat up. Milo's face was redder than his hair, and tears streamed down his face as he lobbed bowling balls down the restored lanes. He tossed them like they were shot puts, and as they landed in the old wood, big craters opened beneath them, dotting the lanes like someone slowly poking holes in Swiss cheese.

"Whoa," I said and scuttled backward off the lanes. "I've got enough holes in my head already, thank you very much."

I jumped to my feet. Milo spun around and charged forward, a neon orange bowling ball clutched in his right hand, ready to throw. I put my hands up in a gesture of surrender, trying to catch him off guard.

I snatched the ball from his hand and simultaneously dodged behind him, grabbing his collar and sweeping a leg under his feet. He landed safely with his ass in one of the white bucket chairs beside the old bar tables, too stunned to say anything.

Still had it. Not bad for someone who was basically dead yesterday.

Footsteps pounded across the room as Neptune's compact body lurched out of the communications room, wielding a machete. "What the fuck is going on out here?" She jabbed the blade at my nose.

"Everyone just calm the hell down. Neptune, I love you, but if you ever shake a machete in my face again, I will make you eat it for breakfast," I said, still holding the neon bowling ball. I used my free hand to pull up the gown—hard to feel intimidating when your tits and ass are spilling out everywhere. I really needed to train naked more often because it was becoming a common problem.

Neptune lowered the machete but didn't drop it. She put her free hand on her hip. "Look, boss, I don't care who's causing trouble. Even if you're the one freaking out, I gotta put a stop to it, *comprende*? And it looks like you got caught red handed ruining my fine craftsmanship." She pointed at the destroyed lanes. "You back on shit already?"

"No, Jesus, give me a little credit. It's not me, obviously." I looked at Milo who had begun sobbing, his head buried in his hands.

Neptune came forward a step. "Milo, dude, what's wrong man? Is it Trina?"

I set the bowling ball down and put a hand on Milo's back. He knocked it away with a quick smack that echoed down the lanes. Neptune raised the machete again, but I motioned for her to drop it.

I shook my head. "Just give him a minute." But she was right—it had to be Trina. Nothing else would set him off like this. If she was dead, Neptune might have to turn the blade on me My brain couldn't handle entertaining that possibility. Good thing my addict sensibilities were prepped and ready with a healthy dose of denial.

We waited, but Milo wouldn't even raise his head, and the sobs were coming in waves that traveled through his body like little earthquakes.

"You think we should give him a sedative or something? He's fucking lost it." Neptune poked the machete at him.

"Stop acting like he's going to go all slaughterhouse on us. It's Milo."

Neptune shrugged. "He might not look like much, but he's got some fighting chops on him. I've seen people go crazy in this desert and start stabbing people for no reason. I don't let anyone get the drop on me—not even my own mother. Hell, I trusted you, and you turned out to be a goddamn junkie."

Ouch. "Fine, just watch where you point that thing—Milo's going to have a hard time sewing himself up if you get twitchy and run him through."

Milo seemed to be oblivious to both the machete pointed in his direction and the conversation we were having. I tried to get his attention several more times, but he just sat there, his sobs growing more hysterical by the minute.

"Keep an eye on him but don't stab him." I walked into one of the back bedrooms and came back with a soggy Radar in tow. Bastard had snuck into the shower.

"You really want me to do that?" he said. "What's gotten into him?"

I dragged him across the floor until he was adjacent to Milo. "Not sure, but this needs to stop."

Radar scratched his head. "Okay, if you say so."

Neptune cocked her head, trying to figure out what we were talking about, but she kept quiet.

Radar put a hand on Milo's shoulder, and before he could knock it away, his body jumped, then stiffened. Radar grabbed Milo's other shoulder and laid him across another chair so his upper body was supported between the two seats. He wasn't unconscious, but stunned enough he had stopped crying.

"Did you just shock him?" Neptune stared at me. "You're

worried about me stabbing him, but you tell Mr. Robot here to light him up like a Christmas tree?"

"It was just a mild shock. He'll be fine," I said.

Milo was breathing at a more regular pace, and after shaking his head back and forth a few times, he tried to sit back up again. Radar went to help him, but he shied away from his touch.

"Thanks, I've got this," Milo said in a quiet, shaky voice.

"Sorry about that," Radar said.

Milo ignored him and looked straight at me. "It's not working. It won't work—it can't work. I don't have the equipment."

"The Ketacillin?" I said.

He averted his eyes before answering. "The two reagents are authentic, but I can't finish the synthesis. We need equipment they would only have in a big fabrication lab, like they have in Domes that still have a manufacturing industry."

I squatted down on my heels till I was eye level with him, trying not to let the desperate relief show on my face. "But she's still alive, right? It's not over yet. We can find a way. There's always a way."

Milo hung his head and shook it quickly, his hands shooting up to clench tufts of hair. "That's not the only problem. Her lungs are too damaged. She'll slowly die if we can't repair them."

Which reminded me. "Where is she?"

Rage was in his eyes again as he jabbed a finger at Neptune. "She wouldn't let me stay with Trina, and I can't bring her here—without the ventilator she'll expose everyone."

I thought Neptune was going to explode again, but she just rolled her eyes. "Don't be stupid. We can't let Juarez waltz right in and take everything just because our friend is dying. Get your shit together. Techs are down there watching her, and you said it yourself—nothing more we can do for her now anyway."

Right. Juarez. I think it was safe to say I still wasn't thinking quite right.

When Calavera abandoned Juarez to take over the Nogales territory, that whole area went rogue and started taking pot shots at us. Wouldn't have been dangerous, but then Albuquerque and Calavera joined the fray, and fighting everyone off suddenly became expensive. Very expensive.

I swallowed. "Just slow down. Bring me up to speed. What's the deal with Juarez?"

Neptune rested her machete on the table. "Last night we had a few attacks at the border, right around our weak spots. Like they knew where to hit us. This evening, we got big action on the radar. Lots of movement. The few guys we caught from the first wave were from Juarez, so the rest gotta be from there too."

"Who the hell is leading them?" I said.

Neptune scowled. "I was hoping you'd know. I don't think it's Calavera. Maybe robot boy over here has an idea."

We all stared at Radar. He was missing his usual trench coat, and his wet hair was pulled back into a messy ponytail.

"It's not Copper, that's for sure," he said.

My eyes got big, and I mouthed at him to shut up.

Neptune shifted to glare at me, her boots sticking to the freshly waxed floor. "Yeah, that reminds me, what the fuck? You just went and killed Copper without talking to us first? Then you lied about it?"

I scoffed. "Never thought you'd get mad at me for icing a traitor."

She picked up the machete again. "Not the point. Now we have no tech officer. We're stretched thin as it is."

Milo stood up. "Exactly. That's not the point. You got high and killed someone. One of us. You had no proof he was a snitch, but you killed him anyway! Whatever happened to us being a family? I thought we were important to you. You killed Copper, you've lost Argon, and it's on your head if Trina dies."

Every single one of his words hit home, but my shame just turned into anger. I ground my teeth together and tried not to do something I'd regret. "Look, I'm sorry about the drugs. I have a problem, I get it, moment of weakness, it won't happen again. And high or not, I wasn't wrong about Copper. That's how Juarez is getting past our security now—Copper ratted on us, left holes in our armor. Radar knows that, Roja confirmed it, and I found Mexican money on him before I sent him on a one-way trip back down the *rio*."

Neptune pushed Milo back into his seat and stood close to me. "Fine. But if you ever dust someone important without running it by me, I'm out. Same goes for the drugs. Better not catch you powdering your nose again, you know what I mean? We clear?"

I smirked. "Crystal."

If Neptune was schooling me for murdering indiscriminately, that was a bad sign.

I was about to say something else when pain stabbed into my skull, right behind the eye sockets. I stumbled, leaned down to grab my head. Radar and Neptune jumped to support me and guide me to one of the chairs. Radar's wet hair trailed across the back of my neck as he made sure I was steady.

I opened my eyes and blinked.

"What's wrong?" Milo said, his voice filled with worry. Least he didn't totally hate me yet. He reached over the table to feel my wrist's pulse.

"Give you one guess. Thanks for the rapid fucking detox."

His fingers tightened around my wrist. "I had no choice. I'm not the one who shoved your face in a trough of Alphadrine and Vinicodone and then washed it down with a bunch of psychedelic Albuquerque trash."

I snatched my wrist back and put my hands on my aching head. "You had a choice. You knew how dangerous that was. I could have died, but you couldn't wait. I'm the only one who can save your precious Trina, and you know it."

"Fuck you, Xero. I know what I'm doing. I'm not like you—I don't risk the lives of people I care about just for fun."

My head throbbed even harder and some sick part of me wanted to strangle him. Partly because I thought he was right. I'm a killer. That's what I am, and killers aren't supposed to have families.

Still standing behind me, Radar put his hands on my shoulders and pulled me back from the table. Smart guy.

"Let's not make things worse. Bad things have happened. We need to move forward," he said. "Everyone take a breath, sit down, and we'll figure this out."

At least someone was rational. I knew it was a good idea to keep some outside help around. Radar and Neptune took seats around the table, making sure to stay between me and Milo.

"Good thinking. Hard to pass up a fight, but I don't know how long we have until Juarez makes a serious move," Neptune said.

The pain subsided a bit, and I was able to think better. I put my hands back on the table. "We have a lot of problems here. Juarez, Argon and Calavera, Trina and the Ketacillin. Plus all the other issues—we still don't know what's up with the Skeletons and Yuma exploding."

"Might be time to dip into our reserve funds and throw some serious cash at this clusterfuck," Neptune said.

My heart could have stopped. No anger this time, just shame. I swallowed. "What do we need, exactly?"

Milo's face brightened. "That would solve one problem. We

could buy the equipment we need, or maybe bribe our way into a lab somehow."

Neptune stared at me. "I see that look on your face. There's no money, is there?"

I laughed nervously. "Fighting wars is expensive. We've got a lot of revenue tied up in inventory out there. There just hasn't been time to push it."

Milo threw up his hands. "I should have known. Is it because you've been shoving the inventory up your own ass to get high?"

"No, and fuck you for suggesting that. You both knew we were having problems, but neither of you wanted to deal with it. I told you to spend what you had to get Trina better, and to beef up security. Money doesn't grow on cacti. I said that I'd handle it, and I will. We just don't have the capital right now."

Both of them started shouting over each other, and Radar put out a hand. "You guys can argue about the past later—it is what it is. What we need now is a strategy."

"I swear, as soon as this all shakes out, we'll be back on top again. I know I've fucked up, but you have to trust me. I'll get us through this," I said.

They started to respond, but then pain, more excruciating than before, raced up my spine, and I screamed. Milo jumped to my side, checking me for a blown pupil. Nothing says fun like a detox aneurysm.

"You're okay. It will pass, just breathe." He put his arms around me, and I let him. I shook in his embrace until it was over.

I breathed in deep. Drugs are bad, kids. "Please tell me this isn't going to last."

He dragged a chair next to me so he could sit close. "We shouldn't have moved you so quickly, but there wasn't much of a choice."

He picked up my hands gently and looked at my savaged forearms, bruised and chafed from the handcuffs and all the needle sticks. "You shouldn't have taken out your IVs. I can't give you any pain medication but more fluids might help. Your wrists need to be cleaned up too."

"I need to take a shower and put some real clothes on. I think the entire desert is up my twat."

"Real sorry you're in pain, boss, but we don't have time to fuck around," Neptune said.

Radar looked concerned, but he nodded.

I put my head on the table for a second, inhaling the sharp plastic smell, letting it clear my head. Even with all the yelling and bullshit, this was home, and I wanted to keep it that way.

I sat up. "I have a plan. It's not a good plan, but it's a plan." Everyone paused, silent while they waited for me to continue. "We need reinforcements. Xed. And Roja."

"Why Roja?" Milo asked.

"Hate to admit it, but we need a sugar mama. We need money. We need her fabulous armor. And if she joins back up with Juarez, we're toast. Without Calavera around for backup, we're going to get hit. Hard," I said.

Neptune shook her head. "I'm into that sexy bitch Roja, but you straight up heard her. She won't help us if you're still fucking around with Xed. She said she told you that before you seized out."

"Xed's the only one I know who can get us access to the Dome labs we need to make the Ketacillin. Roja can't help us there—she doesn't have that kind of power. You got another idea?" I said. Silence at the table. I hate it when I'm right. "Okay then. Roja's just going to have to compromise."

"You gotta convince her in person. She said she wouldn't deal with us unless you had another face to face meeting," Neptune said. "If you survived."

"Same with Xed. He'll want me in the flesh. We still need to figure out how to fix Trina's lungs once the infection is clear, but I'm not willing to give up yet. Without the Ketacillin there's no chance of saving her at all, and Xed's still our best chance at getting it," I said.

Neptune crossed her arms. "We can't all leave base this time. Milo and I need to be here to defend Tucson and patch up the wounded if Juarez tries another hit."

"You're not exactly in good shape to be roaming the desert alone," Milo said.

"I've lived through worse. Think you can pump me full of fluids and get my system clear before daybreak?"

He sighed. "Not enough time."

Radar fidgeted. "I'm going with you. Robot lungs—incredible endurance. No one is better at traveling long distances than me."

"Speak for yourself. I don't need a babysitter. They don't call me queen of the desert for nothing."

"He's right," Milo said. "This is too important for anyone to do solo."

What he didn't add was how none of them trusted me not to get high and like, burn down a stadium or have a seizure in a mineshaft. As if I'd ever do something like that.

I shrugged. There were worse travel partners. "Buddy system it is. Now I need to get cleaned up, maybe eat something, and get ready to go. We're going to be off the grid for this, so be ready for shenanigans."

"I'm always off the grid," Radar said.

I was about to give a snappy response when the ground shook hard enough to knock bowling balls off the shelves. Knocked the snark right out of my mouth too. Seconds later, the lights flickered off.

"Shit," Neptune said.

Radar and Neptune were both ready with emergency flashlights, and Milo pulled a lantern down from the nearby weapons rack. At least we were prepared. He flipped on the lantern, and the white tablecloth glowed like a full moon.

"You two stay here while Radar and I check the infrastructure," Neptune said.

The dull thud in my head told me not to argue.

When they came back, Radar said, "Main power grid is down, but I should be able to get a generator up and running in a second."

"Bigger problem—water's out too. Juarez is hitting our utilities. That fucker Copper probably told them how to shut it off," Neptune said.

I could have cried.

No water.

No power.

No hot shower.

Sand so far up my ass it was about to come out my mouth.

Juarez would pay for this if I didn't have a stroke first.

CHAPTER THIRTY-FIVE

A BLACK car dumped me in the desert, fake red sand at my feet, real old world cacti reaching up over my head, pointing at all the bright star holograms. A yellow light glowed on Xed's porch, and he opened the door just as I was about to knock. He wore another button up shirt, but this time he dressed all in black, save for a plain white tie making a long skunk stripe down his chest. His expensive black shoes were shiny enough to see my reflection.

He pushed his square glasses up his nose. "Nice of you to join me again."

He held the door open, and I followed him inside. The bright white decor and faint smell of bleach bothered me more than it had the first time I was there, and I wrinkled up my nose, squinted my eyes to filter some of the sensory noise. I missed Tucson already.

I'd expected epic hassles at immigration, but getting inside the Phoenix Dome had been disturbingly slick. We didn't even need a cover story. Just had to look presentable, and we waltzed right in. Xed had total control of Phoenix. He'd practically taken over the entire damned Southwest right under my nose.

The door clicked shut behind me. I folded my arms. "Just to be perfectly clear, if anything happens to Radar or my Ketacillin reagents, all bets are off. And I don't just mean the deal. Your goons might take me out, but I'll make sure you come with me to the afterlife."

We had only brought half the reagents, just in case Xed decided to ice us both and keep the antibiotic for himself. Half would make enough to save Trina, and that's all we needed for now. Xed was allowing Radar to supervise the technicians down in the lab, make sure everything was kosher, but he insisted I come home to chat while it cooked.

"You don't trust me?" he said, and I laughed right in his face.

"That's a good one. Pardon me if I'm not really in a trusting mood."

"Ah, I heard you're having a little more trouble down in Tucson. Rival cartels?"

I had to bite my tongue. I was so not into playing innocent with him, but I didn't want to piss him off so bad I turned this into a suicide mission. My leverage still sucked. With Tucson compromised, we were at a real disadvantage.

"You wouldn't know anything about that, would you?" I said.

"No, but I bet Calavera would. Any luck finding her?"

"If she's not dead, she's doing a great job of hiding."

"That's too bad. And your team member is still missing as well."

It occurred to me Xed could have both of them tied up in his basement for all I knew, but somehow I didn't think so. Call it a hunch, but I thought he really would have paid some serious cash to uncover Calavera's whereabouts.

"Real bummer. Just like a lot of other things this month." I flipped my annoyingly long hair over my shoulder.

"You look quite lovely still, despite such turmoil."

Wasn't exactly much time to put together a good Dome disguise. No power and no water back in Tucson didn't make that prep any easier. I ended up wearing a ridiculous wig, and its straight, dark brown strands came down past my waist. A dark blue dress with a tiny pink flower print, black pantyhose, and dainty blue flats tied the goofy outfit together.

I knew Xed would like it.

"I aim to please." I couldn't keep all the sarcasm out of my voice.

He didn't seem to care and smiled. "I have a surprise for you. You deserve something nice after such a difficult week. Follow me?"

Did I even want to know? "Sure, why the hell not."

I followed him through the maze of his mansion, realizing I hadn't gotten the full scope of the grounds on my first visit. The place was enormous. After passing through countless rooms, all white and sterile, we walked down a long, narrow tunnel made of more white marble. Hackles on the back of my neck went up. It felt like I was walking right into a trap, but there was no turning back.

Xed pulled out a big brass key and unlocked a thick wooden door covered with intricate carvings. The door slid open, and what looked like a ballroom was on the other side, bigger than any of the other rooms we'd been in before. Seemed like half of Tucson could fit inside it.

The large white room was dimly lit by fake candles built into sconces on the walls, and the floor was empty save for a very long white table lined with red satin chairs. I looked up, and the ceiling was several hundred feet high—his power bills had to be a bitch.

He gestured at the table. "I figured you must be hungry, so I put out a nice spread for us."

The table was covered with piles of food, like it was motherfucking Thanksgiving. I was starving and eating real food did sound amazing, but I would never admit that to him.

I curled my lip. "So this is your plan? You think throwing some food my way will smooth everything over?"

He raised an eyebrow. "Is there a problem? Am I not giving you everything you want? I've managed to get you access to a top notch facility, and I have confidence they will be successful synthesizing the Ketacillin."

"Which wouldn't be necessary if you hadn't fucked with us in the first place. Enough bullshit. What do you want?"

He smiled, walked the rest of the way into the cavernous room, footsteps echoing, and sat down at the head of the table in front of a whole roasted ham. He waved for me to take a seat next to him.

Lured by the food, I plopped down on one of the red satin chairs. I sat on my long hair, and Xed chuckled as I yanked it out from under my ass.

He laced his fingers together on the table. "I'm sorry you're thinking of our relationship that way. Perhaps we can make amends. I heard you were out of water down there. Maybe I could interest you in another hot bath after we've eaten?"

He held all the cards, and we both knew it. I should have hated him and hated myself for letting him have the upper hand, but I couldn't deny it—the power was sexy. He was manipulating my crew, but it was like looking in a mirror, and it was narcissistically appealing.

And fuck if I didn't want that hot water. Wiping myself down with a damp rag just didn't cut it, and I still felt like I had sand crammed into places god never intended.

I looked back and forth between him and the food, thought of how good it would feel to slip into that big fancy tub again, and I almost didn't care how he was exploiting me. Guy was probably about to jizz in his pants, the way he had me wrapped right around his dick like cheap pussy. But, for the moment at least, the juice was still worth the squeeze.

I crossed my legs, wishing I wasn't wearing the uncomfortable nylons. "If Trina dies, you can forget about any amends."

"In our line of work, certain compromises are inevitable, right?" He began piling ham onto my plate. "I'm sorry about your friend, but it sounds like she was still going to be in hot water even if you'd gotten the Ketacillin delivered in a more timely fashion. Correct?"

I took a breath and suppressed an automatic flush of rage. Just thinking of Trina made me imagine Xed's head on the platter next to the ham.

"Doesn't matter. If she dies, and you had anything at all to do with it, I won't have to kill you. Believe it or not, I'm not the biggest psychopath in my crew."

He smiled, barely blinking. "I can certainly understand your frustration. As a token of my appreciation, I will also think of ways we might be able to get your friend a lung transplant. I can't guarantee anything, but I will do my best."

A lung transplant. He may as well have promised me a unicorn horn and butterfly wings, but the thought was so seductive, I wanted to believe it was possible.

"If you could do that, there are many other things I would give you in return." So many things.

"Have a bite, then maybe we can discuss what else you'd need to feel comfortable with a permanent business arrangement."

"Why did you bring me here?" I said. "You wanted to pretend like we're having a nice business lunch or something?"

Xed poured himself a glass of water and took a swig. "If you wish to call it that. Now, I know we haven't seen any profits yet, considering the...creative way in which you handled the situations in New Orleans and Albuquerque, but there are huge profits to be gained. The load of Alphadrine you brought today alone will bring in several million."

At least he didn't bother to mention my whole drug relapse

issue, which he clearly knew about. I respected him a bit more just for that. Hazard of the trade. As part of our deal, Xed asked for another shipment of Alphadrine, and I was proud of myself for not touching a drop of it on the way up.

I bit a finger. "And you would like to expand your reach out to Domes across the country."

"That is correct. You could be the figurehead of it all."

Dollar signs flashed in my eyes—we *needed* that cash. Xed was a lying, manipulative asshole, but his skill at coercion was impressive, and he had gotten us access to things we never would have been able to get on our own.

And I wanted more of those things.

Xed took another small sip of water, his eyes empty. "Please, eat something."

I bit my lip. "I think I'll just skip to dessert."

His eyes came alive. "As you wish."

He strolled to the other end of the table and came back with a serving plate heaped full of chocolate eclairs, creme puffs, tarts, cookies, and slivers of cake.

He held the plate in front of me, leaning in so he was close to my face. I remembered his smell, how he was more muscular under those shirts than he looked. Hard to keep hating someone who was only doing the exact same things I would to stay on top.

"What would you like?"

"I think I'll take it all." I snatched the plate from his hands.

He smiled, and it almost looked genuine. "I recommend the eclairs. They're fantastic."

I picked one up and ate the whole thing in a few bites. He wasn't kidding—tasted like eating angel babies. Forbidden delicacies.

"While you're savoring those, allow me to add a little entertainment to our evening. I'll think you'll enjoy this."

I eyed him suspiciously but kept cramming eclairs into my face. Once you start, it's hard to stop. Excess is kind of my thing.

A quick jog across the room and he was at the wall, flipping a bunch of switches. I tensed, ready for things to go sideways, but all I heard were some whirring sounds. When I looked up, I realized the top of the room was actually a giant dome, and the two semicircular halves peeled back to reveal a swirling planetarium.

"It's still not real, but it's better than that excuse they call a sky out there," he said.

He was right, the projected Dome sky was bullshit, and I was suddenly sad for him. "When's the last time you were actually outside?" I said.

He stiffened. "A while. I'm rather busy most days."

I managed not to add that he was probably too scared or too lazy to go outside and do his own dirty work. I was trying to behave myself.

I licked chocolate off my fingers. "Pity. Tucson still has the best skies."

"At least this is an improvement in one way—I can control it." He punched a button and a full moon swallowed the sky.

Luminescent and hyper-realistic, even I was impressed by the projection. I stared, mesmerized by the hypnotic moon and little stars twinkling around the edges. Larger than life.

He walked back across the room and sat down again, closer to me this time. "How are you feeling?" he said.

I froze. "Why do you ask?"

"You've been through such trying times. I was hoping the relaxing atmosphere and the food would...improve things.'

I blinked. And blinked. Moon in my eyes, so big, so pretty. Chocolate on my tongue, so sweet. I did feel better. Much better. Way too much better.

Fuck.

Dosed again.

"Nice, isn't it?" he said. "I wanted to ask you. Do you remember way back when you were just a humble psychiatrist?"

I tore my eyes off the moon. Xed was grinning.

"I can't believe you did this," I said.

He continued anyway, "I'm sure you remember. You were a naughty girl, Xero. You experimented on your clients, tried out new drugs on them."

I swallowed. Those days were so far behind me.

"I'm sure you thought all your early recipes were lost, after the Domes went up and all the poor souls with the resistance gene were kicked out. But that's where you're wrong. I found your old notes. You're quite clever, you know that?"

"You didn't," I said.

"I think I'll keep your name for it too—Phaze seems appropriate. My chemists got most of the kinks out of your original recipe, so it should be much more stable now."

I tried to focus on his face, but it seemed so unimportant. The drug was coming up, waiting to peak.

"Pity we still can't figure out how Alphadrine works—bit of witchcraft you have there with all those beneficial lung effects, but that's okay. I don't want to steal your other product. Like I said, I want us to be partners, and I thought you'd like to try out our new line of dual-action drugs. You basically created this, after all."

Oh god. In the early days, Phaze was a drug I'd never been able to finish. Before the revolutions, when I was still working within the system, developing drugs took way longer, and it was much easier to get caught. I knew how brains work, but I was not a lab tech and having partners was risky.

Phaze was supposed to be the speedball of your dreams, working in three-hour shifts. First, the euphoria of an opiate and then the rush of an amphetamine, with a magical period of perfect overlap in between. I never even made it to the testing stage before I was kicked right out of the Domes, and all my research was supposedly destroyed with it. Guess not.

And it felt.

So.

Good.

So much for sobriety.

I should have been mad, wanted to be furious, but it was impossible with all that synthetic opiate petting my neurons like they were soft bunnies.

"What do you think of it? I can't try it myself, given my position, but I thought you deserved to have it. It's not quite perfect yet—maybe you can help us smooth out the formula."

He wasn't just dosing me. I was a guinea pig.

I fought through the haze long enough to respond, "Fuck you," but it came out weak, a whisper swallowed into the fake Milky Way floating overhead.

He stroked my long hair. "You know, the first one's always free, so enjoy the ride. We're going to make a fortune together."

CHAPTER THIRTY-SIX

I SHOULDN'T have been surprised, given Xed's taste level, but it turned out the rest of his grounds looked like an actual old world dude ranch, complete with horses and cattle. I got a tour of the cheesy wonderland as another black car swerved through the landscape and dumped me off at the edge of the compound, the monolith of his mansion a speck of white in the distance.

It was dark out, the Dome's dawn cycle still an hour or two away. At least I thought it was. I'd lost track of time, tripping on Phaze. Xed did me the small favor of letting me go back to Radar while I was still in the balanced stage of the drug, where it would be easier to hide that I was stoned. Maybe he would still be asleep when I hit the amphetamine quarter—I didn't want Radar to know Xed had dosed me. My team was suspicious enough already.

No evening breeze as I got out of the car, just that unsettling dead air you get inside the Domes. I flipped my wet wig hair behind my shoulders and plodded through a trail of cold red sand. It was weird, the sand not being warm from the day like it should have been in the desert. That'll happen when there's no real sun shining.

Bona fide horses whinnied from a coral beside the expansive guesthouse where Xed was putting us up for the night. Those little authentic elements slapped onto the fake landscape made it seem like I was trapped in an old movie set. Had to feel bad for all the

Dome drones who never even touched the outside world.

Gazing up, the Dome sky was nowhere near as impressive as Xed's planetarium, couldn't even touch what the actual desert sky looked like, but it was still pleasant. In the balanced stage, Phaze made everything glow, like the world was shining with invisible starlight. Just like I'd planned before when I created the damned stuff.

I'd worry about the fallout later. Like the fact I'd originally designed Phaze to be incredibly addictive.

"Are you okay?"

I squinted in the dark and saw Radar leaning against the guesthouse, hat down over his head, arms and legs crossed like he was an actual cowboy.

"I'm alive if that's what you're asking."

He straightened. "That's not what I was asking. I asked if you were okay."

I had that special twinge in the pit of my stomach that junkies get when they think someone's onto them.

I cleared my throat. "I'm as okay as I can be, considering how much shit we're in right now. I'll feel a lot better if you have some good news for me."

He reached into his pocket and held out a vial of white liquid. It sparkled like an opal in the moonlight. "Milk of the gods. Verified and everything. I'm amazed they let me walk out of there with this. Keep wondering when Xed's going to kill us both and save it for himself."

I shook my head. "I doubt Xed would murder someone right in the middle of his Dome. Don't shit where you sleep. Once we're back out in the desert that might be another story. Since I'm moving on to New Mexico alone, once they see you're headed to Tucson, they'll know you're the one with the Ketacillin. When you clear the Dome, use your mercenary tricks or something. Go underground, disappear, make it back fast."

"Always do. ASAP is my middle name."

I should have been ecstatic, but even with the Ketacillin in our grasp, we were sealed in enemy territory. Victory seemed a lifetime away, and mistrust hung between us like polluted river vapors.

We stood an awkward distance apart, and I realized I was afraid to get too close to him, as though he could smell the drugs on me.

I swallowed. "Well. Big day ahead. Should probably get some rest. Um, did you eat?" That did not come out as confidently as I'd hoped.

He stepped forward, closer to me, the sand from his boots hitting my ankles. "You sure you're okay? Let me see your eyes."

I was sweating. What did my eyes look like?

He pulled back my hair, pausing when he realized it was wet.

"I finally took a bath. About time—thought I'd never get rid of all that sand," I said too quickly.

He frowned, neither of us wanting to comment on what else might have gone along with that bath at Xed's. He stared at my eyes and said nothing. Then he started patting me down. I stiffened but didn't stop him. When he found something in the front pocket of my dress, he froze. I held my breath as he pulled it out.

"What's this?" He held up a napkin wrapped around something circular.

"It's a cookie—snickerdoodle. Thought I might want dessert later."

He slipped it back into my pocket and finished searching me.

"See? All good, right?" Now if I could just get him to go to sleep before the Phaze clicked over to the amphetamine stage, everything would be okay.

He put his hands down. "Sorry."

I forced a smile. "So, food. Do you need it? I ate tons already."

"Not sure I'd trust anything in this compound."

I almost laughed at how right he was. One of us was smart, and it wasn't me. I started asking if he wanted any of my field rations, hoping to distract him more, but it was no use.

Bang. It hit me. Hard. Heart thumping in my chest blood rushing to my head, muscles bulging. I inhaled with surprise.

This was no Alphadrine.

This was no perfect drug.

And it did not feel good.

Quick as always, his hands were around my waist, eyes boring into mine. My pupils had to be bigger than the moon in Xed's planetarium. Shit.

"I knew it. I knew it," he said, equal parts anger and worry.

Breathing way too hard, I stepped back out of his grasp and tried to ride the wave.

"It's not what you think it is. Xed dosed me—I never asked for this."

In between big gasps for air, I tried to explain to him how I knew about Phaze without making it seem like I was a total scumbag.

"Christ, you're going to be hooked again. We have to take you back to Tucson so you can detox."

"No," I yelled, surprising myself with the volume. I'm not usually a screamer, if you know what I mean. It echoed across the compound and spooked one of the horses.

Radar inched forward. "Calm down."

Good advice. I closed my eyes, put my hands on my chest, willing my heart to stop beating so fast. "We don't have time for that. I have to be in New Mexico by tomorrow. I came up with the idea for this drug, I know how it's supposed to work—once this third phase peaks, I'll be fine, but there's no way in hell I'd want more. It's awful."

No wonder Xed needed me to stick around and fix it. He knew it was only half finished. Nothing would make him happier than if my crew abandoned me for being a junkie, and I was forced to be his crime lord wife. I opened my eyes, and Radar was in my face again.

"You can't keep making these mistakes."

My muscles spasmed, clenched so hard I was shaking. "I am doing. The best. I can. Back off!"

I pushed him, and even before my palms connected with his chest, I knew it wasn't right. Strength. So much strength. My hands felt like they were going to punch through his ribs and back out the other side.

The impact shot up my arms, and he grunted. I wanted to stop, to pull my punches, but it was too late. He flew backward, slamming into the horse corral and shattering the fence. He landed in the water trough, and sparks arced through the air.

Horses shrieked and panicked, their galloping silhouettes lit up from the electricity surge. For the first time ever, I heard Radar scream.

Then Silence. Darkness.

"Radar!"

I sprinted to the trough. Horses raced past me, out through the fence hole and into the night.

On my knees, I slid to his side and pulled him from the water. I dumped his limp body on the muddy ground and thought I could feel broken ribs where I'd hit him. How did you revive a fucking cyborg? I'm a lot of things, but a mechanic isn't one of them.

I was a doctor, but it didn't take an expert to know that

breathing is good, and he was still breathing. With shaking hands, I touched his neck. A pulse. He had a pulse.

Alive.

I shook him, clutching his wet trench coat, not able to think over my heart that was sucker-punching my chest from the inside out. "Wake up, you have to wake up."

"Stop. Stop shaking me." He twitched and tried to roll away.

I let go. "Thank god."

He coughed and sat up. "Harder to kill than that. Probably just blew a fuse. Easy fix." He grabbed his side and groaned. "And cracked a rib or two—longer to heal, but I'll live."

With knees in the sandy red puddle that looked like a pool of blood, nylons ripped and digging into my skin. I fell forward and hugged him.

And I cried for the first time since Evan died.

He hugged me back, my muscles still twitching from the Phaze. We held each other like that for a minute, and maybe it was from my own thumping heart, or maybe it was whatever electricity was leaking out of his body, but I felt tingly all over.

He pulled back, patting his pockets, the closest thing I'd seen to terror in his face. "The Ketacillin," he said.

The vial. It was on him when he short-circuited. I'm not sure how my eyes didn't actually pop out of my skull in horror.

Radar tried to get up but grimaced when his ribs twisted the wrong way, and he flopped back down.

I flung my arms into the trough, stupid long hair tangling like seaweed in my fingers as I desperately scoured the water. I thought of the explosion, all that electricity. It was enough to shatter such a small bottle—I could be bathing in Ketacillin right now.

Nails broke, skin ripping across my fingertips as I clawed at the wood, grasping for something, anything that might be the vial.

Nothing.

I thought back to it all, everything that had happened since we left that day for Casa Grande. The Skeleton attacks. Losing Argon. Invasive surgery in the Dome. The haboob. The drugs. Killing Copper. The detox. All the pain, all the times we could have died from dumb mistakes I'd made. Radar was right. It all came down to now, to one stupid vial, and I'd failed.

I put my head down into the water, not wanting to kill myself but not exactly wanting to be alive either. I wanted to drift away, forget any of this had happened, and leave it all behind. The pain in my muscles, the horrible throbbing of my heart, and the ache in my chest that had nothing to do with cardiac function, I wanted it all to drown.

I was sinking deeper, dirty water flowing up my nose, when something bumped against my forehead.

Scooping both palms to my face, I sat up, falling backward into a cross-legged pose.

There, floating like a white lily in a pond, the Ketacillin vial bobbed in a pool of water between my cupped hands.

Laughter that was somewhere between joy and madness rang out into the empty corral.

They didn't call it Phoenix for nothing.

From the ashes, it was time to rise.

CHAPTER THIRTY-SEVEN

I KEPT my mouth closed as I glided across the dry plains on an old mototractor, but dust kept getting up my nose even with a helmet on. Taking a page from Roja's book on that one—mototractor wasn't the safest way to travel the desert, but it was the fastest. Except unlike Roja, I didn't have to worry about asphyxiating. Bonus for me.

The terrain in New Mexico was easier to get across, more actual pavement left, and the off-road pathways were made of firmer sand or packed dirt. I wasn't saying that I liked it yet, but I was feeling a bit more favorable toward the state than I had before. Anything seemed great after being stuck in the Dome with Xed. Even a trip to the Casa Grande Breakers sounded appealing.

This was where I was really wild and free—out in the untamed Voids, warm sun on my shoulders, wandering where most of the world's population couldn't survive without respirators. You'd think being the chosen few would have been less of a pain in the ass, but this was America after all, and that's not how things worked.

The Phaze was mainly out of my system, leaving behind the special gift of a dry tongue, red eyes, and another headache. Or maybe it was still the headache left over from Milo's stupid rapid detox and my unfortunate drug combo at the Silver Jackalope. Who knew at that point? Strung out or not, there was no time to rest. I couldn't risk contacting him yet, but by now Radar should have made it back to Tucson with the Ketacillin, and it was my turn to hold up the other end of the bargain.

This time I wasn't headed for Albuquerque—without Xed there was no way I could get into the actual Dome, and I wasn't welcome there anyway. The Silver Jackalope was over, and there was no safe place to forge an alliance with Roja. I'd thought the deal was off and I'd have to surrender to Juarez, or agree to be Xed's evil bride, when Roja suddenly came back with an alternative meeting spot.

Hatch.

Little town, down at the southern tip of New Mexico. I didn't know anything was still there. Hatch never had a Dome, and after the revolutions, most of the stragglers from that area made their way over to Tucson. I thought there was nothing left but dried chilies and tumbleweeds.

What the hell was Roja doing in Hatch? I stopped at the end of a lonely dirt road a few miles from the town's center. Right at the coordinates she gave me, in front of an empty hill, stood a small building that looked like an old Southwest diner. Square and faded but still clearly painted blue: it stood out like a robin's egg against the beige mountains.

Across the front in orange letters, difficult to read under layers of rain-spattered dust, it said "Ximena's" in carefully printed script. X marks the spot.

Interesting. Why had Roja brought me out to an abandoned diner in the middle of nowhere? She was a daredevil, but traveling outside the Domes wasn't easy for her, and if she wanted to murder me in the desert, she could have done that much closer to home.

I got off the mototractor and pulled off my helmet. This area didn't have problems with the acid monsoons, but I still wore a reinforced black combat suit. I thought back to what Argon said about wanting to have field uniforms like Calavera's Skeletons. If things went well with Roja, master of armor, then he might get his wish.

Whether I'd get Argon back alive was another story.

Shaking off that thought, I fluffed out my Mohawk as best I could and tried to ignore the weird giddiness in my stomach that I didn't think had anything to do with Phaze withdrawal. Cooler than Arizona, the day was still warm, yet I shivered. I wasn't afraid of many things, but I was afraid of ghosts.

And that's exactly what Roja was to me.

I had to get past it. Radar said it best right before I nearly killed him: I needed to stop fucking up. Perfect, since every time I confronted Roja it was like coming face to face with the biggest mistake I'd ever made.

I could handle this. I'd survived torture and nearly died too many times to count. How bad could this be?

I put my shoulders back and knocked on the door.

Air hissed, and then Roja stepped outside. She wore a gas mask, which wasn't surprising, but the rest of her outfit startled me. I expected her to be tricked out in every bit of combat gear imaginable, on the off chance I wanted to kill her. Guess she had confidence in my desperation because all she wore was a loose white peasant blouse and a bright yellow circle skirt.

I nearly swallowed my tongue. Evan used to wear clothes like that.

"Come on in," she said over the mask's intercom. "Move quick, we're wasting air."

She shut the door behind me, which turned out to be reinforced with steel and a sealing mechanism on the inside, similar to the one at the Silver Jackalope mine. There was a matching door behind us—we were in a small airlock. Smart.

She waved me through the second door and bolted it shut. I thought I'd seen everything, but New Mexico was just full of surprises. It *was* a little diner, and it was clean. The furnishings were old but well cared for. The tables were made from a heavy wood carved with flower designs, and the cream walls were covered with bright landscape murals. Dried chilies hung from the ceiling, and a red banner covered with kachina doll reliefs went around the top of the walls. Southwest splendor.

She took off the gas mask and set it on one of the tables. "Welcome, welcome. Thanks for joining me—how do you like the place?"

"It's, um, it's great. What the hell is this doing out here?"

She leaned against the adobe, her fiery hair blending into a mountain sunset that was painted across the wall. "Been in my family for generations. I retrofitted it to be oxygen-regulated, so I can use it for little meetings like this one."

"Who was Ximena?"

She smiled. "Why, that's me. Originally my grandma, actually. I was named after her."

I paused. Exchanging real names—not something done casually

with cartel bosses. Even if they already knew your real name, inviting someone else to use it was a big deal.

She raised an eyebrow and stuck out her hand. "Ximena Ramirez. Pleased to meet you."

I hesitated for a second and then shook her hand. "Anastasia Petrovna."

Jesus. All that was missing was a ring and it could have been a wedding. Serious business.

"You're looking a little rough, babe."

"So I've heard. Tough quarter for me."

"But you still look nice in that outfit." She touched my arm, then made a face. "We need to get you in some better gear—way bulky stuff you've got on. I'll get you hooked up."

I got a boner just thinking about her armor. What's more fun than new war toys?

I cleared my throat. "Isn't it ridiculously expensive to keep the air in here breathable?"

"Definitely. But it more than pays for itself. You'd be surprised how many rich Dome drones want to relive the glory days and go on an illegal Voids safari. Plus, I make all kinds of great things in the kitchen. Very profitable things." She twirled, her yellow skirt making her look like a blooming sunflower. "And I get to have a nice vacation too, wear the clothes I want."

I never understood exactly what Roja's cover job was, but I knew she was some kind of corrupt IT contractor for the military. Of course she was—Evan had been an IT specialist too. Life was such an unfair bitch.

"Seems like good business," I said.

She crossed her arms. "It was also going to make a good base for helping Calavera take over Tucson, but I think we've already come to an agreement about that, yes?"

I tensed. I should have realized. Hatch was only about two-hundred-fifty miles away from Tucson. They would have invaded and taken everything.

"If she's still alive, Calavera and I are already square, and after yesterday, I'd kill Xed on sight if I could. So, yeah, I'm on board for a merger with you," I said. Way too many Xs on the playing field.

She looked at me sideways. "Why don't I get us some coffee, and you can tell me about what happened last night."

She pointed to a table, and I took a seat. A minute later she came back with two blue enameled mugs that looked like they were meant to match the diner's paint.

I took a sip of the coffee and closed my eyes. There was a little extra zip, and it was just what I needed. Then I blanched. "What's in this?"

"Chili powder, a little cinnamon. Good, right? Family recipe."

"No drugs?"

She gave me a sidewise look. "Of course not. Sorry about what happened at the Silver Jackalope—wasn't trying to dose you. Figured you knew how I rolled. It was a rave, and I didn't know you'd already swallowed way too much DISC."

I exhaled and put my head down as I gripped the mug "I'm just a little paranoid."

She scooted forward and curled her hands over mine, cradling the warm coffee mug. "You're strung out right now, aren't you?"

I wasn't sure whether I should be embarrassed or annoyed. There was no judgment in her voice, so I settled for exhausted. "Something like that."

I brought her up to speed with a few crucial details about my situation and what was going down with Xed. She sipped her coffee, and I tried to stop flashbacks of breakfasts with Evan from bubbling to the surface.

"This Phaze stuff—any way you can get your old notes and figure out how to fix the formula without involving Xed? Call me crazy, but other than that horrible third cycle, it sounds like a wonder drug. I could sell the shit out of that and make us a fortune," she said.

I smirked and pulled a baggie out of my pocket. "Maybe."

"You jacked one of Xed's desserts. Sure there's dope in that?"

I fondled the crumbled pieces of the snickerdoodle. "Nope. Might be nothing more than an expensive cookie. But if it's legit, then it's our ticket to all the expensive cookies you could ever dream of."

I needed Argon back—if anyone could detect traces of the drug, it would be him. I stared at the baggie.

She tapped her feet. "You want to eat it, don't you?"

"So bad." My toes curled in my boots.

"I've got all kinds of other things in here to take the edge off, if you want."

"No. I can't go down that road again. We need to talk about that."

She stood up. "One second, crucial step coming up."

I inhaled, and it smelled spicy. New Mexico, land of the batshit drugs. "What is that?"

"My grandmother's *mole*—come help me."

Sure, why the hell not. Nothing seemed weird anymore. Cooking drugs, cooking traditional Mexican foods, same difference. I followed her back into the small kitchen area where a big clay pot simmered on the stove.

She dumped a plateful of chopped chilies and spices into the sauce and stirred it with a wooden spoon. "Great, just need to stay back here and stir it every few minutes. What were you saying?"

I leaned against a white tiled counter across from the stove and automatically scanned for weapons—chef's knife lay on a cutting board next to me and a butcher knife hung from the wall next to her. That made things more exciting.

"I want a partnership with you, and I can't pretend like we're not in some deep shit, but I've got a few rules. Rules that are not negotiable," I said.

She put her hand up on the wall beside a bundle of dried meadow flowers that was a little too close to the knife. "Like?" she said.

"No drugs."

She laughed in my face. The steam from the *mole* made my forehead sweat, and the boiling chili fumes stung my eyes.

"I'm serious," I said.

"Bit hypocritical, don't you think?"

"This was all a big slip, and I think it's pretty clear why I have that rule. I nearly ruined everything." I hesitated then said, "My wife died from drugs, and you look so much alike that you could be her sister. I can't live through that again."

She sidled over, one foot right in front of the other, her hips swaying as she stopped close to me. She smelled like cinnamon. "I'm not your ex-wife."

"Dead wife."

"I'm not her, and I'm not you. I try my product, I socialize with my clients when appropriate, but I'm not an addict. I party safely."

I shook my head. "Not good enough. All the drugs need to stop."

She closed the distance, pushing aside the knife and cutting board. She grabbed my hips and pulled me into her. "Relationships are all about compromise, right?"

Her pelvis ground into mine, and I moaned. Hard to argue with that, so I bit my lip and tried to resist the urge to bend her over the counter.

"So let's compromise." She nibbled my ear and whispered, "No drugs when I'm in Arizona or anywhere near your crew. Fair?"

She kissed down my neck, and I hissed slowly through my teeth. Her lips were so soft I couldn't think straight.

"O...okay." Maybe we could negotiate more later when I wasn't thinking with my crotch.

Behind her, the *mole* splashed over the lip of the pot. She let me go and turned down the burner. I breathed out and shook my head, trying to forget how good she smelled.

Once the *mole* was under control, she turned around and smiled. "Fantastic. Now that we've got that little detail cleared up, is there anything else to negotiate?"

"My best friend is still dying. Don't suppose you can cook miracles, can you?"

"Thought you got the Ketacillin."

"We did, but she'll still need a lung transplant. Too much damage. Xed claimed he could get us one, but dealing with him isn't an option anymore."

She grinned. "Xed's a liar—he can't get you a real lung transplant. I can't either, but I can get you something else. Artificial lungs."

"Impossible—that's even more dangerous to have around than real lungs."

She shrugged. "It's true. From your favorite person—Voodoo. With that open harbor and jack shit for security, New Orleans used to be a hub for all that black-market cybernetic work before the big crackdowns. They still have parts lying around. I want a pair myself so I can leave the Dome permanently, except I've never found anyone left alive who knows how to assemble them. But that guy of yours—he knows, doesn't he?"

"You better not be fucking with me."

"Voodoo might not deal with you anymore, but she'll deal with me. Just another benefit of our partnership, eh?"

Nope, not even going there. No energy left for false hope and fairytale promises. Had to put that desperate wish aside until I saw some proof.

I waved her off. "There's one more thing we need to handle first—Calavera. Once Xed realizes what's happening, there's going to be fallout. It'll take a unified front to fight him off. Calavera and whatever's left of her Skeletons—we need to get them back."

She swished forward again and wrapped her arms around my neck. I couldn't stop myself. I grabbed her waist and kissed her hard, wanting to rip that skirt right off her hips.

She pulled back. "Well then, we're in luck. I know where Calavera is, and with those pretty lungs of yours, you can bring her back." She ran her tongue across my lips. "Time to go hunting."

Chapter Thirty-Eight

Stars plastered a night sky so deep and clear it looked like another cheaply animated Dome ceiling. But I wasn't inside a Dome.

This was real.

A vicious wind ripped through the heavy layers of my insulated black clothing like it was lace. I clenched my teeth and gripped my laser tight, trying not to drop it from my numb fingers. As I gazed at the constellations, a bright object moved slowly across the sky. At first I thought it was a shooting star, but it hung in the air, gliding along at a leisurely pace. Not a shooting star at all. A satellite.

A fucking satellite.

Very few satellites were left after the great harvest.

Very few.

"*Pinche cabrón,* stop fucking around and get inside," Calavera said.

"Don't have to tell me twice. My tits are about to drop off," I said.

I followed the white flashes of the short woman's Skeleton armor across a cement patio, past an abandoned observation tower, and inside an old building. I closed a pair of cracked glass doors behind me, rusty metal hinges crunching as they rattled shut. Glass fragments tinkled onto the concrete, but the doors held. Even with wind blasting in through the cracks, I was instantly warmer.

She flipped on a switch and the room flooded with red light. "Red light keeps your night vision going. I learned something up here."

On the walls, ripped astronomy posters dangled above wrecked educational dioramas. Broken glass and destroyed trinkets littered a ransacked gift shop. Battered folding chairs collected in a tangled mass at the center of a small lecture area, dirt and crumbled leaves clinging to everything. A dusty banner that said "Welcome to Kitt Peak National Observatory" hung across the entrance.

"I didn't know this place was still here," I said.

"Had to make some wicked deals to get in—the Tohono don't let nobody on their territory, and even my Skeletons won't mess with them. They've been on these lands longer than anyone."

She stripped off her rigid skeleton helmet, and her sugar-skull face tattoos looked even more demonic in the red light. She took a second to untangle her curly black hair and stowed the foldable headgear in a jacket pocket. "Follow me—safer in the back. Too many windows for snipers out here, and we got a lot to talk about."

She took me past heavy black doors that closed behind us with a thud. She flipped a switch, and the normal light killed my vision. I put an arm up to protect my eyes, but while I was blinded, I heard another door open and close. Footsteps clacked across the room. Calavera was supposed to be alone.

I opened my eyes, threw up the laser, and dropped my center of gravity, tensing for a fight. My finger hugged the trigger, waiting for my sight to come back.

In the center of a black room, spiky tips of orange hair slowly came into focus.

"Long time no see," Argon said.

I exhaled and holstered the laser. "You sneaky bastard." I ran forward and crushed his shoulders with a big hug. I should have punched him, but I was so happy.

"Sorry about the secrecy," he said. "I can explain."

He jumped when Calavera snuck around him and spanked his ass.

"Ay, *papi*, stop fooling around with other women," she said.

I stepped back and gawked. "You two are shacking up? I don't know what to be more surprised about—that you're fucking this chola or that you've been living in a secret mountain hideout for the past month." Really, I was just happy he was still alive.

"*Oye*, watch it," she said. "Don't be jealous because he likes my sweet ass better than yours."

I rolled my eyes. "Fine by me, I've got enough man troubles right now as it is."

Calavera's mouth twitched. "You got a boyfriend? I'll believe that when I see it."

Argon blushed and stuffed his hands in his pockets. 'I'd love to sit here and girl talk, but we have some real shit to deal with."

"Damn right. You guys have some serious 'splaining to do," I said.

"You look like a popsicle. Why don't I bring you something hot to warm up with and we'll go over everything?" he said.

"Yeah, yeah, sit your white ass down." Calavera hooked a finger at Argon. "We need some *chocolate caliente*. Come help me carry stuff, *cariño*."

I shook my head. That was one relationship I never expected.

She pushed him out the door, and I sat down at the bottom of a small stack of theater seats. Must have been a planetarium at one point, but it was gutted and a rear wall had been crudely knocked down for more floor space. Lab equipment—nice looking stuff too—crowded the floor, and something was cooking. Lights blinked on steel vats that leaked little puffs of steam while timers softly pinged.

The lovebirds came back with steaming Styrofoam mugs full of instant hot cocoa. The powder clumped on the surface of the hot water, and I tried to stir it with a finger. The cocoa was probably older than me, but I was grateful for the sensation it brought back to my hands.

"So here's what happened," Argon said, but Calavera interrupted him.

"*Espera*, let me tell it first."

"Experience has taught me not to argue with armed women," he said.

I laughed—least he was well-trained.

Calavera punched him in the arm and some of his hot chocolate splashed onto the floor.

She faced me. "All right, so you know me and you just made a deal, and everything was cool, you know? Then I get contacted by this guy, this Xed. He wants to make me a deal, too."

I scoffed. "I'll bet he did."

She gave me a look. "*Cállate*, lemme finish. He says I should join him because he's planning on taking over the Domes, you know like killing everyone inside like they did in the Australian genocides."

Well, that was news. "What the hell?"

She ignored me and kept going, "Said he's going to use some poison gas you can't defend against. You can't even use gas masks because it goes in through your skin. Said he wanted me to join him because I had good soldiers and we could be partners in the revolution."

I gulped my hot chocolate and burned my tongue. "No way. That's insane."

"That's how it went down. Then he told me some story about oppression and riots and some other history shit. Like he's the only one who's ever had it unfair, you know?" She whacked Argon's leg. "White guys always think they got it so hard."

"I'm assuming you told him to fuck off," I said.

"Yeah, you think I'm some kind of psycho or something? Guy's a real *loco*. I tell him to shove it, so he tells me I'll be sorry and that he'll steal my army. Thought he was bluffing me, but turns out I was wrong." She jabbed a finger at me. "Some bitches were mad about the treaty with you. That's all it took. He stole a bunch of them, and I had to make myself disappear. *Sabes?*"

I took another sip of gritty hot chocolate, savoring the warmth and trying to ignore the texture. "Your Skeletons are tough. Almost took me out a few times."

She laughed. "I train some crazy *vatos*. We don't fuck around. But not everyone turned on me, just the real shit bags. Everyone has a price."

"When you left for the Domes, there were Skeleton traitors in the patrol group that showed up, but the good ones saved my hide, helped me escape from the Breakers and get back to one of Calavera's safe houses," Argon said.

"Picking up dork boy here was a great idea cuz I figured we needed to stop Xed, you know? Some of the Skeletons went double-agent, and I got a sample of the poison from them." She poked at Argon. "So this guy could figure out how to beat it."

"You're a lucky bitch—I can't think of a better chemist out there," I said.

"We're all lucky bitches—a chemical weapon like that could waste us all," she said.

I knew Xed was a total asshole, but I didn't realize what a crazy fuck he really was. This was a whole different level of wacko.

I looked at Calavera. "No wonder Xed kept wanting to know if I had found you—he didn't want you to spill the beans."

She laughed. "No shit. After I didn't bite, guess he realized his little plan wasn't going to be so popular with the cartels after all."

"I wanted to contact you, let you know I was alive, but it was too dangerous. By the time we secured this base, you had already made contact with Xed, and we couldn't risk it. Not until we could figure out how to get you away from him. Roja sniffed us out just before we were going to let you in on everything," Argon said.

I put down the empty Styrofoam cup. "I should be royally pissed that you let me think you were dead, but there's no time for that. Everything is fucked. Things really went off the rails while you two were up here honeymooning."

I spent a few minutes filling them in on my side of all the crap that had gone down since Argon went missing.

Argon stared at the black ceiling. "Trina. She might make it after all."

I nodded. "There's still a chance. Sounds like she has as good a chance as any of us at this point."

Calavera leaned back. "Damn, bitch, that is some shit. Glad you finally made nice with Roja." She tapped her chest plate. "She has the best armor, and she looks real good naked."

I swallowed a momentary stab of jealousy. "Right. With you missing, and your Skeletons compromised, I didn't have much of a choice about bringing her into the fold. Had to make an executive decision."

"Fine by me—you were the one being weird about her. Three queens are better than none."

Argon cleared his throat. "So, this drug problem...what's the story with that now?"

I crossed my arms. "There's no story. It's done with. Get past it."

He looked over his shoulder at all the lab equipment. "Okay."

I tried to ignore the subtext. "This whole time I just thought Xed wanted to manipulate me into being his full-time Alphadrine bitch," I said. "Why waste time dragging me all across the southern United States trying to grow Alphadrine addicts if he's planning on killing everyone?"

"The shit he cooked up is nasty, but you know the Domes all have decent venting systems to deal with chemical leaks. For maximum carnage, a poison gas would need to work quickly," he said.

"Oh fuck. Alphadrine is a bronchodilator."

Argon nodded. "The more people he gets doped up on Alphadrine, the more people die before anyone can vent the Domes, and the easier it is to take over the local government. The intel Calavera gathered says his initial test targets are going to be Phoenix, Albuquerque, and New Orleans—Domes big enough to make a statement but smaller than the real hubs like Los Angeles or New York."

"Yuma. What about that? That had to be Xed, right? Why blow up Yuma if he's planning a takeover?"

Calavera laughed. "It's fucked up, but it's pretty cool my Skeletons had the chops to blow up a whole Dome. Nothing like that's gone down in my lifetime. Think about it—makes sense to take out Yuma. It's the only stop between Phoenix and Los Angeles. Without Yuma, those stupid Dome enforcers can't get across the desert easy. It's one big dead zone."

"Also, Yuma was the only place to get Ketacillin this side of the Mississippi. With Yuma gone, Xed had leverage to trick you into seeding Alphadrine across the other Domes," Argon said.

If I was a better person, I might have felt bad that Xed had killed an entire city just to coerce me, but instead, I was only furious he might have killed my friend. I clenched my jaw.

"Remind me to murder the fuck out of him."

Argon pointed to the lab equipment, and I noticed how tired he looked. "Lucky for us, someone was using this place to manufacture drugs. Probably high-quality shit, and I bet they got run out by the Tohono. Left all their fancy equipment behind. Feels like I haven't slept in a month, but I think I've finally got it. I came up with an antidote that will actually exploit the same pathways Alphadrine does—in fact it's something of an analogous molecule. If you've taken Alphadrine with it, the antidote will actually work better. I'm calling it Betadote for now."

I slowly nodded. "Betadote, clever, I like it. Have I ever told you what a fucking genius you are?"

Argon laughed. "That's not exactly how you usually phrase it."

Calavera stood up. "That's right, don't let her talk down to you, *papi*. You're gonna save the world."

I rubbed my eyes. "There's a lot of shit to handle here, too many moving parts," I said. "We've got the antidote, so we can protect ourselves. What about the people in the Domes?"

All I ever wanted to do was keep my friends alive, hold onto my territory, and make some money. Saving the world wasn't really on my to-do list.

"I know, it's a pain the ass, right? I didn't think it was worth it either, but listen. Think of the cash. We can hit this thing from two directions. We sell the Betadote and Alphadrine cocktail on the black market, and we make a ton of *dinero*," she said.

"Do we have a timeline on this? Any idea when he'll pull the trigger? That's a lot of ground to cover. Just getting someone out to New Orleans will take two days minimum," I said.

"We can't be certain, but the reports we're getting from some of the double agents say we have somewhere around a week. Night of the full moon," he said.

"Not a lot of margin for error. What about the population that doesn't buy shit off the black market? Distribution's going to be the trickiest part of this," I said. Cash aside, the thought of getting involved in another huge revolution was exhausting. One was enough for my lifetime.

"We use connections. Roja knows people on the inside. She can figure something out," she said.

I thought of Sanchez and my other Dome supply mules. "Maybe you're right—they could push a dummy government program, like a vitamin regimen, make everyone take the drugs. The government does shit like that all the time anyway."

"I'm cranking out the Betadote as fast as I can," Argon said. "Fortunately it's extremely concentrated—a little will go a long way. Just a little taste on a carrier material should be enough for it to work."

Something popped in the lab, and the room went dark. He sighed, and they pulled out red-beamed flashlights like this was a regular occurrence.

"Like I was saying, I've got this place running full steam. Fuses aren't real happy about it." His flashlight bobbed across the room to a panel on the wall.

That reminded me. I felt the snickerdoodle bag in my pocket. "I forgot to ask—if we all happen to survive this shit, I think I have a sample of that Phaze stuff Xed dosed me with. What are the odds you can extract the chemicals and work out the kinks?"

He mashed buttons, and the lights came back on. He grinned, hands behind his head. "What do you think?"

Calavera turned off her flashlight. "My baby can do anything. We're going to be rich."

I glared at her. "I'm going to puke if you don't knock that off."

"Make me, *puta*."

I rolled my eyes. "Before we become billionaires, we need to, you know, not die. First, we pull Juarez out of our asses. It's pretty clear who's responsible for that invasion. We can thank Xed for rallying all the stray crews into something dangerous."

"I trained a lot of those *pendejos*, too, before I moved to Nogales. Juarez is a different kind of crazy. That's why I left, you know? We don't take them down, your home's going to start looking like the wrong end of a piñata party but without all the candy."

"Agreed. Which is why the next step is to pull the weed out by the roots. Xed's gotta go. I'll gladly pull the trigger myself, but I need access. He's all holed up in the Dome like a coward," I said.

Calavera bit her lip. "That's a problem. I got all the bad Skeletons still looking for me—I can't go nowhere. It's gotta be you."

I thought through all of my connections, but none of them could get me into Phoenix. The Phoenix Dome was as tight as they came.

Then it came to me.

The satellite.

Had to thank the dark sky laws for giving me such a clear view of the heavens, free from light pollution. Clear enough to see that stray little bugger floating around in space. Important, because before the great harvest the satellites used to control all the inter-city subway lines.

Most of the tunnels into the Domes had been capped off, but there were decommissioned trains that still ran underground through the Tohono territory—the government didn't have the authority to enter their lands and remove them, but we were friends with the Tohono. We literally spoke their language.

With some smooth talking, we might get access to the tunnels. Then it was a matter of blasting open a tunnel and hacking into the routing system. Evan had told me it was possible to hijack leftover satellites if you could get the codes.

It was a long shot, and it was going to take some muscle, some brains, and a lot of explosives. What could possibly go wrong?

"I think I have an idea," I said. "Did you find any satellite control panels up here?"

Argon raised an eyebrow. "Yeah—not in this building but up the hill at the central observatory tower. Not like it's good for anything. All the satellites are gone."

I smiled.
Neptune would finally get to use all those grenades.

CHAPTER THIRTY-NINE

I LEANED back in Xed's chair, three chess sets staged on his desk in front of me like he'd been in the middle of reorganizing all his uptight office decorations when he left for lunch. The office smelled exactly like it had before—too clean, too sterile, full of that chemical odor that comes off new plastic. Over it all, I still smelled Xed's weird chlorine and raspberry scent. I wondered if he really did bathe in bleach.

Footsteps pounded in the hallway, and then the door flung open. Xed stood there panting, wearing a white shirt with a red tie and black pants. The tie was flung over his shoulder, and his glasses sat crookedly on his sweaty face. Seeing him panicked for the first time filled me with a sick joy.

He froze when he saw me sprawled out in his chair, and he forced his typical blank expression back onto his face. He leveled his glasses and straightened his tie as though he was perfectly used to finding me squatting in his office.

"Xero. What a pleasant surprise. I see you met my secretary." His voice was calm, but he couldn't quite hide the anger from his eyes.

I folded my arms. "She's taking a nap."

"I'm guessing you've disabled all the alarm systems and cameras as well."

I slid backward a few inches and threw my boots up on the desk, knocking over chess pieces and smudging red Sonoran desert clay all over his papers. "Why don't you have a seat—lay down on the couch if you'd like, tell me about how your mommy and daddy never loved you enough."

He hesitated, then faked a smile and adjusted his tie again before taking a seat on the therapy couch. Behind him, the mirrored bank towers glimmered, backlighting his glasses so the lenses glowed, and I couldn't see his eyes. The couch had been cleaned, but I thought I could still see faint stains from where I'd bled all over the suede. I liked to leave my mark wherever I went.

"What can I do for you?" he said.

"Like I just said. Tell me about your parents. What happened to make you so goddamned fucked up that you'd want to kill millions of people?"

"Calavera," he said. "She found you."

"I'm waiting. I can help you free associate if you want. I did a whole psychoanalysis cycle in graduate school."

Xed smirked. "Sure. If you really must know, my parents were born in the Domes, but they were kicked out because I was marked for the Breakers. You know how it was in the old days. One family member went, the rest of the family went, too. They died quickly in Casa Grande, and I grew up alone in the slums. So yes, you could say I hold some animosity toward the Domes and how they like to handle things like basic human rights."

Ah, similar to what happened with Radar's family. They said it was just a lag in policy, but many thought the extra banishments were intentional—another way of reducing the population. Thinning the herd. Ugly stuff. I thought back to that little kid in the Breakers, dying alone in filth, and imagined him with Xed's face. I almost felt sorry for both of them.

I pulled my feet off the desk, dragging a stack of ruined papers and more chess pieces with me. "Funny how a guy like you could talk about something like basic rights. Since when has mass genocide been considered humane?"

"New world order. We need a country where people don't get tossed out to die just because they have a genetic difference. Big changes require big sacrifices. You should understand that better than most."

I shrugged. "Ethics aren't my strong point, but I've never claimed to be a humanitarian."

"We're not so different, you and I."

I clucked my tongue and wiped my feet on the light gray carpet. "We are a lot alike. With a few key differences—I'm not a mass murderer and a narcissistic despot. Something's gone kablooey in your head, man. You're over the edge and under-medicated."

"You haven't even heard my offer. This whole time I've been trying to make you my partner."

"Partner? Is that why you lied to me, lured me all across the country, and then drugged me? Pretty fucked up idea of partnership."

"You were an adult when the deportation laws went into effect, so you must remember. How did it feel to be plucked out of your cushy job and dumped right into the trash?"

I swallowed, angry at the memories trying to surface—all my money, all my status, gone overnight.

He continued, "Revenge is sweet, but that's only the beginning of what I'm offering you. How many times have you been fucked over by Dome policies? How many times have you put your neck on the line because of some meaningless law? How good would it feel to be the warden and not an inmate?"

"I *am* the warden already. I won't be your inmate."

He shook his head. "You're a captive, and you don't even realize it. Deny it all you want, but we both know there can be no real freedom while the Domes stay in power."

I liked to think my resolve was strong, but his words hit home a little too hard. Everything started going wrong right when we'd first gotten into Casa Grande, that night when immigration took all our gear. What would it be like to have that level of control? I'd get to say who comes and goes, not just in Tucson, but everywhere.

My territory. My rules.

He got up from the couch and sat in a cushy chair in front of the desk. "Calavera's a handful to begin with, and I know you made another treaty with Roja. How do you really think it's going to work, trying to share power between the three of you? Cartels and democracy don't exactly go together."

I held my breath. It had taken forever to make an agreement with Calavera. Everyone in the Grease Weasels had begged me to do it, but I didn't want to give up my power. My control. Now I was stuck with not one but two people threatening my independence. Between Roja and Calavera, how much would I get to keep?

Tucson was mine—I didn't want to share.

He leaned in and pushed all the chess pieces aside, leaving a king and queen at the center of the desk. "You know I'm smarter than either of them. I'm the better choice. With you and I paired up, we'll be unstoppable."

I shook my head. "Sounds like more lies."

"With me, there will be more than enough to go around. You can have Arizona. All of it. You make the rules."

Arizona. Mine. No one to tell me what to do; no one to get in my way. A true queen of the desert.

Temptation is a terrible thing.

He pushed his glasses up. "And don't forget. The drugs. I like them too. I grew up in the Breakers."

"Ah. You were a dealer." Now it all made sense. I should have guessed.

He smiled. "How do you think I know what clients will like? I'm a professional. I grew up doing this. Had to stop using when I forged my way into the Domes, but it doesn't have to be that way now. Think about it. No more laws. No more judgment from your friends or your crew. Complete freedom. Complete control."

"You want me to give up my alliances so we can be a junkie kingpin super couple? Rolling in drugs and money all day long?" I said. "Okay then. Prove it. Get high with me." I smirked, but my mouth may have been watering, my palms sweaty.

"Gladly. After today it won't matter. New Orleans and Albuquerque will fall this evening, and Phoenix tomorrow morning. It's all automated, by the way. With or without me, this is happening. But don't worry—I have a spray you can use. It will coat your skin and keep the gas from penetrating your nervous system."

"You're so generous."

"Nothing but the best for my queen," he said, stroking his red tie.

What was that in his eyes? Love? Lust? Greed?

All of the above?

I reached underneath the desk and opened the mini-fridge. "I fixed the Phaze." I plunked down a brown dropper bottle on the dark wood, next to the chess pieces.

He eyed the bottle. "Oh, really?"

"And it's good. So good. Do it with me."

"I try it with you, and you're in? Partners?"

I nodded. "We need a liquid carrier or it will burn your mouth. Got any coffee?"

"Of course. I don't usually drink the stuff—addictions and all—

but we always have a pot in the lobby. Small thing, but I will so enjoy drinking coffee again. Once we're in control, there will be no reason to limit ourselves."

Xed was even more anal retentive than I realized. Or perhaps careful was a better word for it—he'd done a much better job of staying sober than I did. After keeping all those urges bottled up for so long, what would he be like once those floodgates were opened? What kind of demons lurked inside?

What kind of dirty pleasures could they bring me?

"Can't believe you've stayed off coffee this whole time," I said. "You're more of a sadist than I thought."

"You mean a masochist."

"I think you enjoy pain of all sorts, Xed."

He grinned. "I'm not the only one in this room who enjoys pain of many varieties."

Something about the way he said it sent a shiver up my spine, and I tried to hide it from showing on my face. I rolled the bottle on my upturned palm, and we both stared at it, mouths open, nearly drooling right onto the desk.

He swallowed and pulled at his tie again. "Be back in a moment."

He stood up and went outside, returning a minute later with two white mugs. "Not sure when this was made, considering my secretary is...indisposed."

"It'll do."

He sat back down, and I opened the bottle. His fingers dug into the chair arms as I squeezed the dropper, filling the tube with a dark brown liquid.

My tongue stuck to the roof of my mouth as we both stared at the dropper. I knew I had to do this. I wanted it so bad, but the consequences were so huge. With the Phaze completed, it would be a flawless high, nothing else would match it, not even Alphadrine. Once I started, I didn't know if I'd be able to stop again. Everything hung in the balance, and it was hard to believe that such a small thing, one tiny drop of a chemical, could tip the scales and change everything.

I closed my eyes for a second, took a deep breath, and dripped the viscous liquid into the coffee. Xed stared at me, breathing hard, red tie on his chest moving up and down like a flag in the wind.

I grabbed my mug. "I'll go first, but if you don't follow me, deal's off." I patted my breast pocket. "Then we get to find out which one of us has better knife skills."

He picked up his mug, and he couldn't hide the slight tremble in his pale hands. "Fair. After you."

I raised my glass in a cheers. Our mugs clacked together.

"To new beginnings." I slugged down the lukewarm coffee in one gulp.

He peered at me, waiting.

I sat there, eager for that first tingle, for that incredible feeling to hit me. When it sparked, I leaned back, closed my eyes, and moaned.

"Perfect, just perfect." I opened my eyes. "No one can resist this."

He sat up. "I knew I could count on you. You're the most tenacious person I've ever met. Together, nothing will stop us." He looked down into the coffee. "Bottoms up."

He only took a small sip, but once the first bit of narcotic hit his lips, that same spark lit up his eyes. I knew that feeling, I knew that look—what it was like for addicts getting their first taste after a long dry spell. He sucked down the rest of the mug.

He smacked his lips. "It's...spicy."

"Chili powder—gives it a kick, actually works as a catalyst. Fantastic, right?"

He started to reply, and then the color drained from his face. He sat back down, breathing hard. "No. No. It's not. Supposed to feel like this."

I stood up. "Sure it is. I thought you might want to get a taste of what you created."

He coughed and grabbed his chest, eyes wide.

I picked through the chess pieces and curled my palm around three of them. "I've already taken the antidote, so I'll just have to miss out on that special pleasure. My chemists are the best, as you know. I won't be needing your protection."

He flopped across the desk, scattering chess pieces as his hand stretched out, grasping.

I caressed his cheek. "You want something inside your fridge? Nothing in there will help you. That's one deadly compound you made—works fast too, doesn't it?"

He smiled weakly, struggling to breathe as his face lost color. "I may die, but it's too late. These Domes will fall. My people will be free."

He sagged back into his chair, and I knocked the rest of the chess pieces on the floor. They flew across the carpet, softly thudding like fat raindrops on desert sand.

I plucked the other pieces from my hand and set them down on the desk—three queens, a figure from each of the sets, one silver piece, one mahogany, and one ivory. No kings.

"Sorry, Xed. It took a little time, but we've already sold all of the antidote to the Domes. Thanks for waiting to pull your doomsday switch. We might not save everyone, but the revolution is over, and we've got a pile of cash for our trouble. This thing dies with you."

He puffed, sucking in air like he was breathing through a straw, a blue cast settling over his complexion.

I grabbed his red tie and pulled him across the desk, bringing his face down to the three chess pieces. He tried to pull away, but his strength was gone.

"The first one's always free, but eventually you have to pay the piper." I kissed him, his lips already cold. "Three queens are better than none. Goodnight, Xed."

Epilogue

"STRIKE!" I SAID. "Looks like I've still got it."

Neptune had restored the lanes, leaving a smooth and shiny surface for the balls to glide down. After the pins cleared, she ran to make sure they would reset correctly.

"No one wants to beat their boss anyway," Trina said. "At least we don't have to pretend to lose."

Radar put down a neon green bowling ball. "Maybe you should take it easy. Are you sure you're feeling okay? I know this takes a while to get used to."

Trina ran a hand through her freshly bleached hair and puckered her bright red lips as she looked at the long scar running down her chest. A full four inches of it were visible before it disappeared into her hot pink tank top.

"I think being part robot is kind of fun. And Milo said I'm cleared for moderate activity now. Right, Milo?" she said.

Milo stood up from behind the snack bar counter, holding a plate of hot dogs and a few bottles of beer. "Emphasis on the moderate activity. You're lucky to have a doctor and the original mechanic in house, but don't push your luck." His voice was serious, but he smiled from ear to ear. Couldn't help himself.

Radar followed Neptune down the lane and started poking at the mechanism.

"I got this," she said.

He kissed her neck. "I know. I just like watching you work."

She elbowed him in the ribs but then turned around and pinched his nipple before going back to adjusting the gears.

"I wish Trina would behave more like Roja," Milo said.

Roja was draped across three chairs, her head on someone's sweater. I sat down next to her, and she moved her head to my lap. I stroked her soft hair.

She touched the scar running up from her blue blouse. "I'm fine. I'm just lazy. Can't say no to someone taking care of me."

I smiled and kissed her forehead.

Argon and Calavera sat at another table near the snack bar. Milo tossed them each a longneck beer.

"How's the new equipment working out?" Milo said to Argon.

Argon used the table edge to pop his beer top. "Amazing. I can make pretty much whatever we need." He smiled at Calavera. "Especially now that all those trade routes into Mexico are open—the sky's the limit. Antibiotics, anything. We're solid."

Calavera used her bare hands to pry off the top of her beer. She took a swig. "I told you all, *mi ángel,* is perfect. We won't need no more robot lungs."

"Don't knock it till you've tried it." Radar came back up the lanes to grab a bottle for him and Neptune.

Calavera took another sip. "Hey, *chicas,* ain't we supposed to be having a strategy meeting?"

Trina finished her turn, and I stood up to get my new bowling ball—it was clear with three queen chess pieces suspended in the middle.

"Fuck it, let's keep bowling." I picked the ball and hurled it down the lane. It rolled in a perfectly straight line over the greased wood, gaining momentum as it rumbled toward the pins.

Strike.